Acclaim for
an

"[Dowell] writes with a superb power of constant implication—always careful, always energetic, always suggestive."
—Thom Gunn, *The (London) Times Literary Supplement* (1984)

"I found it beautiful the way I have always found the works of Carson McCullers beautiful—works to savor."
—John Howard Griffin, author of *Black Like Me*

"Dowell writes in anger, and with a corrosive wit . . . . Above all, however, he writes with compassion. *One of the Children Is Crying* is strong and compelling."
—*The Louisville Courier-Journal*

"Not since James Agee's *A Death in the Family* has there been such a beautifully written and deeply felt novel about death and its repercussions within a family."
—*The (Maryland) Post*

"An unusually powerful and effective novel."
—*The Sacramento Bee*

"No two of the five novels [Dowell] has published resemble each other, but all share a theme which binds them in sequence: the compulsive way we use our imaginations to re-create and distort those we wish to love, and the loneliness and estrangement which result."
—*The Washington Post Book World* (1984)

"Stirring and poignant."
—*The Houston Chronicle*

"With this material, Coleman Dowell could have gone in any direction. He has, in fact, managed a strikingly successful amalgamation of the best in traditional and the best in so-called modern to write a richly textured, deeply thoughtful novel . . . . Full-bodied, mature, satisfying."
—*The (North Carolina) Pilot*

"He is an artist. He has an ability to project even horror with both beauty and tenderness."
—Sumner Locke Elliott

Also by Coleman Dowell

Mrs. October Was Here
Island People
Too Much Flesh and Jabez
White on Black on White
The Houses of Children

ONE of the CHILDREN IS CRYING

Coleman Dowell

Published by Weidenfeld & Nicolson, New York
A Division of Wheatland Corporation
10 East 53rd Street
New York, NY 10022

Originally published by Random House, Inc.,
New York, in 1968.

Library of Congress Cataloging-in-Publication Data

Dowell, Coleman.
One of the children is crying.

Reprint. Originally published: New York:
Random House, 1968.
I. Title
PS3554.093205 1987 813′.54 86-19084
ISBN 1-55584-044-2

Manufactured in the United States of America

First Weidenfeld & Nicolson edition 1987

10 9 8 7 6 5 4 3 2 1

FOR

Bert Slaff and Tammy

AND IN MEMORY OF

Hub Smith, Jr., and Yetta Arenstein

AND WITH THANKS TO

Lucy Kroll, Andrew Lyndon and Lee Wright

The Gathering

God setteth the solitary in families:
He bringeth out those which are bound
with chains: but the rebellious dwell
in a dry land.

Psalms 68:6

ROBIN

Robin was coming home. When Erin called him at four in the morning, breaking a three-year silence with the austere message in the austere hour—"Daddy is dead. Will you come home?"—she had listened without breathing for the sound of his voice with a mingling of guilt and yearning. The sound he finally made justified her guilt; it was child, not man. In momentary panic, more mother than sister, she thought: I spared him as long as I could. Which was true; she could spare him—his presence—no longer. She needed his strength to augment hers, and she told herself that even then she could feel it cutting precisely through his shock, reaching out to her as it had always done. She longed to reassure him, to say something personal and small enough to slip past the huge primitive shape of death, which she imagined as standing spraddle-legged, reared against the sky between farm and city, but she found that she could not. The simple, the small and personal, were beyond her power to use, even for the sake of her brother, whom she loved more than anything. Loathing herself, seated at the black instrument upon which she had learned to play with such skill over the years, she looked into the mirror above the telephone table and saw herself, in her black, high-necked dress, as a bird of ill omen. Unable to trust her voice not to croak, she communicated with her brother by silence and then replaced the instrument. But before she again lifted the telephone—endless, the variations to be played, lasting through the dawn; was she virtuoso enough?—she recalled a ritual and performed it: she covered the mirror with a cloth. With a sense of disembodiment that was close to comfort—the weight of her flesh left behind the cloth, her brain free; for it was the flesh that overburdened the brain—she was able to think, positively: Robin is coming home.

With Robin here, love would once again be possible. For her father, the subtly decaying body lying in the next room beyond red velvet curtains, she reserved her censure: his death at Christmas was an act typical of him, and instead of apology to him or to herself for the thought, she asked him silently if this was not so: After all, she told him, you could hardly have gone on, year after year, behaving as you did—dimming joy, causing pain, so much pain!—without being entirely aware of it. It can't hurt you to admit it.

Of course, the idea of her father's discussing anything of a personal nature with her, much less that he be asked to agree with her criticism, was a sign that she was slipping into sentimentality, and she disciplined herself against more of the same so forcefully that her body—so briefly away—recalled itself to her with a cracking of her spine that was like sleet against a windowpane. She held herself, rocking slightly, welcoming her tired body back, not loving it, but caring for it as best she could. As she had cared for her father; she had been concerned for his needs in health and had taken care of him in his sicknesses. If she could not see the word "love" in relation to him, it could be because love was a reflection as much as it was anything else not abstract, and as such, it required two pairs of eyes to mirror its reality. "Nonsense," she said aloud, thinking that she had not seen her love mirrored in Robin's eyes since his abrupt departure, which had had about it an aura of desertion. "No," she murmured, killing her delusions of three years as casually as she would squash a cockroach, "there was no *aura* of anything. It was desertion, plain and simple. Otherwise he would have answered my letters, at least." She felt lightened of a great burden—though not in the least bereft—and sated with self-indulgence.

She dialed the sleepy operator again and spoke to her with a severity designed to stem a repetition of condolences. To state one's sympathy once was proper; to repeat and repeat it, as the girl would do unless checked, was time-consuming and indicative of a dearth of ideas, or even manners, like someone who praised the soup while chewing the roast. Listening to the alarm spreading from operator to operator in that mysterious code—TC Cleveland plus and a string of numbers—like the formula for an explosive, the appropriateness of the simile occurred to her: "chewing the roast" conjured a table laden with (most ghastly of expressions) "funeral baked meats," and the sound of false teeth clacking as obscure relatives filled up on the largesse of the dead, managing to maintain mournful expressions while savoring the juices of meat, the bite of old and witty wines. She allowed herself the luxury of a solitary snort of amusement at the thought of "witty wines," an expression her gentleman-farmer father used (had used) in parody of Frenchmen whom he (had) passionately disliked.

The phone rang and rang for Millicent, but there was no answer.

Robin lay slumped in the seat of the day coach, hearing the wheels of the train as part of the machinery of his doom. He had not wished to compete with the death of his father—a positive act, at last—by revealing to Erin his own rush toward destruction, but the sense of it rode beside him like a fellow traveler and would return with him, an unshakable companion because of what they had shared at the graveside and in the rooms of his (their?) childhood. He would have lain so indefinitely, and perhaps slept, if a wakeful child across the aisle had not observed to her mother, in a voice audible throughout the coach, "Look Mama, that man is spitting on the seat." The resultant hue and cry of the passengers and the mother's embarrassed *shushing* gave him the opportunity to wipe, surreptitiously, the drool from the plush, to plump his rented pillow and twist and turn, and finally defiant, to unscrew the cap of his flask and drink the good, the burning, the stolen Scotch, keeping his eyes turned away toward the window beyond which snow clouds rode the windy sky.

" 'The north wind doth blow,' " he sang tunelessly, " 'and we shall have snow, and what will poor Robin do then, poor thing?' " He looked into a pair of hostile eyes peering at him over the back of the seat in front of his. He gave the eyes an innocent look. "A drinking song, friend," he said, "but I can't recall the mel-o-dee." He raised a toast to the man, nodding and smiling, who said—to his companion, not to Robin; people did not address Robin any longer—"Some of us would like to get a little sleep around here." The man's companion grunted and whacked his pillow, a clear warning.

"Make like," Robin said, "it's the tee-vee. Betcha you sleep when the tee-vee set's a-goin." Robin felt the man's contempt for him—a dumb, drunk hillbilly—even before the man hauled himself up and faced him again, arms resting on the back of the seat, his face set in a glare of hate meant to strike terror in Robin, who thought: Like a samurai. Robin fixed him with a superior look. "I am sure," he told the man, enunciating clearly, "that you sleep like a pig in front of the tee-vee, even while the dolls of the marketplace croon and sniff at their underwear in scatological jubilation. Do not," he said, as the man began to disappear, "encourage me to such extreme measures. For, exhibitionistic as it would appear, I, too, am wearing undies, and I, too, have a sniffer—" but the man was gone. The child across the aisle giggled. Robin turned upon her a look of calculated hatred, an inheritance from his late adversary. She began to whimper and prod her mother, who made weary soothing noises without opening her eyes. Robin twisted his face at the child until her eyes became glassy with the certainty that life as she knew it, with Christmas and sticky desserts and nice funny strangers, was somehow ending. Robin gave her up to her nightmare and drank.

When Erin's call came he had had to climb up the walls of his drunkenness as from a well, fingers slipping on the slime, to come within shouting distance; even then he had had to shout several times to make himself heard. After she had gone he had crouched over the dead phone and tried to recall her intonation. Had she said, "Will you come home?" or "Will you come?" and how much was implied by her use of "will" rather than "can"? Had she known that if she had asked, "Can you come?" meaning "Can you afford it?" he would have found his way clear to refusal? Because if she knew, she would also guess that he would be coming for the last time, and would try to entangle him once again in the feeling of family that had obsessed him to the extent that most of his forty-five years had gone into it and been lost like coins into a child's bank with a hole in the bottom.

Dialing Tim's number, reaching him—the only person in all the world who looked at Robin, and saw him, and suspected what he had been—he muttered, "Old man dead, Tim boy. Money—home."

"Can you make it over here?" Robin heard the finality in Tim's voice, like death, and he said good-by carefully, so that his friend would know that he knew that they had really parted on the telephone; he imagined Tim's relief at at last finding the opportunity to be rid of him, his gratitude to Robin's father for dying His parting contribution would be generous, Robin knew, and so he was grateful to his father for dying, too. He began the arduous task of dressing. Buttons and shoelaces took longest. He found it endlessly interesting that the flooded brain of a drunk could philosophize, compose poetry and music, remember with terrible clarity, while its servants—fingers, feet—had to be cajoled, with, at best, childish results. He visualized alcohol as the Great Regressor; finally, if he is lucky, the alcoholic regresses to a place of fluids and silence; until then, there are buttons, and shoelaces—but no neckties; he could not take on a necktie. He turned the coat collar up to hide that omission, pulled his hat brim down to shield his vulnerable eyes, and at the door his brain directed his feet to turn and walk back through the dark to the night table, where for once the hand found the flask unerringly as though a compass were centered in the palm.

He took on the four-flight descent as he would have taken on an enemy, once—courteously, but deadly in intent. The streets were sleety, and twice, fooled into the belief that level ground was his friend, he fell, tearing, the second time, a large hole in one knee of his inadequate trousers—five ninety-five in Klein's basement and meant for spring. His overcoat, sizes too large, hand-me-down, flapped buttonlessly open like a cape and icy air centered at his crotch, tearing at the symbol of his unrealized manhood.

With awe undiminished by time or his condition, he thought of his unreleased sperm. Having never had an outlet, pooling in him like a white sea, was it the stuff he spewed from mouth and nose, gagging on in the night? Then it would be children-seed he planted in the aridity of Kleenexes and under-the-pillow handkerchiefs. Billions of possible children dumped into incinerators or sent to the laundry, and he had the image, a new chimera for his collection, of a seed doggedly claiming life in a piece of Kleenex, repeating the process of evolution on the shelf of an incinerator, mutative in the strange womb—pallid, froglike, growing amid smoldering cabbages and grapefruit peels. He had to stop and lean against a tree, glassy eye to glassy trunk like the knee of a frozen confessor. What word, to free him? To banish the horror, what good, clean word? "Erin," he said, and she came, but she was not alone; the others came with her—his fellow betrayers, all but Rhoda, who had somehow never been involved. Lucky Rhoda. Cold, possessed, club-woman, lucky Rhoda.

He saw himself and the others at a game of anagrams, using the letters of each other's names, in a parody—though who knew it then, *who?*—of family containment that is the glory of the Southland and the shield of the Jews. He could remember only the words they had formed of the letters of ERIN. Priscilla—sly, triumphant, the classic schizophrene whose cruelty was, from birth, an absolute—had shown NIER; laughing from face to face she had told them that it meant to deny or disown. Millicent—a dike even then? commenting secretly upon her "difference"?—had presented RIEN. Spur—young brother, son, constant charge, ultimate woe—snorting with laughter, had uncovered IN ER, but Erin had not understood. Robin alone could not make a choice, because Erin's name had seemed to contain for him all words. Recalling the game, he saw Priscilla as the family Cassandra, for they had all denied and disowned Erin, he last of all, which made it the greater perfidy.

His mind returned to the present, the train, as though thrown there; it jolted in his head and pained his eyes with the return of light. Of course, at that point he always stopped: the point at which he was face to face with his perfidy. Even the most extreme, maudlin drunkenness would not allow him to go further, into excuses, or pleas. But he would have to find something to give her—excuse, plea, or the flat of his hand—before he got to the farm. He would have to find the courage. But once again his mind would not let him hurt it beyond endurance. It flung him back to the tree, the stunted New York City tree, to which he clung like a nest of stinging things, returning him to a more bearable consciousness by allowing him to skip over the astringency of Erin's name, like salt in his wounds, to the recollection of his purpose, which was to get to Tim's, and beg, and borrow, and steal.

Tim was waiting for him in a dressing gown; Robin saw that he had shaved. Deference to the dead? Formality of final things? At four-fifteen A.M. one does not wield a razor lightly. Tim saw Robin's torn knee and went to his closet and brought forth a black suit, indicating the bedroom where Robin could change. He turned away to the telephone and spoke into it his first words since Robin's arrival, telling Mike at the all-night deli that he needed a large check cashed for an emergency.

In the bedroom Robin filled his flask, compulsively stealing, from the bottle of Scotch always there, sloshing some of it onto the glass top of the bureau. There was a box of Kleenex nearby but he could not bring himself to touch the flimsy placenta. Instead he bent his face and lapped the spilled whiskey and polished the glass with his tongue.

Suited for mourning, he stood before Tim in the old posture of hand-out, and Tim counted into it the money—generous, as Robin had known it would be; generous old Tim. But flawed. He had not, after all, gotten Robin's message of farewell on the telephone.

"This is the last time, Rob," he said, "I'm sorry."

Robin mourned his friend's lack of subtlety; it could have been so sadly fine, so finely sad—the silent understanding, the wordless farewell forever—something restorative, in a peculiar way, of trust. "You bastard," Robin said, and left.

"I'm drunk," he murmured to the child across the aisle, "but I'm going to get drunker," he said more softly, then whispered, "and then—watch out," and watched her tremble, alone and afraid as he on the sleeping train.

PRISCILLA

Something was fluttering across the street, half in and half out of the scraggly iced-up hedge that separated awful Birdie Criswell's house from the broken sidewalk. At first, when she had gone to raise the blind and open the window and clear the room of her husband's stink, and had seen the white fluttering, she had thought it was a little white dog, but the more she looked the less doggy it became—the less *animal.* A large wounded dove would have made those desperate movements, or a swan. Also a lamb, a goat, a calf. But if any of these were caught in a hedge, they would have called out in their own tongues for help; seeing her leaning from the window, they would have barked, cooed, screamed, bleated to her. Now, after hours of interested vigil, she knew what it was. It was a large bunch of greenish-white asparagus, the kind you bought in cans in the Gourmet Shop on Henderson Street, only, naturally, much, much larger. A monstrous bunch of huge asparagus stalks caught in the icy twigs.

She had gone to the window at twelve o'clock midnight while her husband was still making his sheepish exit from her bedroom. He came once a week, got on top of her, humped and groaned apologetically, and always, just before his little moment, he would say, "Do you love me, Prissy?" and she would answer either yes or no, depending solely upon her mood, because the words had equal value and meaning, which was really none at all. But whether she said yes or whether she said no, he gushed like a fountain, then shudderingly withdrew from her, kissed her hairline (she would not allow her lips; she had never really allowed her lips) and left—no, sidled out of—the room, the filled rubber that she made him wear dangling like a little ball attached to the head of his thing. In the beginning, when they were first married and he swaggered with pride and they shared the same room and bed, he would approach her, insolent with sexuality and misinformation—he believed that she loved him—and say, in his tough truck-driver's voice, "I'm knocking you up tonight, kid. I'm gonna shoot so straight you'll be lucky if you don't have a litter nine months from now." And she would smile softly up at him, the docile little woman, and say, "Maybe, Ed. But prove it by busting the rubber, darling," and he would sheathe himself, actually counting on the force of his ejaculation to knock her up. This went on for about six months. For that period she was interested and occasionally avid. Then one night, as he came at her with his staff jutting foolishly before him, she said to him, "Sit down. I've got something to tell you." The look in his eyes was so incredulous, so wild with excitement and hope, that even she had been affected and had come close to tears of joy. He wanted a child so much that it was like fever, hotter than his desire, deeper than his love of the big, brutal trucks he maneuvered so adroitly between here and Chicago with their locked, secret cargoes; stronger than his love for her. She was reminded of all his other loves by the look in his eyes.

He sat on the edge of the bed, taking her hand and curving it around his big erect organ as though it were a mystic ritual that she should be touching the source of life when she told him about its stirring in her body. She told him, simply and gladly, exploring his eyes with hers for each nuance of expression.

"Ed, there won't be any children. Not ever. The year before I married you I had every organ removed except the one I piss out of. They were diseased and rotten. I'd had three abortions, the first when I was thirteen, and gonorrhea twice. I got the last dose from dear brother Spur."

In her hand his thing had withered away. It seemed, to her abnormally sensitive hand, as though it were trying to withdraw into his body like a turtle pulling in its head. She sat up and kissed his brow and a second later she found herself lying across the room, her head half under the bureau, with blood pouring from her nose.

She lay watching him dress, watching the white carpet turn red, and wondered idly if a nose had an automatic shut-off, like those gadgets attached to bourbon bottles that measure out a shot at a time. Pints seemed to be pouring from her and she didn't mind. However, in case she shouldn't bleed to death, there was something she wanted to say to him. He was at the door when she spoke his name. She kept her voice low, so that he had to strain to hear her. "If I don't lie here and die in my own blood—if I survive this beating and *you* survive *my* survival"—she giggled at the curiosity on his face; he was exactly like a baby when a watch is dangled before it—"just remember this, sugar-man mine: You can never divorce me." She waited, peaceful and drowsy, until the question was forced out of him. She answered, "Because our lovely state doesn't allow a man to divorce an insane wife." She turned face downward in her blood and went instantly to sleep.

Later, that awful Birdie (prying, as usual) told Priscilla that Ed sat in the car all night, hat on and all, under the street lamp, clutching the steering wheel and sometimes resting his head on it. She thought, thought Birdie, that it was *so* considerate of Edgar, finding himself locked out and all, not to wake Priscilla up to let him in. She herself, she said, simpering, had been a victim of the night! She had worried about him *so much,* about his catching cold and all, that she just couldn't sleep and kept getting up and going to the window to check on him. She had almost (titillating herself) offered him one of her own beds, but cooler heads prevailed, thank the Lord!—because *they both knew* what the neighbors would have had to say about *that!*

Priscilla, thinking about it now at four in the morning almost six years later, saw Birdie's face, which you could really see only in profile. Looked at head-on, it was just a narrow wedge that could slip through the crack in a door. Looking at her head-on, you had to use your imagination that there were eyes on each side of that wedge at all. She imagined Ed in bed with Birdie and Birdie suddenly darting up in ecstasy and splitting Ed's skull wide open. She laughed, and her attention was drawn back to the asparagus in the hedge; yes, Birdie could certainly use those; she might even conceive and sprout, in the springtime, the feathery fronds of her peculiar motherhood.

And then quite suddenly Priscilla was frightened to death of the fluttering thing and she knew beyond a shadow that it was patiently working itself loose to come to her. She could hear it squishing across the street and up the stairs, a vegetable octopus, and nothing on earth could save her now. She leaned from the window, gasping and calling, "Go away, please, for Christ's sake, go away." The telephone rang.

The telephone was in the passage between her room and Ed's, at the top of the stairs. She knew the minute she turned her back the fluttering thing would tear loose and whisk across the street and meet her, wrapping her in squooshy slime, entering her while the telephone screamed under her hand.

Ed appeared in the doorway, tacky and bent in his pajama bottoms; on his chest the hair that once had sprung black and cocky as the breast feathers of a mating hawk was scraggly and gray. Priscilla was glad to see him there instead of the asparagus. But why was he there? Had she screamed? No, the telephone had. He came toward her, took her arm and led her to the bed, where he made her sit. She looked at him nervously, thinking: My God, is he going to tell me *he's* having a baby? She began to laugh and the laughter made the bed creak. The creaking reminded her of sex, and out of the blue she wanted it. She put her hand into the opening of his pajamas and took his sex in her hand. Once again she was puzzled. Ordinarily, if she so much as brushed against him, the thing sprang into life; it was practically the only life in him. But it was dormant as a sleeping mouse. She began to massage it, lying back and moving about on the bed. What was that in his eyes? Not desire, not compassion. Something else—ugly. It was a "getting even" look. What did it mean? She knew. She knew.

He told her, "That was Erin on the telephone. Your daddy died tonight. She wants us to come down there."

She heard something moving on the stairs. The overhead light, so bright a minute before, receded to a pinpoint and shadows stood around her bed. Something or somebody whimpered. Priscilla pulled at the clothing in front of her eyes and took what she found inside it into her mouth. She pulled for dear life, trying to contain the growing thing, her hands kneading the flesh around it, a little gurgling sound in her throat. Ed tore himself away, Priscilla's nails scratching his thighs in her eagerness to hold on, and pulled her up and to him until their bodies seemed fused, his ravenous mouth to her mouth, her clenched teeth bruising his lips as she tried to fight him off and find again the comfort of mindless sucking; at last she took the offering of his tongue and drew it into her mouth, fiercely trying to immobilize with suction its nourshing heat as it darted for the first time among the secret places; she bit the intruder and was bitten on her lips until she felt moisture, and whatever it was on the stairs—the thing that had whimpered—went away. Priscilla fell onto the bed, pulling Ed over her—"Cover me!" she cried—and felt his sex between her breasts, his cods to her nipples, life to life. Her fingers outlined bunches of muscles in his back and legs, patting them, thanking and forgiving them for protecting and hurting her. There was laughter in the room, arrogant and male, and she called out to it again and again, "Do you love me—do you love me?" but there was no answer. When he went into her she felt it to be the first time, and in her rage at being made to feel like a woman she bit his shoulder until she tasted blood and salt, and he kissed it from her lips and tongue. "Do you love me?" she begged. "Do you?"

Five-thirty in the morning and she lay with her head on his belly. The light blazed once again in the ceiling, its pinpoint hour over. Drowsily she listened to the sounds in his stomach, squeaking sounds, like swinging on a gate. She looked up at the light and then toward the window. Birdie had gotten an eyeful tonight if she had been prowling from bed to window in her fetid room full of cat-odors that came from Birdie herself, who did not own a cat.

Thinking of Birdie, Priscilla thought of the flutter,

the squish, the telephone. Lying with her head pressing into her husband's hard belly, feeling his hand enclose one of her breasts with new possessiveness, denting the nipple slightly, she began to scream. Ed tried to soothe her, murmuring to her, eventually cupping her mouth with his hand, and still the monotonous sound went on, unmuffled, as if it came not from her throat but from somewhere outside her—from her pores, or the skin of her scalp. No, he thought helplessly, it's coming from her eyes. Like five years ago when she stood and screamed at me with her eyes after she'd found out about Nonie and me. He had called Robin and Erin and they had gotten there quickly and somehow, in spite of Priscilla's avowed loathing of them, they had managed to quiet her.

Of course, he couldn't call them to come to her now, so he'd have to take her to them, the sooner the better. Get her dressed and home to her family. He admitted that he'd have sent her alone, or with Birdie Criswell, if this hadn't happened. He hadn't seen any of them since the wedding trip, except Robin and Erin, and the thought of facing Jasper, death in the family or not, made him sick to his stomach. He hated him so much he could not even call him Spur in his mind—a dangerous name that brought dangerous thoughts.

He began preparations, trying to ignore the sound from the bed. He threw dark-colored things into a bag; he knew about the color of death: he'd been put in an orphans' home when he was nine, so death was like his little brother. Handling Prissy's clothes, he couldn't keep himself from thinking of what had happened before the screaming. "Best damn pussy I ever *did* have," he said, indignant at its aftermath for cutting into his enjoyment, before he remembered, the mourning clothes in his hands, what had preceded it. He could not let himself think too long that she might have taken him so freely, for the first time, as if he were a medicine to make her forget.

He went into the bathroom and rummaged in the medicine chest. Five years ago, during the trouble, the doctor had prescribed some pills to keep her quiet, to stop her screaming. *Why* had she carried on so about Nonie, when she hadn't wanted him herself? He'd never found an answer, at least one he could believe, and an answer you can't believe is nothing. Still—well, go on, think it, he thought impatiently, fumbling a bottle of Bufferin until it dropped into the john. Think it then, and shut up about it. You had the idea she wanted to save you for herself to—he balked a moment, then bulldozed on—to fatten you up like a hog and butcher you (finding the pills) and it worked. At least, she *skinnied* me up with five years of hell; no sir, five years and a half. Because the hellfires started burning the fat when she told me about her and her brother. Abortions—no kids—hard enough, but I could have took that. I got a strong stomach. But—the nightmare rolled into the bathroom and he stood with the bottle of sedatives, watching it, seeing the details as she had told them: the blanket beneath the trees, the possessed bodies, the family just inside the house—He threw up gently, in one gulp, flushed the toilet and remembered Spur's—Jasper's—words when they met: "You don't know what you've got there, old man. Or do you?" And the look that went with them.

He filled a glass with water and went back into the bedroom, forcing himself to think about Erin and Robin and their kindness; they had even understood about Nonie. He felt better, and dubiously reading the directions on the bottle, he decided to give Priscilla one more pill than it said to; that screaming—she'd start bleeding if she kept it up. It seemed as though she got quiet almost as once, and he sat beside her on the bed and watched the bones returning to her body that had been like jelly. Her breasts plumped up and the nipples grew like plant slips as he stroked her. Ashamed, peculiarly happy, he bent down to kiss her mouth, and she automatically turned her head away, which dented his odd happiness, but like a finger on a balloon, did not explode it. He smoothed her hair, then tiptoed over to finish packing.

The faint scent in the closets and bureau drawers of her belongings was mysterious to him, Prissy and not Prissy, as if he were smelling her shadow. On her, the scent of the clothes deepened, plumped out, the way her breasts had under his hands, the way, when she put on perfume, her body changed it from something sickly with a French name to somebody named Priscilla. Her shoes smelled not of leather or of feet but faintly dry and sunny, a little like hay. It was the sunny, windy smell and the look of the country about her that had made him want her on first meeting; he had thought it would be like marrying freedom itself to marry her.

Like most children whose parents are a red brick building, he had wanted warmth and the freest life he could have, the freest job he could find. Those big trucks zooming through the turnpike nights had always meant freedom to him, and making his first haul, he had almost burst with the sense of fetters cast away, of the unmeasurable dimensions of the night that pointed up and out in a gesture of constant opening like a big black rose. He liked the danger, the freedom of the choice of death because it was a freedom. He liked to get drunk occasionally to free his mind; to play poker to free his pocketbook; to fish on vacations—though he didn't free the fish; he ate them—and to have a therapeutic fight now and then. The only thing missing from the realization of his life's ambitions was the warmth of wife and home. He screwed around like any young guy but he kept himself clean. Let the other guys brag about their clap. He wasn't going to take a chance of handing down to some innocent towhead a piece of a nail he'd picked up in a cathouse.

He had met Priscilla in the town where they now lived and where she said she was visiting a friend. She was sitting in the Dog Wagon, one of the town's two restaurants, when he first set eyes on her, and nothing, barring dynamite in his path, could have kept him from speaking to her. She was different, so different that he'd never even heard of anybody like her. The things she said, and the way she said them! It seemed to thunderstricken, helpless and hopeful Ed—who admitted to his buddies that he wanted her so bad he could taste it, and they said they bet he would, too—that she talked the way a kid did, using words for the first time and wondering how they'd sound all strung together. One of the biggest, most serious fights of his life happened when one of his buddies, after sitting over a few beers and listening to Priscilla, had taken him into the john and told him, "There's something the matter with that little girl, buddy." Ed's silence hadn't stopped him. "With her head. There's something loose up there." They had had to carry his friend out on a stretcher and Ed's knuckles hadn't healed for a month. By that time he was a married man. He had not met her family until after the wedding—she had wanted it that way—and he had been a little defensive about his speech and manners, looking for slights, but just one of them had been anything but fine: Jasper.

He finished packing and put the luggage by the door. He would load the car and have it checked at the filling station before he woke Prissy and tried to dress her, hoping as hard as he could that she wouldn't pick up the screaming where she had left off. It had gone on for hours and hours before, over a waitress in a truck-line café. He told himself: You been through all that tonight, but the thought went on, leading him by the nose around the old, old circle. It was such a little thing, the business with Nonie, compared to what Priscilla had told him, which had driven him like a dog to creep into Nonie's bed, trying to get warm once more. Why? he asked silently across the room, his bewilderment, shock and hurt as fresh as new.

The blanket had slipped from Priscilla. He started toward her and noticed that the window was open, the blind up. Down on the street—policing up the area at six in the morning!—was Birdie Criswell, one ear cocked like radar toward the window. He watched as she plucked a flapping newspaper from the hedge. Silently he closed the window and pulled the blind down, grinning: She had sure as hell got both eyes full tonight. And there was the feeling of happiness again, swelling out like a balloon with a big, silly, grinning face painted on it.

Hell, he thought, tucking the blanket around Priscilla's shoulders; maybe today's some kind of beginning, or something; nature ends things and begins other things all the time; may as well look at it thata way; it won't hurt anybody, anyhow. He bent toward his wife's lips but stopped. He thought: Uh-uh, next time we do *that's* going to be *her* idea.

RHODA

Rhoda indignantly drove her small car into the driveway of the small house, where she lived with her husband and three children, at around eleven P.M. She applied the brakes too forcefully, which caused the car to make a quarter-turn on the icy down-grading of the drive; when she had straightened it out, neatly parallel to and centered between the low fieldstone barriers, she switched off the ignition and sat with her hands on the wheel, waiting for the seething, of which the skid had been an extension, to die down. As a rule she drove as she lived, with precision and nerve, kept from charges of occasional recklessness by a supreme assurance that took the outward aspect of pleasantly detached involvement. It amused her friends to speculate upon the various professions in which she could have excelled had she chosen—racing-car driver, naturally; brain surgeon—and Rhoda did not mind in the least the implied doubt of her femininity, because the very qualities so subtly imputed accounted for her acknowledged success in the professions of wife—and mother—and discreet gambler for which she had settled. No, she was hardly vulnerable to cattiness, friendly or not; but there was one form of self-indulgence, in women or men, to which she was antagonistic to an extreme degree: the not inconsiderable one, in her world, of drunkenness, part- or full-time. This was responsible for her present indignation, although it was more than that; it felt to her like a subcutaneous growth, virulent but undetectable to the naked eye in its early stages.

Her partner at bridge tonight, Midge Taylor, had caused them to lose a sizable amount of money because she had arrived at Dodo Wilson's drunk and proceeded to get more and more so, until, looking at her across the table, Rhoda felt that Midge was peering at her from a bottle like one of those full-rigged ships one bought in coastal villages. The others found Midge amusing—they always did because they did not take gambling seriously, which generally worked in Rhoda's favor though she didn't need the gratuity—and even Rhoda had admitted that Midge was a droll drunk. "*Not* droll," she said aloud, letting the anger surface. "Bitchily funny, maybe, but not *droll*. Disgusting and sick—" and thought, as she couldn't help doing at such times, of her first marriage, at twenty-one, to a classmate, a promising law student by whom she had had a child—a bright young man who one day simply walked through a doorway beyond which voices thickly called and did not return. The stock from which he came (she had found it out during divorce proceedings) was rotten with the disease: grandfather, brother, paternal aunt. There were times when she thought of her daughter by Bill, sixteen-year-old Marilyn, and wondered if "like father, like daughter" applied, and she was afraid.

She climbed from the car, the small energetic woman with an adolescent's figure, thinking bitterly that Marilyn had two possible legacies from her father, though she did not know if hypersexuality could be hereditary, and not knowing made it all the worse. Short of discovering a method to split chromosomes and analyze genes, there was no recourse except vigilance, which she loathed, and worry, which she entrusted most of the time to Andrew. She glanced up at their bedroom window, and fear and anger began to drain away as if drawn out by a syringe. Andrew was at home and waiting up. She had not expected him to be here when she got back; there had been a meeting at the plant, and because it was the Christmas season, she had thought there might be some extended jollity afterward. But he had come home and waited for her instead, not expecting her back so early but wanting to be there when she came. Humming a snatch of Christmas carol, she cut across the rimy grass to shorten the distance to him, thinking that these little pleasures—an extra, unexpected hour of companionship, the simple ease seeing the light in their window gave her—were more appropriate to their lives than the larger things, because their lives were scaled to the small by intent and need. The "larger things" included entertaining his superiors, which she did with imagination; included, also, her gambling for economic reasons (and by natural bent), though Andrew believed that she did it because it was the expected thing in her "circle."

When she had had to abandon the idea of being the wife of an important lawyer, she had embraced, without whimper or cavil, the prospect of this life with a man whose expectations were, at their peak, less than impressive. He presently made eight thousand a year; their combined energies, cunning and plots could lift him to the round plateau of ten thousand, period. She managed another several thousand a year with her cool skills; a few times, when she had gotten to a gaming table, she had almost matched Andrew's yearly salary but had quit before she could overtake, or exceed, that figure. She did this not only because she wished to preserve Andrew's role as major breadwinner; she did it also to keep within reasonable bounds her instinct for games of chance, which could, she suspected, unless severely disciplined, cause her to throw herself, and her happy life with her husband, onto the green baize like a pair of dice. Still, she played every game that presented itself, demanding only that the stakes be as high as possible. Losses, such as tonight's, were rare enough to cause no real anxiety. She would simply, next time around, double the ice of her logic and, if absolutely necessary, cheat.

Her fellow club women—and victims—referred to her, to her face, as a "con woman." The name fit, she admitted. She had conned her way through life by inventing a system whereby failure could be parlayed into success. She was too bright to ignore her failures, being fully aware that, ignored, they stockpiled themselves in secret crannies of the mind until one day—boom. *She* looked at them squarely, broke them into component parts as she would a revolver, found the faulty mechanism, reassembled the whole shebang and made it work for her. Her uncomplicated marriage with Andrew was shining proof of her system.

She had conned her way, so to speak, through the halls of academe—mathematics and psychology—by waiting on tables, playing lady's maid to rich girls, and so forth, and nothing she had ever done had touched her pride, which was intact and hard as a new tenpenny nail. Nothing had touched her at all, practically since childhood, except Bill, and she had survived him. She had not, for a time, imagined that she *could* survive him; during the last surrealistic months with him she had reached the point of thinking that his alcoholism was an act of retaliation—that he was willing to destroy himself to destroy her—and she had nearly broken under the continuing onslaught of *déjà vu.* But the key word was *nearly;* from that close call, which had led her to relentless self-examination, which had led to self-knowledge sometimes harsh, she fashioned—was constantly in the process of fashioning—the woman whom she thought of as The Phoenix (Bill had called her Laodicean; they were both right, thank God). Now two things only could threaten her continual palingenesis: drunks and her need to gamble. But with only two adversaries and vigilance, she managed nicely, thank you. When her adversaries occasionally overlapped, as they had tonight, there was admittedly a certain weakening, like the injection of poison into her perfect system, but Sweet Andrew was the antidote; praise be for Sweet Andrew!

She removed her pumps in the living room and went to the door beyond which her two youngest girls slept, opened the door a crack and nodded at the cool air stirring the shadows. In the dim light filtering through Venetian blinds, she saw the outlines of their suitcases in the middle of the floor, tops up, and nodded again: Good girls; they had packed for the early start to the farm. She did not check on Marilyn, whose resentment of such motherly intrusions Rhoda respected, and, duty over, with a sigh, feeling not Phoenix but little brown homing pigeon, she prepared to go in to her husband . . .

"Homing pigeon" did not spring from sentimentality—neither she nor Andrew could afford that luxury—but rather from gratitude. Rhoda was grateful for having been saved—saddled with a child; no beauty—from permanent grass-widowhood. Andrew was grateful to find a woman who did not believe that masculinity depended on the phallic image of "virility" fostered with less and less subtlety by the magazines: It's What's Up Front That Counts. In high school he had been nicknamed "Pee-Wee," and however it was started, or by whom, he had helped it endure for the entire four years by being shattered by it at the onset, having no idea that at least one of his more aggressive classmates warranted the nickname as much as he, or that aggression was a classic response to smallness, whether in Corsican generals or admen. It seemed to

Andy that he moved for four years to the tune of snickers, especially the snickers of girls, not knowing that his furtive way of moving, a result of the persecution, was as much the reason as the name. In the beginning, when the sobriquet was making the rounds, he had tried to get along all day without using the lavatory, but one noon recess when he was cramped and near bursting, an unexpectedly thrown football had slammed him in the kidneys. For a while afterward his classmates had called him "Victoria" for Victoria Falls, and then "Viki," but ultimately that had not proved as cruel, or as satisfying to their prurience. By Commencement Day, Andrew—fifth from the bottom of a class of fifty—had been, he imagined, scarred for life.

Trying to be as self-protective as possible, he attended a small engineering school upstate, where he saw to it that he was seldom addressed by anyone except his instructors. He landed a job on the strength of his academic record alone; his personality did not fall within any of the recognizable categories by which Personnel rated new employees. The only thing the girls in Personnel could find to mention about him was the word he had written beside MARRIAGE on the Word Association test: Misogamist. It had been a defiant gesture, wrenched from him by the strength of his phobia; better an admission of hate than of fear.

He had met Rhoda on the street of the town where he worked, on a holiday afternoon. They were introduced by a woman who worked in an office at his plant, someone to whom he had barely spoken, though he knew her husband slightly; she had startled him by calling him by his first name and by her breezy air of confidence that he was someone whom Rhoda—smart and wonderfully attractive—would want to meet. He had stood passively with the women until released, the only way he knew to act with the opposite sex, thinking that a mistake had been made.

Soon afterward, to his suspicion, surprise and alarm, he found himself being courted by Rhoda—or perhaps he had only imagined that she had been the aggressor, for at some juncture—he could not, even when he tried, recall whether it occurred before or after they slept together—he became the ardent suitor, and then the husband, and then the father. The events seemed in retrospect to have occurred simultaneously, in that the fine, natural order of his married life produced a sheen that overlay his past and, as it were, effected coalescence. If he thought of the painful nickname at all, and the empty years he had spent as a man before he and Rhoda found each other, he saw them as working in collaboration to keep him unattached until she came along.

Rhoda's knowledge of how their life together came about is much more sophisticated than Andrew's, but she does not allow it to get in the way; the important thing, she knows from experience, is not method or process, but result, and the result of her calculation is a man with a solid sense of his own worth because she has been careful to let him think all of it to be his own doing, and that man waits up for her now with pleasure, and an un-neurotic anticipation, and to meet him on equal ground she pushes, she trusts, the last of her own neuroticism about drunks and money lost out of the way and goes in to him, his little brown homing pigeon.

She opened the door to their room and went in briskly, shedding her suit coat and unbuttoning her blouse with the air of the busy, glad-to-be-home club woman. "Hi, A."

"Hey there, Stuff. Home early—you must be loaded. With dough, I mean." They do not skirt the issue of her vulnerability. They serve drinks in their house and use all the terms: swozzled, blind, crocked . . .

"Uh-uh." Kissing him. "Midge was tanked up until it ran out her ears. We, as the British say, dropped a packet. Damn-damn-damn." She ran the words together in the staccato way she had, which was a sign to drop the subject. Tying it up with rue and playful menace: "Make it up after the holidays, never fear." Slipping out of her skirt: "Oh, how I wish we weren't going to the farm this year." It was a yearly remark, automatic and expected, made on the eve of departure. "Do you suppose we'll *ever* spend Christmas in our bide-a-wee? You and me and babies three?" On with monogramed flannel robe, off with bra, skirt-slip, panties. He gave the yearly response—similar words, but she felt, for an uncertain moment, that his eyes were different. She cocked her head at him disarmingly.

"Aw, come on," he said, "you know the kids love the farm. High point of their year, Stuff. And there's gonna be snow. I put the chains on the big car. Just think—we can build snowmen, skate on the crick—"

"—and freeze," she finished firmly, part of the litany. "Those fireplaces never did heat the old house, even when they were all going at the same time." She shivered. "Fourteen fires in that tinderbox—it used to scare me half to death." She sounded as if she were blaming Andrew; she smiled at him and said, "Oh, well, they'd die if we didn't come."

The exchange for her was deadly earnest, so that her capitulation was generally overstated. She sighed and went into the bathroom, then came out and sat at her dressing table (which Andrew, clinging to odd words and phrases from his hill heritage, called a "vanity case") and took off her moderate make-up—light pancake, pale lipstick, touch of mascara—talking vigorously around the facile fingers that applied cream, massaged sallow skin and wiped the mess off with tissue. She told him about a new committee she had been asked to head, gave him the latest figures—impressive —of their local drive on behalf of a new, non-profit nursery school for children of working mothers, inquired about the outcome of tonight's meeting—had they decided to increase production?—but to the back of her mind there clung like a barnacle the idea to have it out about the farm, to get some definitive statement from him concerning next year. She admitted to herself that her intentions had a scrappy feeling about them, and that this could be partly due to her not having been able to free herself entirely from the effects of the bridge game, but she thought that a little scrappiness might serve her cause, and Andrew liked her spirit.

"I hope," she began, "that Carol doesn't come back with a cold as bad as last year's."

He laughed. "She won't be able to go swimming this time. The crick'll be frozen solid."

She kept on course. "It almost turned into pneumonia, I hope you remember. And Gayle always breaks out from the fatty food."

There was no doubt about it—his eyes were watchful.

"That's your department; don't let her eat too much"—beating her to the draw—"and *I'll* keep Marilyn and the local studs out of the hayloft. That's my department."

She turned to face him while his thoughts were on the one hazard of the farm that he would acknowledge to be one: adolescents and haylofts. "Andrew—" A mistake. She should have called him A. and kept it casual. *Andrew* was reserved for serious matters. Well, what the hell. This was serious. "Hon, let's pave the way this year for staying home next. If we prepare them, they won't mind. Nobody makes the yearly pilgrimage nowadays. Every other year, maybe—"

"You said they'd die if we didn't come."

"An expression, A. Pure hyperbole. I bet they'd welcome a Christmas on their own—no grandchildren yelling the place down. They're old and tired, after all. We forget that, don't we."

Quietly he said, "Your dad and mother, you mean."

"Who else?" Her eyes were startled, she hoped not too artfully.

"Erin—" She turned from him to the mirror, masking her anger. It didn't help. He was in there, too.

"Oh. Yes. Well, Robin won't be there, so it won't matter to her." She plucked a hair from her widow's peak. "Gray, at thirty-eight. Damn-damn-damn." This time the rue was real.

"How old is Erin, Rhoda?"

(Rhoda. Watch it, girl.) "Forty-seven."

A moment of quiet. "Too old to have kids of her own."

She looked at him in the mirror, forcing a smile. "Are you being abstract, or something? Of course she's too old."

He spoke precisely. "She likes our kids and they're crazy about her. You said Spur and Bonny and the boys wouldn't be there tomorrow—"

Her voice rose a bit in spite of her efforts. "I wasn't talking about tomorrow. I was talking about *next year.*"

He broke in. "They weren't there last year, either. If it hadn't been for us, she'd have been alone in that big house except for people she waits on every day of her life."

Rhoda said, with a bitchiness that only mention of her family could inspire on occasion, "I carry the people I wait on with me." She softened it a bit: "I'd rather wait on them here. Surprise."

He spoke quietly, a speech, for all its assertiveness and subdued emotion, without precedent in their easygoing life together. "I want us to go—this year, and next year, and all the years after that, if Erin wants us to. I want our kids to take their kids, but I don't worry about that. They'll want to." Unmoving, she watched him in the mirror, a stranger. He misread her withdrawal as skepticism. "You think it's because I'm sorry for Erin? The ones I feel sorry for are the ones who don't know what she is." He lay back on the pillow and stared at the ceiling.

Rhoda wanted to snap at him, "What the hell *is* she

except a damned old maid who steals children?" She was shocked by his unmistakable attack, the first in all their years of marriage. That he should feel sorry for her was almost insupportable, and for such a reason! *Really,* she thought, *really, Andrew,* and silently demanded that he place the two sisters side by side and then choose the pathetic one. She told herself that he was entitled to hyperbole, too, and began the ritual of inner-calming that she had learned so long ago. Christmas trauma, she told herself. Everyone has it; it's well known to psychiatrists. It's just late in catching up with us: the state of misplaced guilt for growing up, and away. We're oriented to moving forward but Christmas forces us to go back. She started to say this to Andrew, but it sounded too dry for his apparently emotional condition. Later she would find out what had happened to make him so edgy to begin with—what had made his eyes so watchful. For the time being she would be light, and sincere; a bit puzzled, but open-minded. "Why, I suppose I hadn't dug into it, you know—Erin as a special case. So damn many of us to think about—worrying about Priscilla; Millicent and Spur so far away—" Damn. She had left Robin out, but she could hardly stick him in now: and dear Robin *so* far away. She picked up the tweezers, saying, "I'll be through with this futile business in a second," and pretended to pluck a hair from an eyebrow.

"I like big families," he told the ceiling.

"O.K., we'll have another baby. I'm not too old." Had she stressed "I'm" too much? Her hand trembled.

The toilet flushed—Marilyn up at this hour, which

meant she would be querulous at breakfast without her eight hours' sleep. The clock ticked in the aging silence, impersonally measuring the depth as well as the length of time. All at once Rhoda wanted to beg: Please, Andrew, let's go back to where I said I didn't want to go this year—back to just before that. And then she jumped into the silence feet first like a reckless child into a pool whose depth it does not know. "What's the matter, Andrew? What brought this on?"

His answer, full of effort, made her go taut. "I don't know. When you started that about not going, I felt like I'd been waiting for it since last year—" He reached for a cigarette and sat up and lit it, his short legs dangling from the edge of the bed. Rhoda was motionless. He repeated, "I don't know," and then said with some vehemence, "Yes, by God, I *do* know. We've got three kids; could, as you pointed out, have more. But why in hell *bother*—I mean, why does anybody *bother,* if all they're gonna do is grow up and hide from each other, and hate it when they can't." Sullenly he asked her, "What's the use in breeding enemies?"

Rhoda gave him a smile almost arch in its attempt to be amusedly incredulous at his exaggeration, but he would not let her keep it. He told her tiredly, "You and Spur and Millicent and Priscilla—sure, I know you don't give a damn about each other. It doesn't take a brain to see that. Your letters—your phone calls—they're like excuses, or something." He slapped his hands to his knees, scattering cigarette ash, at which he brushed furiously. "Well," he said, "if that's all right with you all, then it's none of my beeswax." He grinned at her, angry but asking her to join him somehow; it was as if she were their common enemy, or part of it, and together they would dispatch her, because she was there, and make ineffectual forevermore the part that wasn't there.

"Darling—" she said, and put out a hand to him in the mirror.

"No, let me finish, honey. What I mean is, if our kids can see the *other* side—Erin and Robin"—he made a dogged gesture—"love, in other words, then they won't grow up—" he stopped.

"Like me?" Rhoda said, feeling perfectly empty.

He slipped from the bed and came to her swiftly and took her shoulders in his hands. She waited, disliking the pacifying touch, feeling that disaster could attend or follow it.

"Not you, sweet nut," he said, and pushed his nose to her neat chestnut hair. She thought she heard defeat in his voice and prepared to assail it if he gave her the chance, but she needed the chance. "The others," he said, "the cold ones—the ones who don't know love, or can't take it." He seemed belatedly to sense her emptiness, and as always when distressed, he reverted to word and cadence of his mountain boyhood.

"When is love such a burden, Rho?"

It was not the chance she had hoped for; it was, indeed, a challenge that she could not let go unanswered, because it touched her where neither he nor anyone else had a right to go poking about. Stung, she answered him in a tone that was near-parody of his. "When does love become tyranny, Andrew?"

They remained immobile, their images in the mirror filling the small bright place with mannequins, like an overcrowded show window. She wanted suddenly to be alone with him, away from the mirror-world that exposed them too brightly, where rhetorical questions about love, in which she did not believe, might be expected to be answered unambiguously. In that turnabout place, people who lived in terms of love could never understand her, a person who lived in spite of it—a literal truth. She could never explain to them why she recognized "need" but not "love"; to that unfastidious mass the great virtue of love was that it was supposed to be endlessly proliferous; how could she convince such sentimentalists that the virtue belonged to "need," which could be satisfied, and diminished, and made, eventually, to disappear altogether without harming a soul? Could love do that?

She turned and embraced Andrew's hips, pressing her face into his midriff. "Sorry, kid," he said, and she hoped his flesh did not register the fact of her frown: people were inclined to remember the occasions of their apologies and what she wished was that he should forget. "Don't be silly, love," she said lightly. He turned off the lamps on the dressing table and she put on her nightgown, deciding against offering her body as she had planned to do, not caring to risk the further emphasis of her infrequent need.

They retired and slept, hands touching, until the telephone buzzed. Both telephone and clock were on Rhoda's side of the bed; she thought the buzz came from the clock and raised up and shut it off. They still had twenty minutes, she saw—time enough for Andrew to diminish the need that had colored her dreams too vividly. She turned to him and the buzz came again, the prolonged signal of long-distance. She lifted the receiver, listened, said "Yes" and hung up. She got up from bed and went to the window, pushing aside the Scotch-plaid curtains and looking down at the pruned stumps of her rose bushes, which yielded prize blooms annually. After a while she said "Andy," feeling him awake and waiting. She looked beyond the roses to the lilac tree, the male one that bore no flower, with acute distaste: it was high time it was cut down. "Robin will be home this Christmas."

He got out of bed; she hoped he would not come to her and he did not.

"Was that Robin on the phone?"

"No. Erin. She said Robin was coming, after all. Wake the girls, will you? It's nearly six. Tell them not to take too long in the bathroom. I'll be out in a minute."

At the door he said, puzzled, "Rho?"

"I'll be out in a minute. Put on your slippers. The floor is cold."

Robin would sit at the window when even Tim's was closed to him and look at the city that was like a huge sponge set to rise under a cloth but too loosely covered, so that bugs and rats had gotten in and stuck there like raisins. Staring above and beyond to the stories of buildings that were alternately lighted and dark, seeing or imagining the activities there as if the splotches of chiaroscuro were ink blots in a sanity test, it would come to seem as though the sight were a straticulate cross section of his life in which reality and dream, past and present, could be seen by the merest vertical rolling of the balls of pain which were his eyes. Even so, he fought sleep, for in sleep there was no possible shifting of the eyes, however painful, from bottom to top of dream: dreams exist only in emotional dimensions; they inhabit the sightless nerves as blood permeates cells, as alcohol the brain. Sitting at the window, despite the horrors it gave onto, he managed the limited illusion of freedom of choice —eyes up, eyes down—and would fight sleep dirtily until it threw its black body on him and bore him to the floor.

He sat at the train window, his eyes clinging to it like still-wet ink to a drawing, and fought sleep and discovered within him, suddenly, a feeling of the exhilaration of change and accomplishment, as if what lay beyond, upon the window, were the work of his own hands: *horizontal* motion, side to side animation, a breakthrough! The present erased by speed, the past being left behind, only the changing drawing made by his will on the glass his fleeting reality. Broadly he sketched, or commanded to appear and disappear, the shifting scene, like a maniacal conductor of cartoon animators, but time and again he was brought back to static awareness by the reflected eyes of the watching child. She seemed to him, at first, to be merely an unwanted audience, then his conscience (had not he made her some promise?), then, because she was unchanging, she became the past, the past to which he was flying, for what was his future except the past grown older, wearier, more embedded in the dust of futility? Like a claustrophobe he saw that he was being squeezed between two walls of the past. Downward escape was impossible, for him: he had chosen his method of death, or it had chosen him, or they had made a pact—his father's method, his father's pact; he would be consistent in trying to become his father, even unto death—would Erin understand, when she saw him, that he was keeping allegiance to their vow?

He flung his mind upward, or was flung by it—upward, the route to salvation, hadn't they told him in nameless churches when he was helpless with youth?—ululating, like an owl into the sky. Looking down, sick with apprehension of high flight and a kind of panicked hope, he saw with his great eyes that could be scalded by light: victorious signboards and motels and prison-factories and gasoline stations and Dairy Queens and drive-ins and Joe's Eats and bowling alleys and used car lots and "homesteads" seventy-by-fifty feet bordered with plastic flowers and hedges and artificial grass, and nowhere a single acre of the land to which he had pledged bone and muscle that was not degraded by the passionless lust of the most vulgar people on earth. Being a bird of the dreadful species *omniscient,* he flew into tomorrow and saw the family standing at the graveside armed with frozen clods, and standing with them, swelling the ranks, were the "neighbors," the "friendly dealers," totting up in their heads the bills to be presented for their roles in disposing of old clay (as they had disposed of the rich land, and charged for it).

Hedging—for it had flown into a hole in space and

was held there as if in a vise, the bird extemporized: What faulty planning on the part of some theoretical Deity that the human container was not redeemable at "your local dealer's," as were cola bottles, at a nickel apiece. The commercial cycle would then be unbroken, and the rapid turnover, speeded up by avarice, would stabilize the economy forevermore. And if bodies were redeemable— But, no! Redemption was the one thing that Robin did not want, for him or for his father, for if someone could claim only five pennies for their casings, those coins would be imbued with some of the trust of new-minted things—like children, like brother and sister who believed the myth of family love and unity—and it would begin again, the cycle within the cycle, the rust within the coin (his father the rust, himself one arc in the cycle). He would not wish that on anyone. And you, Father? Would you?

Fighting sight, he saw himself and Erin, the bachelor father, the spinster mother, and heard his father's benediction to their union and their usurpation of his role in life: I was a farmer, once, when the land was mine; when the house that stood on the land was mine; when the children who lived in the house that stood on the land were mine— And coarsely, his question like phlegm hawked and spat at Robin's back: Where have you planted *your* seed? And, finally, the day of the letter, the insinuation that had driven Robin away, or given him the excuse he had been waiting for, the excuse to desert Erin: Why haven't they married? Unnatural— It was then Robin saw his life for what it was: his death, slightly out of focus.

It was Sunday, near his train time. He was running,

falling, imprinting himself on the earth's white, negative skin, flying through the held-out limbs of trees he would not see again to the barn to say good-by to his horse, old and lame, and useless as Robin. He did not know what to do—he was incapable of planning ahead; he knew only that an edge had been reached beyond which was void. He was huddling against the horse's flanks, his face buried in its hide, when Erin found him . . . Does she feel the void? She does not say, but she is troubled; it has been a troubling weekend. Ah, sweet sister, if only you knew what the mailman brings! Yet in her usual fashion she tries to make their parting a sensible one by speaking of small things, necessities, and to comfort him with the mention of pleasures: "Four whole days for Christmas! Now, don't be extravagant. Mama needs nightgowns, but cotton will do—" He takes her by the shoulders and kisses her roughly and runs for the taxi, meeting Mr. Price at the bottom of the rise on which the house stands. And they leave. He leaves. L-E-A-V-E-S.

He is writing her from New York, in an unfamiliar room. He cannot say what he wants except within the parentheses of their old intuition about each other. He has had enough of smalltown and lonesome countryside (dead land, killed by me), of unproductive land; in concrete cities you are not expected to plant (nor wither inside when you cannot); in cities you only reap (stony harvests to burden the overburdened blood). Because he needs to, he imagines her unsuspectingly pegging away at her duties of salvation, rushing from trouble spot to trouble spot, building, rebuilding, reinforcing the structure of family that they have pretended was a fort, not knowing that the others are chipping away at the foundation, doggedly, secretly— He cannot tell her, even now, what he knows about the others, nor the methods they have chosen to undermine her life's work (his, no more). He cannot think about it himself without drinking.

The weight of ugliness and thirst brought the bird to ground, back to the train, back to the Scotch. Robin drank. God, Erin, how can I tell you? How can I say to you my one discovery of life, now that it is closing its door on me, and has closed on him? We must play our given roles in life. We should not take roles not meant for us, for no matter how fine our intentions, eventually we will wake to find that we have deprived another of his reason for living . . . Death can happen before the brain and heart stop.

In his desperation to be in the present, to know the comparative comfort of present pain, he took from his pocket a penknife and plunged it into the fleshy pad of his hand. In the long moment of silence that followed, he saw that the flask had fallen but had wedged safely between his legs. He saw the fortuity as calculated. With cynicism he observed that it outweighed, through the relief it gave him, the only gift of mourning he could ever afford his father, whose place he had taken in life, which was the pain of his still mortal flesh.

The coach rang with screams. Holding out his dripping hand as though it did not belong to him, he looked into the collective eye of the crowd roused by the waking nightmare of the little girl. He stammered a story about his intention to gouge a hangnail—the slipping knife— Mumbling, the crowd dispersed. No one offered help to the wounded, he saw with satisfaction; no bustling Mom took over with clean linen or Band-Aid and bound up the hand of the hurt little boy. He felt their revulsion at sight of him: a bloodshot, spittle-stained, forty-five-year-old man holding out a bloody paw like a trapped animal. Most of them had been rehearsing their lying roles for the yearly performance at the old homestead (seventy-by-fifty feet with plastic trimmings), mouthing and muttering in disappointed sleep that was haunted enough without the tangible specter of their Christmas-Presents and Christmas-Futures staring at them over a wound that, unlike theirs, could be acknowledged.

For the next few minutes the coach filled with rhythmic sounds as pillows were beaten, and Robin, who had once been musical, tapped his foot to the beat, humming an obligato melody, grinning at the child whose mother had again fallen asleep, leaving her alone with Robin. It was not until the rhythm section rested that Robin recognized the tune as "Oh, Tannenbaum."

He sinks into a glade he knows, where firs breathe perpetual eventide; lying there, a young man with his future before him, he plans a Christmas room to be kept the year round, with decorated trees and the crushed bittersweet of needles to carpet the floor, where his children can play. He is hard and vital, but he is tired from work and vigilance, and sleepy. As black sleep comes at him, he reaches out his arms to the child miraculously nearby; in his life, children are always nearby and it is always miraculous. He sees the child's neck muscles swelling as though it would burst into song for him. Sleep falls upon him, heavy as a sandbag, but wearing, oddly, the face of a friend. Because it wears Handy's face, Robin meets it halfway, taking the thrust as if it were love's own.

He slipped down into the seat and his head, askew on its pedestal, seemed, to the child across the aisle, to be tucked under his arm.

SPUR

Spur put the phone back in its cradle, leaned across the bed to his sleeping wife and pushed the plug from her ear by gentle pressure on the back of the exposed shell, and kissed the lobe, murmuring, "Wake up, gal," and when she opened her eyes, smiling, he said, "We've gotta start for the farm. Dad's dead."

"Goddamn it, Spur!" she said, and the tears sprang from her eyes with such force that Spur's face, a couple of inches from hers, was wetted. She hugged him and then sat up and threw her legs over the edge of the bed, feeling about with her feet for her slippers. "Coffee in a minute," she said, pulling on a robe and starting for the door. At the door she turned. "Shall I wake the boys?" Her tone was brisk, though the tears were pouring freely down her cheeks.

"I'll do it," Spur said. "You put on the coffee and start packing."

"Goddamn it," Bonny said, and again, "God*damn* it, Spur," and left the room.

Spur (the nickname was double-barreled; not only was the sound part of his name, but he was hell on a horse) sat on the edge of the bed and held his head briefly in his hands. Telephones always rang for Spur with great news: "It's another boy!" "Congratulations, old man. The Board of Directors has decided—" And yet—

To begin with, Spur is beautiful. There is no extrinsic material about him, no extra layer of fat for Time to feed upon, so that the lines in his face are as hard as the lines in etchings. He is an important executive in one of the largest aircraft companies in the world; perhaps this responsibility explains why he cannot sleep without the aid of pills, must have pills to wake him up and sustain him. The pills, eating from inside, will eventually meet Time's exterior furrows and then, who knows, Spur may fall into a hundred ivory ribbons no wider than the space between one furrow and the next. He has countless fears and perhaps this is one of them; if it is, he keeps it, as he does the others, to himself. But when he walks into a room it is with the tentative air of someone walking into the dark. Despite the phones that have always rung out glad tidings, despite his success at everything he has put his mind and body to (within practical memory), including bronc-busting and son-begetting.

They had not planned to go to the farm for Christmas; their own tree, a miracle of Neiman-Marcus whimsy, stood in the sunken living room near the fountain that could spurt champagne on occasion. But they had planned to fly down later in the week for a couple of days of shooting. Under the tree was the gift he had gotten for his father: the best, most high-powered rifle that money could buy. The old man would have liked it, even though he was a lousy shot.

Spur shook his head as though a branch had caught on his hat in the woods where the game scuttled. He was tempted to call the operator back and check on the origin of the call, but then, cracked-bell loud, he heard in his ear his sister's dry voice tolling bad news; it was too familiar to be anything but real.

He went into the bathroom with the double everything—two sinks, two johns, the tub that was really a pool with two submerged hard-sponge couches—and splashed his face with cold water. He groped for a towel, dried himself, and was about to look into the mirror when he remembered that he was supposed to resemble his father. Turning away, he started for the boys' room. They'd take it hard. They'd been damn fond of Pops, as they called him, thought he was a character, bragged about him to their friends. Recently Spur had hinted to them (they were thirteen and eleven, old enough for such man-talk) that Pops had been something of a devil with the dames. They'd liked that, and he had been relieved. He wanted them to love everything about his dad; and too, just in case he ever stepped out on Bonny—and who could tell? —and they found out about it, there wouldn't be all that caterwauling that went on in the play they'd seen in Dallas, *Death of a Salesman.* That play, he had told them on the way home, wasn't true to life. Men didn't give a damn about those things. He'd had to reassure them of this over Bonny's sniffling. She had cried all through the thing, embarrassing him and the boys, and hadn't been able to go out at intermission. Of course, she was a high-brow, anyway, compared to him, and probably the play had things in it, symbols and stuff, that hadn't gotten through to him and the boys. (He saw himself and the boys as composing a solid front, a literal picture of combined resistance, and took comfort from it.) But after all, he had married her because she combined beauty and a feeling for animal sex with this other ability to talk about foreign writers, listen to music that made him nervous, and keep up to date on just about everything—politics, the latest discoveries in medicine. She had been working on an M.D. when they met, and it took a lot of persuasion to make her give it up. Naturally, she had never regretted it.

He found his train of thought again: the time he had discovered that his dad was stepping out. He had thought it was funny; it was just one big fucking—ha ha—joke to him. He'd lie awake at night and chuckle about it (other things too), thinking about his old man putting it to half the dames in the county. He was about twelve at the time, somewhere between Tom's and Buck's ages; irrelevantly, he thought: That's when my insomnia started; then: it was *his* fault. He kept coming in my room to see if I was sleeping, like a goddamn mother hen. Me twelve years old, and him checking on my sleep . . . For a moment Robin and his father had been one man. He connected the thoughts and separated the men, for his father's sake: Robin didn't think it was funny about the old man. Looked like suffering Jesus, to tell the truth, which made it even funnier. He never did have much humor; neither one of them did—he or Erin.

Spur leaned against the wall and thought about Robin. They would be seeing each other for the first time in three years—a little over. Spur hoped, with fervor almost childlike, that New York had changed Robin so much that none of them would be able to recognize him. It seemed terribly important somehow, though he could not—did not try to—analyze it. He hadn't thought about his brother since he had beat it to New York. Well, that was not precisely so. Whenever they went down to the farm they'd talk about him—couldn't very well help it with Erin there. She'd get you cornered, and look out! It was Robin this and Robin that, just as if he was going to walk right in the door, just as if he'd never gotten away at all.

He started down the hall again, toward the bedroom his sons shared. They had a whole suite of their own, including a gym, but they slept in the same room for companionship. They were close, those two, equals in everything. Buck never lorded it over Tom just because he was two years older, the way some kids did—the way Robin had done with him. Then he thought, trying to be fair on this sad day: It's not the same. Robin was ten years older—is ten years older. (The past tense kept creeping in, but what he knew of Robin lay in the past, only partly sticking up into the present, like an old half-buried plowshare in a fallow field. The top part was rusted; to find out how the bottom part had weathered, you would have to yank the thing from the ground. He would never have done it voluntarily, but his father's death made it pretty likely that he would have to look, now). Thinking of half-buried things, his mind turned back to his father. "Why am I thinking about Robin—it's Dad who's dead," and shaking his head over the unfamiliar, he walked into his sons' bedroom and looked at them sprawled out in sleep, innocent and tough, and all at once real fear came into some region of his chest as he looked from one to the other and wondered how they would take the news of his own death.

Some of that fear rode his back when he woke them and told them; they felt his fear and took the news hard and he felt relieved. If they'd do that for a grandfather, then he had nothing to fear. With a self-knowledge long dormant he remembered that he used to be frightened by the thought of not being missed, somewhere, by someone; and that this was why he had been thinking of Robin so concentratedly, because Robin had never been missed—not by him, or Priscilla or Rhoda or Millicent. Only by Erin, who had, after all, missed life.

Bonny came to the door and smiled reassuringly at the boys. "Brekfuss, ev' bidy," she said, like the maid, and though the joking tone was subdued, there was a feeling of strength in the room and Spur felt that it had been handled well. Tom said he guessed he shouldn't take his rifle, should he? And what with one thing and another—eating, packing, dressing, calling the field to tell Bob to get his plane ready—two or three hours passed without any more uncomfortable thoughts, and by the time they were in the car driving to the private airfield, they were all back to normal, considering the circumstances.

Spur felt strong and confident at the wheel of the Caddy, as he knew he would feel flying the Bonanza. He was in command again, so that when Tom said, "Will Momma and Aunt Erin come to live with us?" and Buck said, "Hell, no. They'd freeze to death. Remember how they slept under 'lectric blankets in July, cause the air-conditioning was too cold?" Spur brought him up short and said there'd be none of that. Solemnly, feeling the weight of his role, he told them, "A way of life has gone, boys. Pops was the last of his kind. A fine man of the old school; remember that," and the boys nodded, seeing a way of life passing above them and gone like a flock of wild geese. Spur wanted to say something more, something they would remember always, but he could not think of anything and so he repeated, "A way of life, boys. Gone. Remember that."

When they reached the airfield and walked out to the plane, Bob was still tuning her up, and Spur waved aside his apologies and took his condolences for the whole family.

Clark put their luggage aboard and Spur stood looking up at the sky with some anxiety. Weather reports from down home weren't good and the sky here was plain nasty-looking. Bonny came up and stood beside him. He glanced at her and saw that she looked anxious, too. He patted her arm reassuringly, and then she said, "Oh, I do hope Priscilla doesn't have hysterics," and Spur realized that she had been thinking about people's reactions as usual and hadn't given a thought to the weather. She certainly had taken the family to heart when she married him, worrying about Priscilla's head and his mother's arthritis—things like that. He guessed she couldn't help thinking like a doctor after her medical training. He patted her arm perfunctorily, his interest strayed.

Bob jumped down and gave him the sign. He shooed the others in, and the boys were so exuberant that Bonny spoke to them sharply, something she almost never did. Settling into the pilot's seat, Spur once again felt the tightening in his chest that he had felt standing in the room looking down at his sleeping sons. He had been gratified by their genuine display of grief at the news of death, taking it as a sign that they would properly grieve for him when the time came. And yet now when they were actually getting under way, when the meaning of their early start should be even more with them, they were horsing around as if it were a holiday.

He gave his full attention to getting the plane off the ground and on course; once on course, hearing the laughter from in back, his thoughts were forced, like the plane, once more into the lane apparently worked out for them by some complicated set of instruments. Self-knowledge smote him a numbing blow, making him admit, by shock tactics, the truth: that not only did he want his sons to grieve for him and for his father; he wanted them to grieve *for* him. Do his grieving for him, because he could feel none.

His stomach lurched as the plane caught an air pocket and bounced like a ball. He was sick at the idea of being stuck with himself and his thoughts for however long it took them to fly through the bitchy weather and make some kind of landing at that empty lot they called an airport in Roseville. If the plane had not contained the only people on earth he gave his concern to, he would have pointed her nose-down and thrown his head back and howled like a rocket all the way down through the livid air . . . Frightened by his impulse into making an earnest search, he found what he thought was the reason for his extreme reaction.

When he was a kid with insomnia he had played a game with himself that he had called "Pushing." It was a variation on medieval jousting; lying in the dark, feeling cowardly, he would summon every conceivable specter that might destroy him, beckoning them on toward his bed, the grisly horde of them, telling them that he was defenseless, to come and get him. He would lie quiescent, muscles and nerves relaxed, feeling the weight of that company pressing against the walls of the room. And then, at the last possible moment, from somewhere inside him, some center of self, of massed and concentrated ego, he would *push.* The effort was so mighty that once or twice he had blacked out, triumphantly, the knight fainting on the field with the dead strewn around him. For all their horror, they had been manageable because he had invented them: the dragons, the giant pythons, the mountain lions, the grinning things that sat in the cellar by day; but there was one phenomenon—not a ghost or beast, but a prodigy—that had shown up when he was about fifteen, against which his "pushing" was powerless. It was a ring of white light, like an angel's halo, which at first hovered over his bed and then *went* like a blown-out candle. He had tried to trace its source to some metal object that reflected moonlight, without success. Gradually curiosity gave way to fear and one night it came to him what the ring could do: it could encircle his body, and pass his body through it, and when it floated away there would be nobody left on the bed, not a trace of Spur, and no memory of him in the house. It would not be death. It would be nothingness, and it was not possible for him to push against nothingness. His lack of grief for his father was a nothingness. He would not push against it.

His head was splitting and he panicked for a second at the thought of migraine coming on. He yelled back to Bonny, "Aspirin!" and in two seconds flat he was swallowing a couple of pills, washing them down with brandy. He laughed, looking at the thickly falling snow. If somebody had managed to break a leg sitting in the plane, Bonny would calmly pull a splint out from somewhere and set the bone.

Spur turned to look at his wife, his face lit by hope. *He* couldn't push against the nonexistent, but she could! He yelled, "I love you, Bonny-blue-eyes!" and she blew him a kiss which he threw back to her gustily before he turned eyes front again.

Bonny gazed at Spur's head, thinking that grief could also bring exaltation. If only that could be the keynote for all of them during the next few days! She tried to recall if anyone in the family believed in the hereafter, other than the mother. One person, other than the mother, would do, to set the tone; their great diversity as persons, which made them often seem not to be kin, coupled with a sense of loss and possible guilt, might be the very reason why they would be willing to act as a family in the days ahead, taking their lead from whoever proposed leadership, although plain grief might be easier for them, in concert, than joy with mystical indications. The tinge of irony to her thoughts was not pleasing to her; she supposed it was her *own* reaction to shock, as opposed to her reaction as part of Spur to the news of death. She went back to the thought of exaltation as a keynote, seeing herself running in to where the family waited, shouting *sursum corda* or some other slogan, taking them by surprise but planting the seed. Actually, though one could never predict such things in advance, the only one for whom she felt real concern was Priscilla. Rhoda would be sensible and helpful. Millicent, at very worst, could be flippant at the wrong times. Robin and Erin—all sense of irony left her at the thought of them, and a feeling like physical hunger that could only be assuaged by them came over her. Dear Erin. Dear Robin . . . She would keep her mother-in-law heavily sedated through the ordeal. Only Priscilla—

Focusing her eyes from the lax, half-crossed, abstracted look people get when gazing across inner distance, she found that her point of concentration was the back of her husband's head. Deliberately she made her mind go blank.

ERIN

It was past seven o'clock on Christmas Eve morning when Erin left the telephone at which she had been seated since the small hours, sending the brief message to her brothers and sisters, to her father's two sisters to whom she had entrusted, somewhat dubiously, the task of furthering the alarm to relatives less close, and to the local undertaker, who was due to arrive at any moment to take her father away for drainage and a spurious sort of reclamation as though he were a piece of swampland. Who would be comforted by this, really, she thought with impatience. The rot was there, underneath the temporary paint job. Of course she knew the answer, and gave it, as she always did, scrupulously arguing both sides of a question. It would comfort her father's elderly sisters, who had begun praying into the telephone at the news, to be able to say, "He looks like he is asleep"; it would comfort friends and acquaintances in the town, and the distant relatives, and possibly most of all, the undertaker whose professional pride was involved.

She had not been able to reach Millicent in Ohio. This frustration was in part responsible for her dawn debate with herself. The telephone had rung and rung and had finally been picked up by an answering service, a curt, impersonal woman who remained so after the message had been given, thereby earning Erin's gratitude. There was enough deception on the way, with members of the family, without total strangers pretending to something they could not possibly feel.

Now Erin stood at the window and looked down the slope of the lawn where snow slid like a young glacier to feed the not yet frozen brook, which ran, an antique mirror, through the whitened and bone-bare trees, past the barn and away, sluggish quicksilver, doomed to reflect whatever passed above it but blessed with a short memory.

Whatever self-conscious poetry there is in this image of the brook, it is Erin's, for this is what she thinks as she stands at the window of a room her father had called "the morning room" (he lies separated from her by a pair of red velvet curtains, in the bed in which he died at three A.M. of a cerebral hemorrhage), and for once the words do not seem pretentious: it is morning, and someone stands at the window to testify to the fact and give to the words and the room function and meaning. As children, Erin's younger brother and conspiratorial sisters had giggled, bent to their homework beneath the lamplight in this room, and mouthed to each other the words "morning room," after they had exhausted the comic possibilities of their father's red velvet smoking jacket—he did not smoke—and the faded work trousers on the long elegant legs, and the feet shod in petit-point slippers worked in a design of violets and roses.

Erin has often stood in this room alone, at odd hours dramatic and peaceful, and thought poetically and metaphorically about the brook, and the barn at which it appears to stop does not obstruct for her its further meanderings; she sees clearly, with the eyes of a love profound and mystical, its passage through the small wood and out into the open meadow. There is one favorite stretch where it runs exactly level with the grass, even a bit above it (to the observer standing slightly apart, or the romantic—and Erin is something of both), like a wide satin ribbon laid whimsically there for the wind to ruffle, to astound the cows. She sees this and more, as if the room were a camera obscura, but the instrument is either defective or magical because, through the falling snow and the darkish morning, she looks for a moment into summer. It is vitally necessary for her to travel this curve of time back to her twentieth summer of life, to stand in the meadow with Robin and feel on the back of her neck the healing heat of the sun. The present pain in her neck, the stiffness, grows from the seed of fatigue planted in the base of her spine, fatigue springing, paradoxically, from the very strength of her will, which has informed her flatly that she will not be tired in the days to come, so that her unbending spine, symbol of tensibility, has almost beaten itself at its own game. Therefore, in this moment when another person would have applied the therapy of hot-water bottle, heating pad or sleep, Erin applies memory.

It is a memory that she has used over and over again, especially in the past three years, but with such care, adding nothing to it or taking anything away, that it has never become soiled through handling.

She stands once again with her brother Robin beside the brook in the meadow. It is slightly past noon. Dinner has been eaten, dishes washed, and father, mother and young children are napping on quilts spread beneath the oaks and firs on the lawn. In the meadow bees sit on the clover, devoted but drowsy Royalists, and the birds are quiet. Erin holds a pail which she intends to fill with berries, later on to be served with clotted cream or made into jam. She wears a cotton dress the color of the rising sun, a gypsy dress. She has taken off her shoes and she sweeps the surface of the water with the toes of one foot like a little brown broom. Robin, his sun-bleached cowlick standing up from the circular font of his hair with such rebellious vitality that it expresses his eighteen-year-old self exactly, has his arms about the neck of his horse, and their mutual, playful nuzzling and the sun on Erin's hair and neck give her, more than anything else could, a feeling of certainty that God walks on His earth, and that His most favorite hour is slightly past noon of a summer's day, when the children are sleeping.

It is possibly the first and last moment of her life in which God is directly involved as anything other than an abstraction, and even this moment is not entirely His. She has merely a sense of His presence, and a vague feeling of Trinity: the sleeping family beneath the trees, the sun, and God walking His meadow. And she and Robin are the line drawn around them all.

She has never performed an extravagant act in her life, and she does not do so now, but for a moment she is filled with such love that it is like fire and she almost throws herself into the brook, not to quench the fire, but to make it audible—to hear its sizzle.

The snow swirls up, but for a fraction of a moment longer her summer self, returning from the meadow, looks in at her winter self, and then they are reunited and she stands once more at the window of the morning room in the house in which she was born and in which she is reconciled to dying.

The house is old, verging on the ramshackle. ("Disrepair" is a genteel local euphemism which she avoids. When she speaks of the house she uses the word "ramshackle.") But in spite of the wind that comes in gusts, making her think of a giant being revived by artificial respiration, nothing about the house creaks or bangs or shudders. It sits on its rise of ground with dignity, amid oaks and firs and sundial shapes of canna beds, and it and the woman at the window have much in common: they are both receptacles of years, of events, emotions and ghosts. Containing, they are contained.

Erin turns into the room and thinks: The taxi. We'll need the taxi all day long, and once again she goes to the telephone and waits for the dozing operator to arouse herself from dreams of God knows what, certainly not the sound of bells, and says to her, "Lulu, please ring Mr. Price for me. I know it's early, but it can't be helped"; and reaching Mr. Price of the taxi company—another euphemism; there is only one taxi —says to him, "Mr. Price, I want you to refuse any other customers until the family are all safely out here. Meet the train and the buses. I don't know how they're coming or when, except for Jasper, who will be flying his own plane. He will have to be fetched from the airfield. Perhaps if this is too much for you, you might be good enough to enlist the aid of friends of Father's with automobiles of their own. Thank you, Mr. Price. No, he didn't suffer. Yes, it would be a blessing if we all could go that way"; hangs up and thinks with pure passion: I hope I burn to death.

With the image of fire before her she walks through the room where her father lies and out to the kitchen. With no thought about why she does so, she walks past the electric stove and goes to the old iron range, unused for years, and goes through the motions of shaking down ashes that do not exist except as ghosts of wood, and with crumpled and dampened newspaper and one match she starts a blaze. She brings in firewood from the back porch, and when the fire is ravenous enough she feeds it, one stick at a time, adjusts the dampers, fills the water tank at the side, and in these gestures of her girlhood she finds something that is too fierce to be comfort, too old to be peace.

The kitchen in which Erin, forty-seven years old last August, moved, was not untypical of other kitchens in that rural section of that southern border state. It was a long low room; down its middle ran a table big enough to seat ten people, four to a side, one at each end; the table was always laid with plates turned face-downward, and with water glasses, spoon holders, jam stands, one at each end, of identical cut glass, and salt and pepper shakers. There was no cloth, and the scrubbed boards were white and hollowed, the hollows deeper in some places than others, so that each plate rested in its own slight declivity, telling of the collaboration between gravy and strong soap and scrub brush.

The iron range, whose pipes were beginning to roar, faced, across the narrow room, its electric descendant, impressive with such appurtenances as timing devices, heat gauges and whatnot. Beneath a stainless-steel sink—spray hose with brush attachment, garbage-disposal unit built in—was an old corrugated zinc slop bucket, and at one end of the sink, seeming to grow rustily from the rotting wood of its platform, was a little iron kitchen pump that once on frosty mornings needed to be primed with a warm drink before it gave back its gift of sweet, soft cistern water.

On open shelves beside the stove (the spotless Westinghouse one), House of Herbs spices with fancy labels sat beside little jars of hand-picked thyme and sage and mint whose curled leaves were still redolent of the sun.

All of these things and others: electric coffee maker, pop-up toaster—shiny things that were labor-saving to the extent that they were apparently self-polishing—all had been purchased at heaven knew what sacrifice of personal needs by Robin after he had left the farm to work in a nearby town, before he went to New York

City to live. They had been gifts to her, to lighten the burden of her daily work—hers alone, for their arthritic mother could not plug in the toaster—but she would have exchanged them all and more, in the past three years, for one letter, one visit. How terribly ironic that the needs of the living could be ignored by the most tender-hearted, she thought, while the unneeding dead could effect miracles. The dead resurrecting the living.

The others had continued to make periodic visits; Rhoda, Jasper and their families were the most constant—Rhoda and Andrew and the girls once a year, Jasper, Bonny and the boys twice, though their summer visits were generally a stopping-off on the way back from vacations in Nova Scotia or the Gaspé Peninsula, wherever the fishing was reported most fruitful. The boys brought her and her mother souvenirs, usually chipped, of historic landmarks or lighthouses; Bonny brought them lovely woollens, and Jasper brought cases of wine to their father, purchased at heaven knew what prices in those northern climes. Of course, he could afford it. He was, by local standards, quite rich and (therefore?) a reason for pride in aunts, especially, and paternal cousins. "Three vacations a year!" Aunt Tonia would say triumphantly, to anyone who would listen. "Spring, summer and winter! Imagine!" Millicent came less frequently—once in two years was her average—and always unexpectedly. She would show up and leave with the same abruptness, unable to tolerate boredom, but one never knew what Millicent might find boring. This, as her visits were, was always a matter for conjecture. Erin found her stimulating, though she knew the feeling was not returned.

Putting out piles of plates and pots, she told herself, "But wait. You are getting ahead of yourself. Hoard your wounds, maiden lady," and her smile was a touch dour.

Priscilla—she continued, as though describing her family to a stranger, which she would never have done —comes always alone, always in the fall of the year. She wanders, her hair floating Ophelia-like on the brumous air, and sometimes she sits for hours beneath a particular tree on the brown grass. She is here and not here, and that is no dried-up old spinster's fancy. One time, to my certain knowledge, Priscilla felt what it was to *be,* and though it was horrible for her, and for others, I was hopeful. In her childhood she strove to break through to the world by using cruelty, certainly a time-honored device, but until Edgar's affair with the waitress, I don't believe she had ever *received* cruelty, or what she imagined to be. If only Edgar hadn't placated her by dissolving himself; if only we hadn't given her the greater cruelty of indulgence. She might then have brought to us what should have been hers to bring: a woman of fire and anger and the fierce hunger for motherhood that was, is, latently hers— she would never have been, even whole, a placid woman. Instead, because of our lack of understanding, she seems to me to be a frail carrying case of brittle bones and flesh that holds nothing, least of all herself.

Erin ran water over the copper pot she was polishing, held it up and looked at her watery yellow reflection in its bottom, confiding to it with a relish compounded of bitterness and malice, "That was after our apostasy, unacknowledged, following their tergiversation, ditto." She laughed, banging the pan onto the drainboard, and set out frozen meat to thaw, thinking that she could hardly accuse the others of turning their backs on a cause they had never espoused. Whenever they came, bearing gifts, they brought, also, impatience for their mother and for Erin pity and thin contempt: Anachronistic Erin, needles clicking as she knit up the raveled sleave of family; unknowing Erin, thinking, or so they imagined, their laughter to be kindly; pathetic Erin, who sang "Annie Laurie" and other plaints after supper while the children listened wide-eyed and asked for more, and brother and sisters stifled smiles and yawns. It had been anachronistic, unknowing, pathetic Robin, too, until he uprooted himself and left and stopped writing to any of them. Erin wondered if they accorded him the secret grace of their approval then, not caring a whit what his life was, how he ate, loved or hated those about him, how he dreamed; approval only because he, like them, had gotten away.

For a number of years—too many to hurt herself with counting—she had known how she and Robin were despised. Until his departure, she had tried to protect Robin from the knowledge. And then when he left so abruptly, she was certain that he had found out, just as she was certain that it must never, if there was any way on earth to prevent it, be spoken of between them, for as long as he had his secret, however he chose to celebrate its possession in that far-off place, he was a man with a hold on life and could die, when the time came, knowing himself to be no pauper. Wounds were hoardable, too, and could afford something approximating satisfaction when counted in solitude.

Her father had died with secrets he thought himself alone to possess, so that if he had had last thoughts—she did not know if a bleeding brain could think beyond the color red—they would have been of those valuables he carried with him to the grave, and he would have felt triumph. Because even guilt, when it is one's last possession, can be beyond price. She imagined the soul crying into the void, "I made it—it is mine—let me have it," reduced to a childlike clinging to something of *one's very own* upon leaving the house where it had lived for so long, as time was measured by soul or child. That was why deathbed confessions appalled her. Before breath had left the body, the soul, feeling the stripping words like fingers, must flee, howling, bereft.

No, she and Robin must allow each other his silence, and the others theirs. When the day came when she ceased her "meddling" entirely, no one would notice, as they had not noticed her slacking off in the years past. Or if they did notice, they would attribute it to old age, an enforced retirement due to extenuating circumstances, and they might speak kindly of her then—as if she gave a damn.

She felt uncomfortably warm and turned to the stove, whose pipes were glowing red, and adjusted the dampers; the old house was tinder, that was why Robin had bought the electric stove for her. There was a sound from above—had her mother moved about in her swaddling of hot-water bottles, blankets and sedatives, muttering of the loss of something she had never really had? No, it was only the house, which, like Erin, had allowed itself a moment of giving-way to the elements, perhaps identical to her own—feeling the weight of snow and ice, heavy as her bitterness, and the blasts of wind like her thoughts from which there was no refuge; perhaps the old roof had spoken to the cellar: I hope we burn to death.

Erin went into the pantry, once the creamery, now a storage place and laundry room with G.E. washer-dryer, and rummaged about until she found an old enamel coffee pot, capacity twenty-five cups, a relic of days when there were farm hands to be fed breakfast and midday dinner six days a week during the seasons of planting and harvesting. She washed the pot, polishing it inside and out, and mixed in it water, eggs and coffee, over which she poured boiling water in the proper amount to make a strong brew, and put the pot on to boil. This done, she pulled out a chair from the table to sit down and think about the design of her day, which she would visualize, frivolous or not, as a croquet game with its wickets and obstacles and strategies, but now, standing at the table, one hand on the back of the chair, she heard the wheels of a vehicle spinning on the icy driveway with its uphill approach.

"That will be the hearse," she said aloud, for courage, "or whatever they carry them away in." Them. Not him. The doorbell rang and still she stood, unmoving. Was her desire to be strong responsible for such impersonality? When she had thought about him a moment ago, it had been only of his guilt. She tried to remember him laughing and carefree but she could not. And now they were going to carry him away for good.

She ran into the room where he lay and looked at him with wild eyes, crying aloud over the gentle tolling of the door, "My God, am I going to be the one? My God, am *I* going to be the one?" Whoever was at the door began to knock, thinking the bell to be broken. Erin looked at her father's face and at the clenched hands and rigid arms lying outside the cover as she had left them, because he would be covered over soon enough. Her throat ached as she said, "Your arms held me when I was a baby. I hope you knew that I could tell it was you, even then."

The knocking at the door grew more insistent. Lifting her head high to push the ache in her throat downward, she walked through the morning room and into the hallway. Beyond the door she heard the stamping of impatient feet on the snowy steps and the gloved slap of living hands warming living arms. She opened the door, asking silently that they be businesslike and swift, and they were. When they went from the house with the body she told them good-by, but in a moment, before she had gone more than a few steps, there was again a knocking at the door. She opened it to the youngest of the men, who said to her respectfully, "Burial clothes, Miss Erin. Everything—you know, underwear, socks, shoes—everything."

She nodded and went into the empty room where her father had lived and slept since gout had made the stairs too difficult to manage. Opening the wardrobe, the first article of clothing she saw was the frayed red smoking jacket and on the floor beneath it, dusty and sagging, the petit-point slippers. She wished that she had the courage of her maudlin impulse to give them to the young man, saying, "Here. These *are* my father."

She found what the young man asked for, but when she took her father's best suit down she saw that it was badly wrinkled. She asked him if he could wait until she pressed it. He said, "My mom can do that, Miss Erin. You'll have your hands full," and because he was young and it was Christmas Eve and he should have been at home by the fire with his family, but instead, when he got home (she hoped he would not have to assist at the embalming), he would be carrying his busy mother a dead man's suit to iron, the tears rolled down her face but the ache went from her throat. She nodded her thanks, not sure of her voice until they reached the outer door, when she asked him, with a slight quaver, how long it would be before the family could see her father.

"We'll work fast, Miss Erin." So this child was an embalmer. "Lemme see—cerebral hemorrhage—oughta take seven, eight hours—" Checking his watch, "It's quarter after eight now." He called softly to one of the men engaged in closing the back of the battered vehicle, "Hey, Plez, what time you figger the fam'ly can start comin by?" Plez answered, " 'Bout five. Any time after five this evenin, miss," and climbed into the front seat. Erin and the young man said good-by again and this time she watched them down the incline and until they disappeared beyond the trees, driving slowly.

When she reentered the hall her mother stood halfway down the stairs in her billowing nightgown, which had miniature raised tufts from neck to waist where she had restlessly plucked and twisted the material, an act made doubly hurtful when Erin considered the arthritic fingers that had performed it. But the hurt which could have gotten out of hand at that moment was leavened by the comic side of the pathetic. Her mother wore a mushroom-shaped cap, as she always had because her mother and her mother's mother had done so as protection against the morbid night air (Erin could remember when the caps were entwined with ribbons and edged with lace, but that was long ago); the cap was askew, the angle rakish; the unkindly funny tilt of of the cap, and the fact that her mother had left her teeth upstairs in their glass of water, so that her nose and chin almost met, gave her the look of a caricature by Cruikshank, all she lacked was a candlestick. She stood looking at Erin vaguely. Erin thought, with an effort to be dispassionate, that to describe her mother's eyes as lackluster would be merely to say what they had been for thirty years or over.

The widow took a couple of steps down, letting her forearm slide along the banister. "I heard the racket. I watched out the windah and saw them take Murdoch away." She spoke clearly enough, although it seemed to Erin that she paused because she expected a refutation.

Erin said, "Yes, Mama," and walked to the foot of the stairs and waited tensely in case her mother should topple, but the sixty-three-year-old woman came down the steps with dignity unusual to her, and only when she stood beside her daughter did she put out an arm for help. The two women walked through the morning room and the death room, neither of them glancing at the empty bed, and entered the kitchen to have their coffee. When they were seated at the table and the mother had taken her first sip of coffee by bending over and drinking from the unlifted cup with a little slurping sound, she raised her head and said, with a firmness that took Erin by surprise, as did the color heightening to liveliness in her cheeks, "We'll need to be specially considerate of Editha and Antonia. He was their lone brother." Antonia, at least, had been the widow's lifelong antagonist, often critical to the point of open enmity. Erin rested her face on her hand and gazed at her mother, thinking: It has begun.

When Andrew left the room to wake the girls, Rhoda let the curtain fall back into place by dropping her hand. That was her only move. Standing eye to eye with the plaid she had bought because she thought it was masculine and did not wish to subject Andrew to a frilly bedroom—standing so close to the pattern that it was like looking deeply into a pair of plaid eyes, she found the idea of plaid eyes strangely attractive. She could have it done with contact lenses—BE THE FIRST IN YOUR NEIGHBORHOOD—BLINDNESS ABSOLUTELY GUARANTEED—It would be, before blessed un-sight set in, like having your eyes propped open with a latticework of toothpicks, the colored cocktail kind, or dyed straws—they served drinks through those, daiquiris and rum things. Bill had liked rum. Bill was a rummy. Bill is a rummy, wherever he is. Daddy was a rummy, too. Daddy is— I lost last night at cards, seventy-five dollars. That seventy-five bucks would have bought one hell of a wreath. Splashy, bad taste, appropriate (who for, Bill or Daddy). I'll take some of my roses. Fool. Dead of winter. Lilacs, then. Double fool. It never did bloom. If male lilac trees' not blooming doesn't prove anything else, it proves that female lilac trees are of some use in this world, if you like lavender blooms with an elegaic scent. Like old ladies' clothes. Like Aunt Edie's —lavender dress, lavender hat, lavender shoes, lavender stockings, lavender gloves that buttoned a half-mile up her arm. Little mother-of-pearl buttons that she wore to my graduation. I was ashamed of her because she wore lavender stockings and had dyed her hair purple. I'd never seen purple hair before. Now I never see anything but. Aunt Edie didn't walk. She sashayed. As absurd as the debutante slouch would be today. She gave me a diary for graduation—a ten-cent-store diary, and I wrote in it that very night: I, Rhoda M., being of sound mind, do hereby depone that I will marry a rich man and have rich children and never have to see any of my family again. That was high-school graduation. Aunt Edie didn't come to my college graduation—one diary is enough for a plain girl—and neither did anybody else because I wrote them that I had flunked out. So Robin and Erin were there the next day to comfort me and take me home. I wriggled out of the lie by saying I knew they would spend money they couldn't afford on presents, that never in their wildest would they have done otherwise. They behaved beautifully—when didn't they?—so the triumph was theirs, after all. All the triumphs, including Bill, because I had to introduce them and they took us both back to the farm. God knows I invented reasons for not going, about a million reasons, but Bill wanted to, so we went. He was so animated, so goddamned boyish, so gee-whiz and gosh and back-to-the-soil. I couldn't warn him *how* soiled—I thought he'd see for himself—all those old-fashioned things and people, fossils—Aunt Edie, Aunt Tonia; no, you could hardly call Tonia a fossil, having to sit on two chairs and then lapping over each side like a flabby sofa cushion on a baby's stool. I was so chagrined when he liked it. *Liked* it. Hell, he loved it so much we had to be married there on the lawn with the farm hands and washerwomen, black and white and clay-colored, and every last sixteenth cousin, all of them carrying on like Peasant Week. The opposite of what I wanted. No, opposite isn't strong enough. Nothing is. There is no word—are no words: Robin as best man, Erin and Millicent as bridesmaids, Priscilla my flower girl. She refused to carry the flowers she was given. She gathered her own. I don't know what else she scattered before us, but I did see something that looked like deadly nightshade and stepped on it deliberately. It was all ruined anyway. That awful shivaree at four in the morning. Everybody crawling on the roof, blowing horns and beating pans, staring in the window, hanging upside down. They thought I cried for joy. How could they know I would have shot them down like weasels. Suppose Bill and I had been—but he was too drunk on our wedding night. Thanks for that, rummy. Thanks for putting off tearing my guts out *that* night, though I might as well have screamed there at the farm, where I would have liked screaming, rather than later, when I didn't like it, couldn't help it, couldn't stop it. Police! I thought he was murdering me. Nothing had prepared—nobody had prepared—me. I told him, I said: There was so much of it all around when I was little, and then not so little—sounds in the night, cheating on each other, tapping on doors, so furtive and slimy that I had to block it or go nuts. Even my major in school, I told him, mathematics, so cool and balanced—but he wouldn't understand. So I tried. I took exercises for him; we worked at it together, hours and hours of "preliminaries," exactly like two animals in a field, trotting around and around. Nothing worked. I told him: Once in a while, then I can endure it. But no. *All the time.* No "preliminaries," then; jump, gallop, scream. I got pregnant just to keep him off. But afterward. It was worse. Of course I knew when he started drinking heavily. People in his profession—lunches and things. But then he began coming home earlier and earlier, and then he wasn't going to the office at all, was staying home all day, as if he thought my watching him go to pieces could change things. It was hopeless. Even Robin and Erin couldn't do a damn thing. At least I managed my divorce alone. I picked Andy out by myself and took his virginity and married him by myself. I'm indebted only to gossip—Jenny's husband saying, new man at the plant, "built like a calf"—how she laughed, telling me. The long road to my happiness is paved with dirty laughs. But here's the point, Rhoda McChesney Laughton Pritchett,

Phoenix-lady: *You made it. You made it by yourself, and it's yours, and you don't have to share it with anybody. You're home-free, laughing your doggone head off.*

And then she thought: Mother was at the wedding; gray silk with a brooch. Like a dressed-up mouse. Daddy gave me away. Now he's dead. We won't have to go to the farm any more.

And then she thought: It was *Bill* who loved the farm. It's *Erin* my husband loves. This death will make them closer. Trips to the farm all year now. I'll never get away.

She stared at the plaid curtains with loathing, the McChesney tartan that she had assumed could no longer brand her when she bought it.

I'll never, never, ever get away.

She began to beat at the design of her family, which included death as an interwoven motif, like a moth caught in its green and orange web; her fists drummed a tattoo on the windowpane.

She heard the door open, felt Andrew in the room, became calm—outwardly, at first, for his sake, then inwardly, for all their sakes: she felt that if she turned loose the despair that had overwhelmed her she would not be able to catch it again and squeeze it away; it would dart out and sting the children and scar them as she had been scarred by the undefinable emotions of others when she was her children's ages. But she released enough of her despair to pass for natural grief in her husband's eyes.

She turned to him, went into his arms and told him the news. She said, "I had to be alone with it for a few minutes."

He held her close, thinking of her not wanting to go, their almost-fight, and the remorse she had been suffering alone. The thought of her penitence nearly managed to obliterate the feeling he had had more and more lately, that had almost come to an explosive head last night: that Rhoda's emotional involvement lay, or was beginning to lie, on the outside of her family—of him and the girls. He had amassed a collection of small signs that seemed to comprise a volume when he read them in loneliness; he had tried to build up to telling her about it last night, to say that neither he nor their three daughters were ready for the cutting of strings, the lonesome launchings, the farewell wave, but that he *felt* that Rhoda *was* ready, and did she know it? Much worse if she didn't, for then he couldn't talk to her, couldn't say: We're not that old; for God's sake, this perfunctory business, this weaning, is for *later*. Come back before you lose sight of us—or we lose sight of you.

But feeling the pain in her, the lostness that was right for the occasion, he told himself that the trouble might be in him—might be male menopause! Eagerly he soaked up her grief like a sponge, but he was either too parched or there was not enough of it; when they left each other's arms he was still thirsty.

Ed got Priscilla into the Pontiac by seven-thirty. She was a dead weight in his arms, knocked out by the pills, and he was a little worried. But, he thought, hell's fire, three pills wouldn't kill anybody or it would have to say so on the bottle, by law.

He had had to ask Birdie Criswell to come over and

sit with Prissy while he woke up Rabbit Johnson down at the filling station and got the Pontiac tuned up. She had had just enough gas in her to get to the station, because he and Prissy hadn't planned on going anywhere except down to the Dog Wagon tomorrow for the Christmas Special, the way they did every year. Prissy wouldn't cook very often but now and then she would pay three or four dollars for a little can of something that looked like coal, or buy some other peculiar thing at the fancy store on Henderson Street, and they would eat it and drink a bottle of wine and act like people in a magazine. She would talk French at him and he, knowing the fun wouldn't last, would gabble back at her in a kind of talk he made up as he went along. Crazy, but it was grab your fun when it came along, and even the coal didn't taste bad after a few times. It was called truffles, and Prissy said only pigs could find it. Then she would laugh and say what pigs could find, two hillbillies ought to be able to find, considering that they were the same thing, and she would take the empty wine bottle and drop it out the window, saying she was a hillbilly and didn't know any better. Anyway, when he got to the station where Rabbit worked and lived in the back, screwing every woman in town, white and black, it had taken him about a half-hour to wake old Rabbit up from the one he had tied on last night. So all Rabbit had been good for was to unlock the pumps and sit there groaning, holding his head, while Ed checked everything from spark plugs to tires. Except for needing gas, she was in A-1 condition. She was old and had more mileage on her than she ought to because of Prissy's tracking down Nonie, but she was a good car and he was going to prove it by driving like a bat out of hell to get his wife home.

Birdie helped him get Prissy dressed, for once not acting coy with him or trying to be sexy, and Ed thought, more than half-serious: When we get back from the farm, I'm gonna blackmail old Rabbit into putting it to Birdie, as a token of my appreciation for her help in a time of trouble. Could be Rabbit would even be grateful, because, as he had said, he never looked at the face, anyway, and Ed was willing to bet that Birdie was a virgin, probably the only one over ten years old in H-town.

As he pulled away from the house he waved to Birdie out the window and yelled, "Thanks, honey!" and saw her blush. He headed up Indiana Street for the nearest entrance to the turnpike, which would take them to within eighteen miles of the farm. The speed limit was sixty-five in good weather, but he was going to keep steady on eighty, and, he thought: Screw the trooper dumb enough to be out looking for trouble.

Entering onto the turnpike he had that feeling of inexplainable awe he always felt when he thought that this road, the pride of the state, was connected with New York City and Boston and Cleveland and every damn place in the country, practically. It made them all—the H-towns with 5500 population and the big ones—all part of each other, like one enormous body: the thigh bone connected to the hip bone; or it was like the trunk and limbs and twigs of a great family tree, connecting all of them, making them all at least cousins.

He grinned at the idea of such a big family and him part of it. And then, naturally letting thought follow thought to his wife's family, and what he knew about them and how he felt about them and what they might be feeling now, and perhaps because it *was* Christmas Eve, and a sorrowful one, at least in its central event, he did something he had stopped doing long before he met his wife, so that she was ignorant of that part of him, and had never been curious enough to ask: he thought about his own family.

He began with the best part, or the part that had been good once upon a time. He thought about his two brothers and two sisters, all younger than he. He hadn't seen them for twenty-one years, and yet they were as bright in his mind as yesterday, now when he let them back in. That sounded mean to him, as if he had locked them out on purpose. He never would do that. Once he had had a big plan, when he was finally free to do what he wanted, about getting in the car one day and going family hunting. It was nice while it lasted, exciting to think of going up to a house and knocking on the door and asking did so-and-so live here, and one great day—but he had somehow never done it, and now he was thirty years old. He counted back: Willard would be twenty-eight, Rosey Lee and Posey Bee, the twins, would be twenty-six, and little old Townsend would be twenty-two. When he saw them bright in his mind, it wasn't as men and women but as towheaded kids. He probably wouldn't know them, after all, and Tow—Townsend—wouldn't even remember that he had had a family, him being one year old when they had all been put in orphans' homes, scattered around like little brown leaves caught in a whirlwind, no two landing in the same place. The others would remember him, but hazily, like somebody maybe they had dreamed. He was glad to recall that he had been a good brother, so that when they thought about him like somebody they had dreamed once, it wouldn't be a bad dream—like the end of their being together.

He wanted to put off that part, though he knew he would have to get to it now that he had started. But, he thought, by damn, if a man can't push his own thoughts around he might as well give up. All right, he said mule-headedly, it's Christmas Eve. We had Christmas like everybody else, didn't we? We didn't have a tree like they do now; there wouldn't have been room for one—but we each had a chair with presents on it. I got a French harp one year and Willard got a juice harp. We learned to play them—"In a Far and Country Village." "Little Maggie." "Red Rosy Bush." All the old songs, and Dad and Maw would sing two-parts and the twins would dance.

We always got up before daylight on Christmas morning and shot off firecrackers and Roman candles —whatever happened to Roman candles? Great balls of colored fire spitting like cats fighting, colors like the beginning of the world; to hold one of them and feel that colored fire jumping out, bucking so your hand shook, was to feel like the Almighty Himself— And there'd be nuts, nigger-toes and pecans, and hard candy and sometimes oranges or tangerines; we'd squirt the tangerine juice at each other's eyes, squeezing it out of the hides, fooling around— Once there was a Milky Way that weighed a couple of pounds anyway that Dad won on a punchboard. Maw would slice it like cake and we'd each have a slice every night after supper. It lasted about a week. Once I made enough money cleaning the schoolhouse and the church and stoking the fires in the winter to buy her a set of dishes at the Company store and she bawled. That was the last Christmas.

Having thought it, he had to go back there to the final year and the night his young coal-miner dad was killed in a union ruckus, shot through the neck and brought home, as far as the doorstep of the two-room shack, and laid there. Ed was sitting inside with his mother, feeling her nervousness because she knew there was a meeting and it was getting late. It was warm enough to have the door open, but they heard no sound of the body being put there, six feet from them; what they did hear was a catcall, mean and ugly, from the dark. They went to the door and looked out in the direction of the noise. There were scuttling feet, men running, and the catcall again, growing faint. Then his mother looked down at the doorstep. She whimpered just once.

Ed hit a strip of icy road and the car spun around and around, four or five times. He sat back and turned the wheels in the direction of the spin, lightly pumping the gas but not touching the brake, until the car righted itself and purred ahead. Priscilla did not stir.

The reaction of the car to the ice, coming when it did, was as supernatural a thing as had ever happened to him. It repeated the movement of his insides that night when his mother whimpered just once.

Between them the young widow and her nine-year-old son had gotten the body of the dead man into the house. They put him in his bed, and then Ed's mother kissed him on the forehead and said, "Be good, now. Don't wake the young'uns," and when he started into the next room, she picked up the sleeping baby and put it in his arms.

Ed sat in a corner holding the baby until along about dawn, when he heard the shot. He put the baby down beside Willard on his pallet and went into the next room. There were the two bodies side by side on the bed, both shot through the neck. Ed never did blame her. When he thought about what she did he had a picture of her running through locust trees and jumping gullies to catch up with her husband, who had had a five-hour start on her, her using the short cut, yelling through cupped hands, as she got closer and closer, "Wait for me, honey," and her finally catching up with him and taking his hand, out of breath but happy.

Priscilla woke to a merry-go-round motion, twirling and dipping but without music, and she opened her eyes and saw white cotton falling from a mottled gray field onto slanting glass where a black knife moved, carving a semicircle of zero which did not remain zero. As quickly as the windshield wiper pushed the snow aside, the snow returned like a gentle answer to a rude question. She knew where she was and where they were going almost instantly. There had been only that moment of abstraction, merry-go-round without music, zeros created by black questions that asked, "Whoooooosh?" which had seemed, to her drugged brain, to be someone saying to her, "Shhhhhhh." They were skidding she knew, without a trace of anxiety or interest, and closed her eyes. She was in her autumn mood, and that was fitting because she went to the farm in autumn and they were going there now. Her father's being dead changed it somewhat, because her autumn mood was one of deep disinterest, of merely feeling without reacting or thinking. Autumn was when she did not impose Priscilla upon things and things did not impose upon her. They simply *were*. But now that was not so. She would have to react to her father's being dead, somehow. Even an insane woman, if she was possessed of Priscilla's type of insanity, was expected to do those things, especially, perhaps, the Priscillas. That was why she occasionally had hysterics: it seemed to gratify people, even when it frightened them outwardly. That was about the extent of what she really knew about people. She had taught herself not to know them, just as she had taught herself French, and for the same reason—both increased distance. But she did not know how she would behave in the presence of the coffin surrounded by family any more than she had the vaguest notion of how they would behave when reduced to the lowest common denominator of emotion. She had never tried to descend to grief because it did not interest her. Of all the emotions, simple or compound, she found fear most worthy of attention, whether self-induced, imposed upon others or spontaneous. Her hysterics this morning were spontaneous and caused by fear unconnected with her father, as far as she knew. (She viewed the qualifying clause with chilly eyes; it seemed extraneous in all senses.) Lying with her head on her husband's belly she had made a discovery, sudden as an electric shock, which could destroy forever her right to autumn moods and the dropping of wine bottles from windows and returning cruelties doublefold to a world that gave them so abundantly; a discovery that could destroy the Priscilla she had always known and never especially liked or understood, but felt comfortable enough with. (There was another girl named Priscilla whom she didn't know at all except to wave to, coolly, from a distance.)

The discovery was two-branched, forked, like roads or rivers: one branch was that she loved her husband, insofar as she understood the meaning of the word—she wanted him near, and wanted him to want to be near her. The other branch, potentially destructive, was that she felt compassion for him. Not at the moment. At the moment she was hanging for dear life onto her autumn mood, which meant that it had fled her.

Gone gone gone. Already some of me has gone and I am part-stranger to myself. My father went all at once but I am going in pieces. I have felt compassion for my husband and I will probably feel it again and then other pieces of me will go because I will be forced to face what I have done to him and then I will feel sorrow and then I will have to tell him things to dispel the sorrow and that will be the end of me as I know myself. Yes, I see what is happening. That thing—road, river—is forked, but last night I was still on both branches, able to be on both. There we were, the two of us, each traveling her own branch, keeping out of each other's hair, but now we are getting—Good Lord, is this grief?—terribly close to where the branches come together and become like this turnpike, one long unending sameness, next exit a million miles.

She imagined she saw the other Priscilla smile at her turmoil and tried to withdraw to a distant place. How dared the stranger smile at her so intimately! She spoke to her: I'll think about Nonie. You were so far away you couldn't have reached me by long-distance then, those foggy nights I spent looking for Nonie without a clue except that somewhere between Hendersontown and Chicago there was a waitress who went to bed with my husband.

When the telephone call came last night—*late one night,* I mean, of course—oh, very well. I *said* I'd gotten a call because it was crueler for Ed to think that somebody was informing on him than to tell him I had gone through his wallet and found that carnival picture with the name "Nonie" on the back. It could have been a cousin or an old sweetheart or a sister; I never asked him about his past because it would have spoiled my brief experimentation with the present, and by the time that was over I didn't care enough to bother. But the picture looked recent. It wasn't yellowed or torn.

I waited until he made three more trips. Three, because of its connection with nine, which, multiplied by anything at all, adds up to itself. I was interested in this because it was the only thing I knew that added up to itself.

Shall I simply report the conversation as it happened? Ed's reaction didn't matter to me at all. Whether he would act guilty, or bluster or swagger. I add this so that when you kill me you will have it straight. Just stop smiling. It looks silly.

"Who is Nonie?"

"A girl who gives me something you don't."

Gives, you see. I knew that he meant sex, but we were having pickled quails' eggs for supper, all briny and tough-skinned but expensive, so I said, "Food?" like someone randomly sticking an old dead seed in the ground just to get rid of it.

"How did you know she's a waitress?"

The random seed, dead as it was, had sprouted. Does that prove immortality, or that I have a terribly green thumb? (I talk this way to myself and you'll have to take it whether you like it or not, Smiling Lady.) Waitress. That eliminated H-town with its two restaurants and middle-aged owners who did their own cooking and serving. I was curious enough to want to stick more seeds in the ground but I had none and so I was forced to invent. Most inventions are potentially destructive; if nothing else, you can swallow them and die. That is not an excuse, merely an observation.

"They told me, the person who called last night." Ed looked stricken. Correction. Men like Ed do not look stricken. They looked *betrayed.* Stricken looks are for persons who read Proust in French. You might remember that. It could be a *bon mot.*

Anticlimax, but I'm afraid I don't really recall the rest of it except that he began to get belligerent about his "rights as a husband." I started screaming. I had to stop eventually because I was getting sleepy, but I started early the next morning. At some point Father and Mother—I meant, of course, *Robin* and *Erin*—appeared. Ed had called them. I let them soothe me and sedate me and so forth, the way they had always done, because I knew—as I had always done—that it was the quickest way to get rid of them. They stayed overnight anyway, so I was more or less compelled to give an eerie performance—floating white robe, knife, shadowy room and so on—vague to me now, because they believed it and it became real and took over. Or was it *you* who took over, protecting them by forcing me to go on with it and lose myself rather than laughing in their faces, making them feel like fools, as I had planned to do?

Priscilla moved and had cause to regret it, because Ed touched her tentatively on the cheek; in his fingers she could feel concern and relief and the new possessiveness that had begun her torment earlier that morning. She had to make a great effort to keep from wrenching her head violently away from his hand, or opening the door and jumping from the car. The woman in her mind had stopped smiling and wore no expression at all. Ed took his hand away. Priscilla was motionless.

After a while she continued her story in a superior tone because the other woman seemed to want her to tell it, very badly.

Robin and Erin left after they had all agreed that Birdie should stay with me while Ed was gone. Ed told Robin—"privately"—more intimate details: Nonie was divorced, she was "lonesome" for a man, she had "made the pass" and so on. That was when I learned that she worked in a place with accommodations for sleepy truck drivers, somewhere between Hendersontown and Chicago. If he had been specific, naming the place, the nearest town, that would have been an end to it. But the idea of Nonie and Ed suspended, wound about each other like vines, above a four-lane reality in a self-created limbo—I don't know. That's a fragment of an image I had; I don't know why it was provocative enough to cause me to go searching. I could have limbo whenever I wanted it. I don't know why I wanted theirs. Maybe you do?

Robin and Erin left, Ed left, Birdie arrived with her cat-smell and knife-face, and I left. Ed told Birdie there had been a prowler—his reason for asking her to stay—and she was all atwitter, ready for woman-talk about brutal rapes until the small hours. She went to the bathroom, which she does a lot, saying she had the nervous pees, and I went down the stairs, got in the car and left. I stopped at a gasoline station and asked which route large trucks followed to Chicago. The attendant got sexy and asked if I was interested in trucks or drivers. I told him I was trying to catch up with my man because he had left his rubbers behind and would need them for screwing. A "lady" saying a thing like that immobilizes a man; it's true; it's more effective than a kick in the groin. *Ça c'est peut-être la même chose.*

The night was the color of river water when a storm has reached down deep enough to stir up the gray putty that seals the river to the planet. — One day, after there have been enough storms and earthquakes and bomb explosions, that putty will become loosened and all the rivers will fly off into the sky like crepe-paper streamers. There was mist with drops the size of small rain. The road was slippery with it and I played the radio at high volume to drown out the sound of tires going squish, a bit of onomatopoeia I can do without. Murderers walking on grass make that sound; asparagus caught in hedges and old people having sex and other unpleasant things so squish. The fog was like old rags signaling *Help* from the trees. The road was long and curved and it pierced through mountains. The tunnels thundered and were horrible, as though they were wounds kept open and runny by cars, and the mountains bellowed in pain. I was afraid and talked and sang and shouted. You were nowhere, nowhere at all. You didn't exist those nights, whatever you may think, because you can't prove it and I am the only one who can verify your existence. You did not exist, so remember this when I am dead and you are prone to smugness: *I* am responsible for you, not you for me, though you may at times in the past have influenced some action of mine. I have said that you will kill me; I am not so sure at this moment that that is true, but if it should happen, I will have to help you. You cannot do it alone. *Vous comprenez, Madame?*

I drove. What else do you do in a car except wait for someone or let yourself be fumbled. I drove, I stopped at lighted places and went to counters and inquired, "Does Nonie work here?" and always the answer was a two-fifths echo: No.

Chicago sounds far away; it isn't. I stretched out the

distance by sleeping all day in motels off the turnpike because Ed would be on his way back. I drove late at night, limiting myself to one stop, one inquiry: "Nonie?" "No."

I found her on the fourth night. She was handsomer than the three-for-a-quarter carnival picture in which she had been all black lipstick and plucked eyebrows. She had eyes in person. She seemed to like her work; she joked with the drivers and laughed as if she meant it. She did not look tired. I supposed she had been rejuvenated by Ed within the past three nights. The stools at the counters were filled with lingering men. I watched from the doorway for a while until one of them, laughing, offered me his knee. She seemed to see me then for the first time and pointed to a table. I sat and she brought me coffee and put it down without looking at me. While she stood beside me a good-looking young driver asked for a room and she said they were all taken. He was rueful and good-humored. Another man said, "What about your bed, Nonie?" and another said, "Ain't you heard? It's been took, permanent." She walked back to the counter primly, through the laughter.

Eventually the men left and we were alone. She had forgotten about me, or didn't care if I saw her sag when the last one had gone. It was not relaxation, as she drew herself a cup of coffee, but *sagging.* If you have missed the point, *she* pretended, too. Did she pretend with Ed? How lonesome can you be for a man? Perhaps you can answer that.

"Why don't you sit with me and drink your coffee?" She looked surprised. I don't imagine she saw many women, or cared to, or got offers of camaraderie from them. She brought her coffee and came to the table. She didn't say "Thanks" or "I don't mind," or anything at all, and I found that I had no plan. I might have walked out if she hadn't said, after a few minutes of sagging and sipping, "You look beat." I am always given these openings. It may be because others sense emptiness and have to fill it with something.

It was easy from then on. I told her that I was on the verge of collapse, that I had driven long hours and was too stony to afford a room. Could I sleep in my car in the parking lot? That was what I really wanted to ask, I said, but had felt *mortified,* afraid she would take me for a tramp— I almost added "the kind who screw other women's husbands," but something in her appraising look told me to wait. She was deciding, apparently, that I was a good egg, because she said that I could share her room. I am crazy, but I would never have taken a stranger in; couldn't she *tell?* How extraordinary. She deserved what she got. Oh yes, she did too. I almost repeated what the driver had said about her room being taken permanently, but I didn't need to. She told me, leading the way, "I got a guy stays over two-three times a month. This ain't his night. I got two more hours to go, but I'll come in quiet. Anyway, you'll be sawing logs by then."

In the room she said, grinning, sure of my understanding, "You sleep on the right side. The left's his. Kinda personal, capish?"

When she left I sat on the edge of the bed and looked around at the "feminine" touches she had added—the usual: white ruffled curtains, artificial flowers. After a while I locked the door. On every article of clothing I could find—underwear, uniforms, flounced blouses, stockings, white shoes—I wrote Ed's name in lipstick and with her own eyebrow pencil. The ruffled curtains, pale pink walls, pillowcases, sheets, furniture, towels, mirrors, bathtub—all were transformed into a monument to Ed. A gift for Nonie.

I unlocked the door, turned off the lights and listened to the monsters arrive and leave. Who could possibly have slept through the noise? I thought about a lot of things and forgot about the monument and gift.

She came in, tiptoed to the bathroom and turned on the light. I suppose it was only a moment later when we were facing each other under the glare of the overhead bulb. She looked older, I noticed. She didn't ask "why?" or "who are you?" If she didn't know exactly, it didn't matter. She was no virgin to such experiences. I could tell by something she gave off that soured the air, an old something. I had left the curtain of her closet open so that she could look inside and see that, too. She half turned toward her bureau, but decided against it, taking it on faith. She sat on the bed—the right side—and looked at the floor. After some time she said, "Is that all," but it wasn't a question and so I left. I waited in the car until Ed got there shortly after dawn, in a car he had borrowed from Rabbit Johnson. I took his hand and led him like a child to her room. The door was still open and she sat as I had left her hours before on the lipsticked bed, looking at nothing in particular, feeling without responding or thinking. Odd to think we were alike in that respect. Ed and

I left his car—this one—sitting in the foggy parking lot to be towed back. He cried on the way, driving and crying. I don't know why—whether for himself or for Nonie or for their limbo.

Priscilla told the other woman: I'm tired. I can't remember why I told you that story. It hasn't proved anything. What happened afterward—his melting himself down to a lump with a penis—was not because I asked any sort of satisfaction. I didn't think his sleeping with Nonie was wrong. I didn't say so, but wouldn't you think my indifference would have told him?

Look, Priscilla, *pleine de tristesse,* if Nonie had done that to me I would have laughed or told her she was silly— I don't know if that is true or not. I am no longer able to judge myself.

She was startled. She told the other woman: The *word judge was yours. I* would have said *remember.* Not that it matters. Whether or not you think I killed Nonie doesn't interest me beyond the fact that you obviously do think so. Is that what you are waiting for, my confession of guilt as a moral murderess because I have tampered with Pride? I can see it in your eyes capitalized: Pride. Then I am a murderess many times over. I have killed brothers and sisters and mother and Birdie Criswell. But I did not kill my father. I used to run to him. And I have not killed our husband because last night—oh, fuck, she said, smiling at the word's exactness, and fell asleep.

She dreamed that she slept with her head on the belly of someone important to her and inside the belly children swung on a pasture gate in a place composed of past, present and future she did and did not know. The belly was hard as the ground of the world and inside it was another world with children who had fathers who had bellies which contained worlds with children and fathers, worlds without end. It was a strange and at the same time familiar dream, so much the latter that it was like a presence she had always been aware of but had not, for some reason, bothered to look at, as if she had dreamed it with her eyes shut within her dream, but now had opened them and was seeing something as familiar as her own blood coursing through her veins, too vitally close to allow objectivity. She tried to step back, back—away from her body and her blood—and she stepped back so far that she fell out of her dream, and perhaps out of her body as she had known it. She sat up and saw that they were leaving the turnpike, which meant eighteen miles to the farm—the only thing she was sure of at that moment; all the rest was implication of ordeal, she felt, though without her usual responses. She felt Ed looking at her, but she would not return his look in case she should smile at him. After a moment he reached over and took her hand firmly, as though he had the right, and steered the car on the frozen hilly road one-handed, with sureness. Priscilla let him hold her hand for a mile or two and then took the initiative and held his.

Tom was asleep. After the excitement of flying two hours through the snowstorm and imagining himself as every kind of bird caught up here, fighting the winds, and the different ways each bird would feel—scared, safe (from hunters like him and his father), plain lost, fierce—he was exhausted inside. He had fought his drowsiness with an old, old trick: wondering how it would be to be any bird and fly head-on into the propeller of the plane. The grisliness of this usually woke him up for good, practically, and he would have to take pills like his father for the splitting headaches that resulted. But this time it had been too awful, because it wasn't the bird or himself with the bloody head, but his grandfather. Bonny had explained what a cerebral hemorrhage was, and the thought of his grandfather with shattered brains was too much to dwell on. Would they have to look in the coffin? Would his grandfather's head be wrapped up in white bandages like a mummy, with the eyes looking out? Tom had started to tremble and had to soothe himself with babyish thoughts that were his secret, having to do with God. Maybe when he was as old as Buck he wouldn't need God any more. He hoped so, because he didn't like having baby secrets at his age. But just this once, and maybe tomorrow. He fell asleep.

Bonny had gone from the blank-out she had learned to use during animal experimentation classes at the University of Texas, which allowed her to observe facts without fainting, to a state of mind which she had privately dubbed, long ago, as "the over-all." In that state she was able to observe the behavior of those around her, do automatic, necessary things with her hands—apply Band-Aids to skinned knees, pass coffee or cocktails—employ stream-of-consciousness, which allowed her to sort the valuable nuggets from available data by the expedient of leaving nothing out, and to relax. Normally functioning people did it every day without knowing what they were doing. The only difference between her "over-all" and theirs was that she was always in control. As arrogant as it sounded, her wires never got mixed. It was one of her gifts to Spur that he did not know about, that made her the perfect wife for him. She saw the tenseness in his neck and massaged it, her fingers sending him messages of soothing and promise, saw by the expression on Tom's face that he was probably fighting a desperate gun battle or the gales of a typhoon, guessed, by Buck's dreamy lost-to-now gazing from the window that he was photographing the earth from the moon or Elizabeth Taylor from up close, and all the while the mind's underscoring ran on like an experimental work by Varese, composed of fragments of conversation, bits of audible youth, scored silence with the throb of things imminent such as storms or sexual climax, sorrow and joy like light and shadow, and which was which? She had known dark joy and blinding, blazing sorrow. So, surely, had everyone, but terms stick. Blazing sorrow. Who would blaze for her father-in-law today and tomorrow as Lara had, addressing the dead Yurii in "unsolemn words": "Farewell, my great one, my kin, farewell, my pride, farewell, my swift, deep little river—"

Massaging her husband's neck, seeing Tom fall asleep, his lips moving, she thought: I knew dark joy when my sons were born, knowing the possibilities of the world they came loudly into, yelling advance warning to a future that might not want them, in which they might be expendable after so much effort. I knew dark joy when I took Spur, because I brought him something precious by renouncing a way of life that had almost become fanaticism: my *idea* of medicine that was far greater than its parts—the idea Lara expressed to Yurochka of the riddle of life, the riddle of death. But I didn't really renounce it, after all. The riddle remains and we plug away at it by living, by dying, by having sons, by making love— If it was the riddle alone that intrigued me, then it is larger now than ever before.

She felt the tenseness go from her husband's neck and stopped massaging. He turned and smiled at her, looking at her for so long that she pantomimed panic, and he turned away, grinning.

She told him silently, "I know so much about you, darling Spur, and paradox or not, it is that knowledge that enlarges the riddle. Some of it is beautifully simple, such as knowing I can increase your pleasure in love by stroking the lovely long sartorius muscles of your thighs—"

But before Bonny met Spur she had learned to *see,* and the roughest part of their fourteen years together had been to try to make that vision selective where their life together was concerned, which was every second. She had learned many tricks—how to push unwanted bits of insight into the corner of her eye and out, like cinders; to use blanking-out when she had to. She had learned to be wary of the context in which she used certain words to him, in relation to whom. "Generous" and "loving" were especially difficult. They could not be applied to any member of his family. "Kind-hearted" could be used if the tone was right. It was best, though, not to speak of them at all except in terms of illness or trouble. She knew her marriage was not so different from others with respect to concessions, adjustments, tolerances and tolerations. She was hardly a docile wife; she imposed her will on Spur frequently and he took it like a prince. If only today—tomorrow—

The prospects of her own upper-middle-class future had begun to frighten Bonny by the age of ten. She loved her parents and her four grown-up brothers, grown-up when she was born to her forty-two-year-old mother and fifty-year-old father. They adored her and tried to spoil her. She was high-spirited; she rode and swam and shot—targets—expertly; she was beautiful and desirable enough, pre-puberty, to make Humbert-Humberts out of most men. A great future as a belle and ornament to society was predicted for her by all. But more and more frequently she would blaze with a flame none of her kin could fathom because it was more of anguish than anger. She was desperate for life but could see none ahead, she told them, in the cozy Texas future mapped out for her of dating and country clubs and coming-out parties and marriage-to-the-right-man, and children and young matronhood and chauvinism, Texas-style, running through it all like a thread through the inevitable "grandmother's pearls" she would inherit at the proper age. Aunts and uncles said that late children were always a little different, that she would grow out of it.

When she was thirteen the war broke out and her brothers enlisted en masse. The city was flooded with soldiers, and girls her age went whirling about on not always properly chaperoned dates. She offered her services to the Red Cross, but the kindly ladies considered her too young, and frankly, too odd. She became a recluse, with books and music for company, and wrote to her brothers every day. When she was fifteen she again volunteered for war work of any kind, and was accepted by an understaffed hospital, where she emptied bedpans, learned to take temperatures and roll bandages. Except for going to and from the hospital, she did not enter the war-wild atmosphere of the city. Alone at night in her room, she began to feel a kind of peace, and then a hotter blaze than she had known before. She talked to her father somewhat inarticulately, but a combination of the two of them and four o'clock in the morning brought the answer. It had a special radiance because her father had helped her find it, assembling from her groping to express herself the components that, put together, made up the logical shape of her need, her future. It was a shape austerely beautiful, and so right that she could not believe any other had ever existed.

At sixteen she was accepted by the University of Texas. She plunged into her studies with a vehemence that astounded her instructors. From then on she moved in a straight line, which achieves its purity only through total concentration and discipline.

In 1947, when she was nineteen and in her first year of medical school, she met Spur, saw his beauty with her clear eyes, and forgot him. He could not forget her and began to haunt her. Wherever she was, he was. She changed the route of her accustomed walks and his feet would follow. She was openly annoyed. Annoyance did not affect him. After a while she was amused; the only words they ever seemed to exchange were "Marry me," "No." His intensity began to cut through her sleep, her preoccupation with work and study. His face with the eyes that *wanted* would rise from a test tube or gaze up at her from a blank X-ray plate. She knew what it was to want; how could she ignore his? She slept with him, thinking that her virginity would balance the scale. It did. She began to want him. Before long, incredibly, it was Bonny and Spur vs. Medicine, and even before she weighed in for the championship bout she knew that she would be disqualified for overweight because she carried his heart in her body. It had taken only a year for the right man to cram her into the mold prepared for her by her family.

Bonny became aware that she was muttering the words that had been in her mind: If only today—tomorrow. She stared very hard at the base of Spur's perfect skull and sent wave after wave of will and word to that cradle in which his subconscious sat like a dictatorial baby: Feel feel feel feel feel.

Buck focused on an imaginary house and spiraled down, down, using his mental camera as though it were a snowflake. When he was about fifty feet above the house, he used a telescopic lens covered with gauze and began to pick out figures: an old lady in a long dress to her ankles doing something with a knife —hold it long enough to establish that sawing motion. Now pick up the girl coming out of the door of the house holding what looks like a pitcher—zoom! A pair of chicken feet, huge, tied over a clothesline; now the girl's face, close up, eyes dreamy and thirsty. Sure, eyes can be thirsty. Eyes can be anything. Now the back of the old woman's head, bobbing with a steady rhythm. Follow the rhythm down her arm to the hand. Close-up on the knife handle sticking from her fist. Now the chicken feet again, including the legs; now the girl's mouth, tongue licking out; back to knife, remove gauze, follow knife blade to neck of chicken, which is being very, very, very slowly sawed off by the old woman. A drop of blood hits the lens. Girl runs over with pitcher, holds it under chicken neck (all photographed through drop of blood on lens), head falls to ground, girl squeezes neck for more blood like she's milking a cow, turns pitcher up to her mouth and—Aw, shit. That wouldn't scare a cat. Not even a goddamn kitten.

He yawned. We been flying—lemme see—three hours. Oughta be there soon. Wonder if I'll cry again like I did this morning? Hell, he scared me half to death, that look in his eyes. Sometimes I think he's nuts. I hope I take after Bonny, or somebody else anyway. I think he hates too much. I don't want to hate, but sometimes it's hard not to. I'd like to be a nice, sane, upstanding homosexual when I grow up, and wear Bonny's pants.

He almost giggled aloud. This had been homo year at school, all the guys mincing around talking with lisps, and he and Tom had practiced at home in the gym in front of the mirror. One night when Spur and Bonny were out bowling they got a couple pairs of Bonny's lace pants and put them on, letting their dicks hang out the side. They told the other guys about it and it caught on like a prairie fire. Guys started bringing their sisters' and mothers' pants to school and doing it in the john.

He sat back and eased his neck, turning his head from side to side and walling his eyes: I'm gonna watch real close this time and see if Spur sure enough hates everybody.

Closing his eyes he brought his grandfather's face into enormous close-up in death, then Aunt Erin, alive, singing that song he liked with the strange words:

When the wheel of autumn makes a turn
Across the field of summer—

Maybe she'll sing it this time if I ask her. It always makes Spur look like a horse about to be shot, his nose all spread open. Uncle Robin usually looks like he was expecting something that didn't come—a letter, maybe. How can a song make everybody act so different? I'll find out this trip.

He leaned against the plane window, rubbing the glass to make a view-finder, and slowly, slowly, his camera circled, looking for what it could find down there.

The Darkest Angel, drunkards and babies share a memory and a fear of falling headlong from a place of love. The Angel, alone, knows that He was pushed, and why. In certainty there is comparative peace; in His dreaming reenactments of the fall the Angel, alone, does not cry out.

The child across the aisle from Robin had kept her vigil for hours. Occasionally she lifted her mother's limp wrist with the watch on it and tried to decipher the message of dots and numerals at which the hands pointed insistently, but she could make nothing of it. Her mother murmured and made anxious sounds without waking. Nobody came into the car and nobody left it. The train sped on, its *clackety* as exterior and automatic as the blubber-and-snort of sleeping people. The noises, the snow, the child's sense of fatalism—all eventually made a silence of their own, a void through which no meteor could flame, an incorruptible constant. Robin, falling, screamed.

Everything shattered, exploded at once. Doors flew open, passengers flew up from their pillows and seats, the snow flurried on the wind, up and down, as though driven by an erratic pulse, and the child began to cry in desperate relief at the top of her lungs. Conductors, men with boxes of sandwiches and milk, porters with brooms, the slowing train, the crying child, the darting-up people—all seemed to be converging on Robin where he lay with terrified disoriented eyes staring from the position of his dreaming fall, and the clamorous language they spoke was as fragmented as his vision. They seemed to be demanding milk of him, offering him tickets, shouting to him to Damn God, and a child-soul went howling around reproaching him for betrayal. He mewled in answer to their accusations and demands, saw the eyes try and condemn him.

"Sandwich, sandwich, drink, drink?" With effort his hand felt for the lifeline he had let go when he fell. Clumsily the hand scrabbled about the seat with a sense of its own—sniff sniff sniff—and found the flask; knew, with its own feeling for sorrow, that what it held lacked weight and shook it, asking the ear to testify to its mourning: the lifeline had come unfastened.

"Drink drink drink?" The eyes were knowing above the voice. Robin sat up and gazed into them with a hope he felt to be dreadful: he was that near sobriety. "Drink drink drink?" One of the eyes winked and the head inclined, indicating a direction, then withdrew. Carefully Robin stood, stuffing the flask into his jacket pocket, and followed the man.

The train wrenched to a halt as Robin and the man stood between cars and hurriedly transacted their business. Robin knew he paid an extortionist's fee for the pint but he did not protest. People were crowding behind him with luggage, pushing more than was necessary when they recognized him. He lost his balance and went hurtling head-first toward the iron steps, but his extortionist threw his weight upward from a crouching position and caught Robin with his shoulder and bore him to the wall and pinned him there. Robin gazed at the man's sardonic grin, the cracked lips so near his own veined with tobacco stains, and smelled the man's sweetish tobacco breath and the acridity of his skin that was like the smell of a barn where tobacco is being fired. He felt the man's heartbeat; his leg, pressed between the other's two legs, felt the lump of his manhood, felt it stir. His savior drawled, "Don't wanna feed that good stuff to the ground, do we, buddy?" Robin hunched his shoulders like wings and shoved. The man tottered backward, colliding with the little girl who had been Robin's victim, who was coming through the door with her mother, her eyes searching for and finding Robin. "You bastard," said the vendor, and picked up his basket of sandwiches and shoved past the passengers into the car.

With his wounded hand Robin dug down in his pocket and came up with a handful of change. As the child and her mother pushed past him he shoved the hand with the dried blood at her. The child struck his hand; pain splintered his arm, and in anger at her misunderstanding he raised the throbbing hand against her, fist clenched around the coins. The mother, seeing the gesture in disbelief, struck out at Robin with a small bag and caught him in the groin. Robin fell back against the wall, both hands spreading to comfort the assaulted virgin. The small rain of silver upon the iron floor coincided with the shout of " 'Board!" The child darted at the blood money, knowing it to be hers. She gathered the small harvest as carefully as though she were picking four-leaf clovers in a summer field. One coin lay half hidden beneath Robin's left slipping foot and she dug it out with little picking movements of thumb and forefinger, oblivious to her mother's tugging, the impatient porter, the man who had kept her sleepless and terrified. She had learned, in a few hours, all she needed to know about life to make a success of it: all things have their price; one waits for the payment. When she at last descended the steps she had left her mother far behind: the woman made a gesture half-horror, half-entreaty, toward Robin; the child made none, nor did she cast him a glance. She had given and she had been paid.

The porter lifted the steps and clanged the door shut and locked it. The train jerked forward and the porter left without a look at the man clutching his privates: everybody *knew* the toilets were locked when the train was in the station.

Robin tried out his breath, released his wounded groin, reached into the lower of his two sagging pockets and brought out the bottle, cracked the seal and drank, sliding, back to the wall, down to the floor, where he sat alternately drinking and resting his forehead on his drawn-up knees. After a while his breath came regularly, its thin whistle timed to the rhythm of the settling-down train. His groin hurt from the blow and the pressure in his kidneys, but the cold floor gave some relief. He looked at his watch with watery eyes. Thirteen hours to go. Which, he asked the bottle, was the unlucky thirteenth hour—this one, or the one at the end? Erin, counting from the other end of time, beginning with one, would find him, if she found him at all, sitting in the middle of the thirteenth hour. He wondered if he had ever really been elsewhere. The bottle winked at him, its dark-sherry color reminding him of the vendor's eyes. He scrubbed and scrubbed at the knee that had felt the man's stirring animal nature, as arrogantly indiscriminate and boastful as that of most men bred and raised by the soil. Its proximity excited them, an automatic excitation, whether in the form of a dark field or the clay of a racked and ruined body. It was earth speaking to earth—a signal like a Masonic handshake; a variety of *love.*

Having found the word to justify his rejection of the man, Robin scrouged down within himself as though huddling over one dying coal of warmth; he had found to his bitter amusement that even hate required vigilance. He must tend the coal and blow upon it, or else go empty-handed to his father's death.

The Clan

I rose because he sank.
I thought it would be opposite,
But when his power bent
My soul stood straight . . .
Emily Dickinson

The first carload of people arrived at nine A.M., *just as Erin was sticking the last tortoise-shell hairpin into her mother's coiled braids.* In the past hour Erin had stripped the deathbed, aired the room, remade the bed—for someone might have to sleep in it—bathed her mother, sponged herself quickly, and gotten both of them dressed and down to the morning room, where the widow was now ensconced by the fire to receive condolences in comparative warmth. The car, a Model-T with flapping side curtains, was crammed with people. They have brought the children, Erin thought, knowing the house would sound like a steam kettle with all the *shushes*—needless *shushes* from polite mothers to silent doe-eyed children who would stand as far away from the fire as possible because that was "manners." Except for the gentle, siblilant admonitions, the mothers would be as silent as the children. The men, from her mother's stock, would say the few words necessary and then join their wives and children in the colder regions of the room, where they would stand ruminating.

Erin ran to the hiding place beneath the stairs and fetched forth an old brass spittoon, giving it a whack with a dustcloth. This spittoon was brought out only when her mother's people came to call. The word "ruminating" had reminded her that the women would have lower lips ridged with snuff and the men would be chewing tobacco. Both sexes could score bull's-eyes across the width of a room with their dark streams. She barely had time to place the spittoon centrally on the hearth when one of them called "Hello" from the doorstep. They would not use doorbells, and knocking, however soft, was thought by them to be rude.

"Your cousins, Mama," Erin said on her way to the door, and her mother nodded, knowing her people had the best manners, no matter what her husband had thought, nor her children, for that matter. Called them "white trash," she knew, though they bore the names of kings and nobility: Stuart, Raleigh, Essex. True, they let their houses fall down and lived through the winter with rags stuffing up the holes in the windows, but for all that they had dignity and a sense of what was fitting. Generous folks—if they grew two tomatoes on a vine, some one of them trudged through the dust of summer to bring her one, a thing her husband's side never thought of doing. She heard them scraping their feet carefully and the "Shhhh" to the children, heard

Erin murmuring, and she drew herself up into a position of sternness that would help lighten their burden when they saw her. They would know she hadn't forgot mourning was for the heart's privacy. Death was a time of iron, and only the youngest bereaved—the bride of less than a year, the child too tender to know—could bend in public. She had dreamed last night that she was a young bride, without get, and had wept in her sleep, wounded to her heart's marrow. (In her thoughts she pronounced the words the old way—wounded to rhyme with sounded—and would do so openly today and tomorrow. The children would not mock her today and tomorrow, and she would find strength in being what she had never stopped being within, whatever they may have thought: a hillwoman with a sense of what was fitting.)

Her kith and kin came into the room and their eyes spoke to each other's. Randolph, her dead father's dead brother's youngest, came forward and told her they were joined with her in grief. She nodded, looking from one to the other, not slighting the children, looking as directly at the arm-held baby as at the others. They took their places around the room and "Shhhh" went the mothers and *splat* went the snuff and tobacco juice with never a drop falling short of the mark.

Others arrived from neighboring farms and the town until the room was densely packed and almost hot with body heat. This presented a problem for the cousins: between them and the spittoon there was a solid bank of humanity. They began to edge out into the hall, one by one, fanning the door open and spitting out into the snow until there was a perfect semicircle of discoloration hemming in the house like half of an elfin ring. The fanning door began to lower the room's temperature and the visitors shuffled their feet for warmth until it sounded as though a dance were in progress. To eliminate the problem, Erin brought tin cans from the kitchen and handed them about. The close-range spitting tolled like bells and smiles were passed around. The cousins, oblivious, continued to ruminate and spit, and soon the various levels of juice, when added to, were producing an almost recognizable melody. One town girl, who had been two years behind Priscilla in grade school and who was noted for her high giggles, was overcome with her specialty and struggled from the room, red-faced and gasping. In the hall she gave vent to her mirth, leaning against the newel post of the stair; Priscilla and Ed walked in and were greeted by the sight of hysteria. Ed thought she was crying and put his arm about his wife protectively. Priscilla, who had always been infected by the girl's idiotic giggles, joined her. Ed stood aghast as the two of them stammered and giggled.

"Oh—Prissy—I'm—so—sorry—" but she was again overcome, horrified and trying to stop but unable to; doubly horrified because it was Priscilla, who had always frightened her with her unexpected responses to everything.

Priscilla thanked the girl, and despite Ed's efforts to stop her, went into the morning room still giggling. Erin was just entering from the room in which her father had died, where she had been considering setting up more chairs but had decided that a fire must be laid there first; it was her intention to ask Randolph's help, but her eyes met those of the mortified Ed, who had followed Priscilla in a vain attempt to salvage the moment. Erin smiled at him faintly in reassurance and went to her sister through the sudden total quiet. She took her hand and turned, saying, "Mama, here's Priscilla."

Priscilla, only smiling now, went to her mother and kissed her cheek. Straightening up, she looked about the room. "Mama," she said, "Where's Daddy?" A look of alarm spread around the room, communicated from the corners of eyes. The girl had come laughing in here like she expected a present, said the eyes, and now this question! She had plain "gone off" again, to ask a question like that, like she didn't know he was dead!

Priscilla, impatient at the silence, said, "I mean is he laid out here? I want to see him."

Erin took her elbow and spoke formally. "They are preparing him for burial, Priscilla. The funeral will be at Owen's. We can see him after five-thirty this evening." She was leading her sister away to help her out of her coat. She nodded to Ed, indicating that he should speak to his mother-in-law.

"Owen's?" Priscilla said. "Why not the church, even if he didn't believe in God?" The changed quality of the silence kept her in the room and egged her on, as such atmospheric changes had always done, to get to the bottom of it. She looked around at the people watching her, picking up cues from their eyes and their tensions. "Half the people who flock to church every Sunday don't believe . . ." She felt herself separating into parts, as she had in the car. One Priscilla was suddenly bored, finding tiresome the effort to say something shocking; the other Priscilla was shocked at the idea of wasting such a perfect opportunity to leave a mark. That should have been all, but a third sensibility arrived and stood to one side, namelessly observing the struggle between the two, finding the second Priscilla, who wanted to leave her mark, terribly pathetic: it was as if (thought the observer) a fierce little cat, dying of its wounds, tried to unsheathe its claws for one last swipe at its killer. The second Priscilla, loathing sympathy from a stranger, murderously angry at the suggestion that she was like a dying *anything,* battled her way free of the other two and finished her sentence with spite prepense: "They go there every Sunday without believing, so there's no difference . . . except that Daddy's *really* dead . . ." and she swept through the red curtains like an actress, feeling behind her the applause of the shocked and gratified audience.

She knew, the minute she entered the old dining room, that her father had died there; it was as if he told her so himself and wanted her to say something about it. "In a minute, Daddy," she said, respectfully impatient, and heard the stirring on the other side of the curtains.

In her mind she tried to repeat the act of gazing from face to face—the faces of herselves—but the others, the bored Priscilla and the mysterious observer, were gone; and yet the girl who stood in the deathroom looking at a section of herself—the left side, from waist to knee, and two hands pinned to the hip like a corsage—in the part of the mirror that had come undraped, felt a certain shame for her words, which the second Priscilla would never have done, and it was she who had spoken the words. She stared in confusion at the fragments in the mirror, wondering to whom they belonged. From the gloom behind her a hand materialized—large-boned, ringless—and moved slowly forward as she watched in perfect stillness. It covered her clasped, reflected hands as though, the girl thought, to join them in holy matrimony. The main confusion she felt about the hand, however, was willful and short-lived; no matter what she wished to think, it was obviously Erin's hand. It was too uncared for to be her father's.

Ed's ears were burning as he went to his mother-in-law, the old lady he had seen only once, six years before, sure she would not remember him and afraid of saying the wrong thing, but she gazed at him directly, a strong supporting look, and her firm voice was supportive, too, as she said, "Edgar, I'm proud you could come. You'll want hot coffee after your drive. Give your wife some, too. Her cheek felt half-froze to me." Grateful at being freed from the obligation of staying in the room where people were beginning to whisper about Prissy, Ed bent forward and reached out to touch the widow's hand, but seeing the twisted talons, he froze in the supplicating position, struck with a feeling of grief that was like paralysis, like the result of a heavy blow on the back of his neck. As sudden as the grief, the reason for it came to him: this was how his mother's hands must have knotted and swelled and strained at the gun as she lay torn between husband

and children. He recalled having heard mention of his mother-in-law's arthritis, but the tears were already on his cheeks; as if she knew they were not for her, and that he was sorry they were not, the widow said, in sympathy, "There, son. It's all right, now." Ed crossed the room, his face averted from the crowd, thinking that, after all, in his experience of death it was kids that got left; he didn't know how bereft wives and husbands felt—did he? In the next room Priscilla and Erin stood with their backs to him. It looked as if Erin were comforting Prissy. In mourning for his own parents, Ed wanted to share his wife's grief and he wanted her to share his. Before he could decide how to tell her, in the morning room the widow's voice rose, clear as a girl's.

"I'm beholden to you all for coming and will be proud to have you come back, but we'll need the room and the chairs"—she said "cheers"—"for kinfolk who have commenced to arrive." Over the scraping chairs and embarrassed murmuring she added sternly, "My own folks was the first to come."

Erin and Priscilla turned about slowly, seemingly not of their own volition, as if each word of their mother's advanced their propelling mechanisms one notch. Their faces were blank as wax dolls' (Ed saw, with disappointment and yet some relief, that Priscilla's eyes were dry) until their mother finished speaking, then identical expressions of disbelief revealed their strong family resemblance. Breathless, Priscilla said, as if she had to make Ed believe her somehow, "She's never—Mama's never—in all our lives, she never *has.*"

Ed shook his head in companionable bewilderment,

wondering what Prissy meant. Erin nodded as if something was clear to her. Fanned by departing callers, the door sent gust after gust of icy air to part the curtains, through which the widow could be seen bobbing her head in regal dismissal. When the curtains were finally still Priscilla walked over and pushed them aside, gazing into the room that now contained only her kin. "Mama," she said. "Mama—"

"Go have your hot coffee," her mother rapped at her. "You're half-froze. I told your husband to see to it that you had your hot coffee."

Priscilla said, "Yes, Mama," and let the curtain drop. She pressed both hands to her mouth and walked toward the kitchen like a sleepwalker, except that her eyes were bright with the actual moment. Erin and Ed followed her, and in the kitchen she stood half-turned from them, hands still pressed to her mouth, her throat trembling with laughter or tears; neither the watchers nor Priscilla knew which until the tears began to fall, rolling down her cheeks and hands and wrists into the cuplike cuffs of her sleeves, though she made no sound. The silent flow of water was a wonder in its way; another wonder was that neither Erin nor Ed made a move toward her. She was on her own in her emotion; possibly for the first time in her life in front of family she was allowed to be alone, unled. In a while she took her hands from her mouth and said, "I'm glad you've got a fire in that stove, Erin. Mama was right. I'm half-froze—" She hung onto the word for a moment, then settled for her mother's version.

Almost boisterously, Ed said, "Well, where's that coffee? I'm *plumb* froze, myself."

As Priscilla poured coffee, Erin found it hard to stop

staring at her. She felt distinctly cotton-headed as she thought: Here is a woman I do not know, but have suspected, and luxuriously let the thought go unextended. Her light-headedness had begun in the morning with her mother's concern for Editha and Antonia, a stranger's words expressed in a stranger's voice, and yet words and tone had been somehow expected, else why had she thought: It has begun, and why was she staring at Priscilla as though waiting for further revelations? Fatigue, she told herself, watching Ed put five spoons of sugar in his coffee, and the admission surprised her as much as anything. In a moment she would be back to normal, but the light-headedness was not at all unpleasant; it was like a new and sudden perspective of an old vista, none the less breathtaking for her having heard, somewhere, sometime, that the vantage point existed.

The doorbell rang and Erin started the tiresome circuitous route to answer it—they had always talked about cutting a door straight through to the hall—but when she reached the door of the morning room she heard Randolph's murmur in the hall and the (always) strident voice of Aunt Antonia asking, unsoftened by tearfulness, "Where are the family gathered together in their sorrow?" and Aunt Editha's soft voice, almost extinguished by tears, saying something about the Lord in His infinite wisdom . . . Instead of making her way to them and taking their coats and trying to subdue the one and comfort the other, she stood curiously, like an eavesdropper, bent slightly toward the curtains, waiting to hear what her mother would say to them, that meek woman who had lived in awe approaching terror of her husband's family.

"Randolph, do the kindness to take Murdoch's sisters' overcoats. I'm proud you could come, Editha, Antonia. Take the soft cheers there." Erin felt laughter rising in her: Even if her mother had *forgotten* that Antonia required two straight chairs, improbable as such forgetfulness would be, couldn't she *see* that the woman could never fit in one of the soft ones? Immediately she felt chastened. Her mother was simply not pointing up the fact, leaving Antonia to choose her own seating arrangements, sparing her feelings by not requesting that Randolph "put forth two cheers." In her mind she heard Randolph solemnly chanting, "Rah rah." With a kind of wildness she thought: Is this the effect of death, to change everyone into someone else, to bring ludicrous images to mind? Is it our protection against death's bareness to become what we aren't, to panoply our minds in alien clothes like actors playing parts, confusing ourselves as to who we really are until we can creep back into ourselves, too late to do more than feel foolish for having been hypocritical? He is the first to go in death from this house in my memory. I assumed, I suppose like everyone else, that the only response to death is honesty . . . She stopped and repeated Priscilla's gesture of hands to mouth. She heard her mother's voice controlling the situation of the two sisters, who were determined to mourn as loudly as possibly. Suppose, she thought, that *this* is honesty, and all the rest has been pretense? Robin, hurry home and help me! You're the only one I can trust!

She got herself in hand and walked back to the kitchen, where the task of cooking large amounts of food awaited her. There she found Priscilla—who had never cooked when she was at home, and according to

Edgar, did not cook for him—deeply engrossed in the preparations of a ham for boiling and baking, surrounded by spices and implements. Erin poured herself coffee with a hand that rattled the coffee pot with its trembling and sat down across the table from Edgar before she should fall.

"God," whispered Editha, "in His infinite wisdom has seen fit to take our only brother from us. We must not question him, Tonia, but oh, it is hard." She sniffled and searched in her patent-leather pocketbook for a fresh handkerchief.

"He was stainless." Tonia spoke harshly, as though to warn those of argumentative bent. "A God-fearing man if there ever lived one. I can see him, accepting his True Saviour when he was a lad in his teens, lying beneath the waters in the arms of—"

"Tonia, Murdoch never was *immersed.*" Editha was shocked at the fabrication, thinking that a lie at this time might do her brother more harm than he had done himself.

"I can see him." Tonia was implacable. "Beneath the waters, held in the arms of Reverend James like an infant—the infant Jesus." She had begun the story aimlessly, not expecting to be contradicted, but now that she had been, she was determined to have the last word if it took all day.

"Tonia!" Editha's voice rose in distress. "We *sprinkle* in our church!"

"*Your* church," snapped Tonia. "We *duck* in mine and Murdoch's." Editha began to weep in earnest.

"Randolph," said the widow, "fetch some coffee from the kitchen for your cousin-in-law's sisters," and remembered to point the way to her cousin, who had not been welcome in her husband's house. When he had gone she looked from one old lady to the other, enjoying the feeling that her eyes glinted. "My husband was a man of strong will, as I reckon you all know, or some other woman would be here in my place today—" She faltered. "Here by the fire—" All at once it seemed not to be worth the effort. Her mouth, in which the upper plate of her false teeth had slipped, slacked open, and her shoulders curved forward and down, as though to protect the cavity of her chest where one precious secret might still be buried. Millicent, she thought, I want Millicent. Why isn't she here with me? A fire seemed to be glowing across the room: Tonia's eyes, waiting for her to finish what she had to say, waiting for a fight. Nobody had ever stood up for her, against Antonia, except Millicent. If she could just wait, just hold off finishing her words to her husband's cruelest sister, until her beautiful daughter got here to stand with her, bracing her with her laughter that acknowledged no man or woman better than herself—no, nor her equal. Foreigners paid her to let them photograph her face and put it in magazines; she had watched men looking her daughter over, in the flesh or in magazines, and had seen their britches stirring as if they carried live animals in their pockets; the way they had looked at her when she was Millicent's age and before, before Murdoch took her and bent her like a child's crossbow and strung her so tight that she could only sound one note when plucked: Millicent.

Randolph came back with coffee, cream and sugar on a tray, and the tired old lady found her resolve returned to her. A gnarled hand made a slow journey to her mouth and fumbled there, pushing at the slipped plate of teeth until a little sucking sound announced its engagement to the roof of her mouth. Pushing her shoulders back against the wings of the chair, lifting her chin, she said to them, as Randolph stood with the tray on which not a spoon rattled, "We was fourteen and seventeen when we said our words to each other in the church up yonder. We growed up together as man and wife, and to my certainty, though I'd as lief one was true as the other, he was never ducked nor sprinkled. God was a name that come to his lips if he mashed a finger or one of the young'uns spoke back. You loved your brother, Tonia, I have no doubt, recalling the fight you put up—" She paused, regret plain on her face, then forged on. "If you *knowed* him, too, you'll know he wants his rest." And then, because she felt her heavy bones as her enemies —more so than Antonia—she spoke to her as an equal, with neither rancor nor awe, "Now you just hush up, girl," and Tonia, famous for her temper and last words, was momentarily moved and silent.

"Miss Edie," said Randolph softly, placing the tray on a small table beside the lady, "will you do the kindness to sweeten and cream the coffee." The shaken lady began to do so, the spoon clattering against the cup. Tonia regained her strength of purpose at the slight and bore down heavily to deliver some telling reminder of herself. She was thwarted by her sister.

"Don't the rest of you want coffee?" Edie asked

timidly. "The women look cold." Despite her kindly intentions, "the women," in her delicate voice, sounded like "the cattle."

"Thank you, ma'am, but we won't partake," said Randolph.

Tonia found her opening. "How could you, with your mouths stuffed with that ungodly tobacco!"

"That is one reason, ma'am," said Randolph, with a touch of amusement which Tonia found intolerable. He continued, "As for being ungodly, it grows in the earth and bears a flower." He handed her a cup and withdrew to his place at the back of the room; once there, he drew a bead on the spittoon and let fly a perfect, arching stream. The spittoon responded to the artist's touch with a note so joyous and prolonged that the baby gurgled and flapped a fat hand in a kind of acknowledgment at this lovely preview of its future.

Tonia felt defeat. How could she, without making a scene, answer any of them tellingly? To do so, she would have to bring up her brother's infidelities, which would be more of an attack on the dead than on the living. And the words "he wants his rest" made her nervous, as did the throng behind her, despite her having lived surrounded by these people, or others like them, for seventy-five of her eighty years.

When she was five and Editha three, their parents had brought them here from Scotland, plunked them in the midst of the alien corn, proceeded to have a son, whom they named Murdoch, and then died—a series of events which Tonia saw as leading up to, and falling away from, the birth of her brother. It seemed entirely fitting that the climax of her brother's birth should have been followed closely—within ten years or so, she thought vaguely—by the death of her parents, but whether it was brougham, buggy or buckboard from which they were thrown to the rocks beneath the old bridge spanning the Rose River, she could not now begin to recall. No shred of their personalities, which might indicate their choice of vehicle, remained with her, though she chose to believe that her father had not been a sporting man; to have believed otherwise would have imposed a strain on another, more basic belief of hers, which was that for the parents to have lingered on until their son grew up would have been a kind of bad taste, in that they, by imposing upon Murdoch their narrow Scotch ways, might have blighted the one perfect bloom of their union. As it was, she had raised him, instilling in him facts (she could not remember if they *were* facts) of his ancient lineage and blood rights, tracing for him the line (if invented by her, then most thoroughly and cleverly) that stretched back to castle dwellers who had owned villages and consorted with Scotland's kings and queens. He had taken seriously only the parts which suited his temperament, such as his right to drink royally and visit his virility upon any available female. She *thought* she had taught him to share her dislike and distrust of the hill people. She had stormed and railed bitterly when he chose Eula Marie Raleigh, a near-illiterate with a terrifying family who lived like beasts of the fields. Editha, younger and less family-proud—Tonia and Murdoch had excluded her from their lives as much as possible—had not seemed to mind. She believed in marriage for love alone, she *said,* and argued that since Murdoch plainly loved, and since Eula Marie was handsome and pliable and plainly loved in return, there was nothing for it but the altar with flowers decked. Poor Edie—she was probably incapable of vindictiveness, which left her an ineffectual romantic who waited for love that never appeared and so took to eccentricities such as purple clothes and hair. Tonia married and buried a man of good name and property, and watched, more or less from afar, as her brother sired by the hill woman a pride of children who happily inherited none of their mother's traits of family or taste. Periodically Tonia paid visits of state and saw with satisfaction that time, her brother and the children had relegated Eula Marie to her proper place in the background. Her good looks had faded quickly, and Murdoch, the high-spirited laird, had wandered openly afield, seeking the rose with the dew still on it to pluck, finding it in plenty and plucking, plucking.

Tonia's religion was verbal; inwardly she was a hedonist who delighted in bawdy thoughts. She bought paper books with lurid covers, read them, invariably disappointed at their tameness, and burned them. Her walnut glass-doored bookcases displayed sets of Walter Scott, Dickens, Goldsmith and Thackeray to the scrutiny of visitors. Even Edie, something of a snoop, did not know the paperback side of her sister. Only with Murdoch had Tonia been her true self.

But here, now, was this same hill woman, this brood

mare, sitting regal as a queen by her fireside attended by her motley court of juice-squirting kin, and the McChesney jewel, Scotland's transplanted light, the lifelong object of Tonia's pride and despairing joy—her blue-eyed Murdoch, her son, her dream lover—lay beyond expanses of snow, separated from her forever by the overabundant flux of the fine blood in which she had taught him to glory.

"By God," she boomed, startling herself. "It's too much!"

Edie was solicitous. "Is the coffee too strong, dear? Have some more cream." She smiled tentatively at her sister-in-law in case the remark should be taken as derogatory. "I think the coffee is delicious, but Tonia, you know—her stomach is weak." "Shhhh" went the mothers, as though this statement might be too much even for the children, who had barely shifted positions since their arrival, and the deepening juice plinked reassuringly in the cans.

Tonia sighed and gave up. Pulling the insulation of her fat about her like a downy comforter, she settled her chin somewhere in the vicinity of her bosom and dozed, her stomach muttering an interior monologue of perpetual hunger.

Edie set her cup carefully on the table, hoping no one would notice that she had taken only a tiny sip—she was a tea drinker; coffee was about as palatable to her as tobacco juice would have been. She folded her hands in her lap like a little girl in church, listening vaguely but sweetly to the sermon of the fire. A delicately chiding smile soon touched the corners of her mouth as the carefree past came into the room, a windblown child with a hatful of wildflowers. Edie had left the child at home, where they had lived together for a great number of years, sharing secrets and games, neither of them growing any older, telling her where she was going and why, and why she thought it best to go alone, and the child had agreed; and here was the naughty creature as demure as could be, acting just as if they had agreed the opposite! She really should be angry, but her little friend had put on lace mitts and her best slippers, and her dress, except for a smudge on the sash, was spotless. She could not be angry; was, indeed—let her admit it!—grateful. The child settled happily on the floor beside Edie, and as the older of the two girls listened, began a most amusing story about a large dog and a runaway pony cart. They clung together, laughing until they were breathless.

Eula Marie looked at her husband's sleeping sisters—Antonia grunting and twitching, Editha smiling—and thought: Poor old things. He never was theirs, either, and wondered if they knew, and hoped that they did not.

The clock ticked and whirred and struck in the silent room. All at once the house was shaken by a roar that filled the sky. Antonia awoke with a frightened snort, Editha with a small cry. They all sat and stood in stony wonderment as the roar grew, descended from the heights and emanated from the level field behind the house, the treeless field that once had nurtured and brought to fullness crops of value but had lain fallow for years. Whatever thoughts the listening people had, whether of the Angel of Death or a great speckled bird, were interrupted by Ed bursting through the red curtains, his face aflame from the kitchen heat, his eyes plainly seeking something he would not find here. He stopped just inside the door, took a deep breath, looked at his mother-in-law and said in a voice that cracked, "Jasper just landed in the back field in a airplane, the damn fool!" and added lamely, "He'll have trouble getting her up again. It's a sheet of ice back there—"

Tonia rose in quivering fat, so incensed that she did not recall that she required help for the maneuver. "Who in God's name are you to call my favorite nephew a damn fool?"

Ed's color deepened. His mother-in-law, sharing his anger and reading his thoughts, said, *"Antonia, set down."*

The command so startled Tonia that she fell back on the two chairs, where she teetered, arms wildly waving, seeming at one moment to be destined to fall forward on her face, at the next to be aiming for crash-landing on her back. Randolph and his oldest son stepped forward and steadied her. She offered them no thanks. She was heaving fearsomely, her bosom like the swells of a tidal wave, now touching her chin, now agitating her stomach. Before she could get herself in hand there were "halloos" sung out in children's voices, echoing blithesomely around the house, and reprimands, and a clattering on the back porch, and a stream of bitter air like a river that rushed through the house and held the red velvet curtains straight out like banners on its current. The widow sat waiting—not for her son, it was felt, but for a chance to clear up the matter at hand, and for once Tonia wished there were some way to divert her sister-in-law's attention from her, but there was none. She subsided and waited to be chastised. The widow said, "Antonia, Editha, this is Priscilla's husband, Edgar." It was a command which was acknowledged, if grudgingly, on all sides. She continued, "There have been enough aspersions cast here today. Ugly words don't belong in a house of mourning. I'll thank you to recall that hereafter." Tears fell from Tonia's eyes and Editha joined her, sniffing and dabbing. Ed walked to the back of the room and stood with the cousins.

After a time the curtains parted and Spur came in slowly, followed by Bonny. He looked at his weeping aunts, patted their held-out, beseeching hands in passing, and went to his mother. He surprised everyone by kneeling before her and taking one of her hands in both of his. Bonny stood just within the curtains, gazing at the back of his head with held breath. Feel feel feel, she willed him. After a while he got to his feet, dry-eyed, and looked around the room, nodding coolly to his cousins, who returned the nods. His eyes came to Ed and got stuck there; the barely clothed hatred on the man's face shocked Spur deeply; he was helpless before it. Bonny went to the widow and kissed her cheek, murmuring, "Mother dear, we're so sorry." Covertly she looked for signs of ravagement, and finding the opposite, sternness with even a touch of anger, she truly felt like shouting "Rejoice", as she had wanted to do when they found Priscilla serenely cooking in the kitchen. She was not misled, knowing the worst was always still to come, but for the moment she breathed easily. She shook hands with Tonia and Edie, walked between the eye-locked men without noticing, shook Ed's hand and the cousins', murmuring their names as she did so, hoping she got them all straight.

"Where are my grandsons?" the widow said.

"I'll bring them in, Mom," said Spur, and wheeled about. At the door he stopped, without turning, and asked in a curious voice, "Where's Rob?"

"I don't know. He may be sailing down. Would that bring him soonest? Ask Erin. She will know."

Spur walked to the kitchen, thinking: *Sailing.* She's crazy; that explains it. I though she looked too—but he could not finish the thought. He went in to his sisters and said, deadpan, "Mom said Rob's sailing down from New York." He did not get the reaction he sought.

"She doesn't know geography," said Priscilla in an engrossed voice. "If I remember, you're not so hot at history." She lifted her head and saw that Erin was smiling faintly over the bowl in which she stirred a batter. Spur saw the smile also, and felt humiliated in front of his sons, who believed he knew everything. Looking at them, he saw that Tom's expression was defensive for his sake, but Buck's was enigmatic.

"Go see your grandmother," Spur said, aiming his words at Buck, biting down on them.

"Me, too?" said Tom, and once again Spur saw on Buck's face the look that was related to amusement or insolence. He pushed the boy toward the door, a little too hard, so that Buck stumbled. To cover his motive, whatever it was, he gave Tom a shove, too.

When the boys were gone, Erin, frowning slightly,

said, "I imagine Robin is coming by train. If so, it will be midnight before he gets here."

"Why in *hell,*" said Spur, feeling his disgusted tone to be warranted, "didn't that so-and-so take a plane." What he really wanted to say was, *"Train.* I bet if there was a horse and buggy for hire, he'd take *that."*

Erin, in a faraway voice, said, "He hasn't got a private plane, Jasper, and I imagine he couldn't afford the fare." She seemed to be speaking to herself. "Whatever money he has made, he has spent on this house to make it comfortable for occasional visitors."

Spur felt as though he had been slapped twice; of course the *occasional visitors* was aimed at him, as was the implication that money harder-earned than his kept the old house from falling down. He started to ask her why in hell he should put money into an old dump that wasn't worth the burning. He began to sweat. As soon as he could, he'd ask Bonny for a tranquilizer. Otherwise he couldn't tell what might happen. He looked at Priscilla for another of her smirks and felt a tingle of anger at her calmness.

She looked out the window at his plane, nesting where corn used to stand. "Most impressive," she said, sounding as if she meant it. Spur felt easier. He pulled a chair from the table and straddled it. If they wanted to hear about planes, the time might go quickly and even pleasantly. Funny, he thought, that they had never asked him about his work. Priscilla turned to him, smiling. "A virile thing, isn't it."

"The horse of the space age," he told her drolly. "Still takes a man to break one of the varmints. And do it *right.*" He bucked on the chair to illustrate.

She watched him merrily. "Goodness. Don't tell me you feel sexy about a *plane*."

"Hell, I don't need a plane for that—" He began in amusement but midway had the feeling of having played into her hands. He finished unenthusiastically, "I'm just plain made that way—" and waited.

She gave him a full smile "A chip off the old block," she said, and he saw where she had led him. Softly he told her, "Watch it," and glanced at Erin, and heard with surprise the pleading note in his voice.

Priscilla leaned against the counter, arms folded, facing into the room. "Sometimes I've thought about those girls and wondered if the honor of being deflowered by our daddy was enough to make up, you know, for not finding husbands. It was common knowledge, you know, where their flowers went." Spur could not find a word to fit the occasion that was fit to say.

Erin stopped what she was doing and looked at Priscilla. "How did you know, Prissy?" She had not called her sister the childish name for years, but neither woman took notice of the intimacy.

Priscilla answered angrily. "You and Robin couldn't keep everything from us, though God knows you tried." Erin was silent. Priscilla turned and looked out the window. "When that was a cornfield and I was a ten-year-old loony, I found him and a young black girl —she wasn't much older than me—"

Spur got up, letting the chair fall. "What the hell kind of talk is that today of all days—"

She replied without looking at him. "I wish you wouldn't say 'hell' so much. He may be there, 'today of all days.' "

"Can't you shut her up?" Spur's appeal to Erin was more frightened than angry, but it was Priscilla who answered.

"His being dead can't change the truth. Part of the truth was that he was proud of the way he was. The day I found him with the girl, all he said was, 'Go back home, Prissy.' He wasn't mad. He didn't stop. He—oh, I think he smiled; no, grinned." She looked at Erin. "It didn't affect me at all. I never did hold the way he was against him, the way I think you have. Somehow, his weakness—if it was one—was a kind of strength to me." She smiled. "I guess it was having proof that even *Daddy* was—flawed. You had your own strength," she told Erin, "you and Robin. And Millicent, I think. The rest of us got by on tricks. Mama's trick, obviously, was to *hide* how strong she was. But the rest of us cheated. Crazy Priscilla, icy Rhoda, hollow Spur." She looked regretful and seemed about to say more, but Spur did not give her the chance.

"Tricks," he said, hackle-risen. "You've always turned everything around, Priscilla, damn it. You call that old woman in there strong, and me"—he changed it rapidly—*"him* weak? Oh, sure; he's helpless now, and that's your meat, isn't it?" The awful image was there, highlighted by Priscilla's small, choked laugh. Remotely, Spur wondered how he could go on making so many mistakes. It was as if some basic part of himself were no longer operating.

For a long, shattering moment, Spur looked inward and saw an unsuspected connection between himself and his father that was distinct from forms of address and traditional expectations. The connection was composed of influences and motivations which ran along something that looked like a wire, or a vein; as he watched, amazed, a forked thing—which could have been scissors, or man, or woman—edged through the fog and severed the connection. He felt the pain as mortal, even as the image began to fade, and he fought hard against crying out affirmation of what he knew to have been the death of the part of him that was his father.

The easy use of words was not a gift that had been bestowed upon Spur. He wrestled daily with the most simple articulation. Faced with the need to speak a eulogy for himself and his father, he could manage only words he had heard spoken about other newly dead, and because they were ready-wrapped, they came out fatuous. "When he was alive he was strong and good in the ways that count in this world."

Priscilla was infuriated by the words "the ways that count," imagining that goodness, at least, did not need to be qualified. Her fury outweighed her regret at classifying Spur as hollow, since she did not really know whether or not he was. But she suspected, once again, because of his words, that he *was,* and "hollow" led her to "hallow," and she struck her opening notes from that string. "I can't stand hallowed speeches full of lies. I can't stand your hypocrisy. All I've ever felt from you is hypocrisy. It comes out of you like diarrhea. I don't think, whichever Priscilla wins—I don't think I'll ever look at you without wanting to hand you a roll of toilet paper." The other Priscillas, entering as a theme, threatened to change the motif of her song. She tried to dilute its power by including Spur in it, as a cluster of sour notes. "That is, unless you're fighting for your life with another Jasper—" But somehow the tune got sadder and sadder with Spur in it. She felt that the strain of her malice was the only one major enough to be safe and she strummed it eagerly, waiting for the usual release—"a Jasper who isn't a coward and nickel-plated big shot with nothing inside but smelly stuff, like one of those dirty tricks you shoot for in carnivals—" She made a pushing, warding-off gesture, seeing Nonie and the weeping Priscilla superimposed on each other. "Get away," she said. "Get away."

Erin saw the change from fiery but possibly truthful girl to lost and mad one with a feeling of sinking. She put her arms around Priscilla and held her close.

Spur, after the initial shock of misunderstanding, straightened up and went toward the two women, manful and sure of what needed to be done. "We'll have to get her upstairs to bed," he said, and began to lead them toward the morning room.

Erin held onto Priscilla, resisting with all her might Spur's direction. Between them they played tug-of-war with their sister. "Not through the morning room, Jasper," she said, dry-lipped. "We'll have to go around and come through the front." Her old impatience with her father over the matter of the door through to the hall covered her knowledge of Spur's motivation like a tattered blanket.

Spur stared at her as though she were a fool. "The snow out there is hip-deep in places!"

"It can't be helped," said Erin, tugging her sister toward the back door.

"Goddamn it," Spur said, "she'll catch her death of

cold!" His impulse to strike Erin in the face was nearly overpowering.

"She, she, she," said Priscilla derisively. "Are you really worried about *her?*" She began to laugh. "Poor old Erin, can't you see? He wants me to go through there to reassure everybody that I'm still crazy! That some things don't change!"

Spur dropped her arm and rushed from the kitchen by the back door. If anyone had looked they would have seen him running through the snow toward his plane, but no one looked. The two women stood together, unmoving except for Priscilla's trembling.

"Erin," she said, after a while.

"Yes, dear."

"Do you feel sorry for me?"

Erin, thinking that she would be truthful, too, and surprised at what the truth was, told her, "No. I don't think so. No."

Priscilla gently freed herself from Erin's arms, patting her for a "Thank you," and walked toward the massed family. Her trembling was discernible from a distance, and still Erin, to whom anything trembling was too poignant to ignore, would have answered no if Priscilla had repeated her question. She felt inexplicably grateful to her sister. Priscilla left the room without looking back, leaving something hanging in the air—a confidence, perhaps, something important—where she had paused at the doorway.

Erin went back to her pots and pans, her stove, her batters and roasts. She saw the three of them as they had been a few minutes before, heard their words in her head, felt their purposes in her blood, and said softly, "Why do we hate each other?" The inclusive "we" made her feel closer to them than she had for years. Running water over a mound of potatoes in the sink: I wonder if I have been wrong all these years to think that wounds should be hoarded? If they are one's only riches?

Rhoda and Andrew arrived at two. They had left at seven-thirty but the increasingly dangerous roads had added two and a half hours onto the normally four-hour trip. When they got to the house fires had been lit in the twin parlors across the hall from the morning room, and this domain was given over to the children, where they could play word games, tell stories or look wistfully at the snow, thinking of other Christmases when sled rides and snowmen were possible.

The young hill cousins, with some prodding, joined Tom, Buck, Gayle, Carol and Marilyn, who, as the oldest girl, acted as chaperonc and flirted with Randolph's eighteen-year-old son. She calculated that he was too far removed to be considered a relative at all, and decided to seriously consider marrying him. She was, she told herself, dangerously aroused by his pointed ears and slanty eyes and muscles. He was too polite at the moment, but she vowed to kiss him before the day was out. She tossed her Brigitte Bardot hair, kept her sisters and Buck in line with womanly authority (Tom was asleep on a window seat, unable to take the air of death in the house, made all the more unbearable because they were not told which room he had died in; it could have been in this very room), and all the while she plotted the simple, casual way in which she would request this darling boy to accompany her to the barn. She had lost a locket there last year, she would tell him—lost it in the haymow and had found herself unable to think of a single other thing all year: *that's* how much she loved that little old locket! She toyed with the idea of surrendering to this faunlike boy her virginity—a thing Brigitte would have found irresistibly attractive and decadent, under the circumstances, with death ringing them in like Apaches with knives. Of course, Brigette would have done it on the bed where her grandfather died, but Marilyn felt she was not quite that French *yet*. She had better confine herself to French kissing, which she would probably have to teach him how to do. But if they got carried away and he *demanded* the other, what on earth could she do but moan and give in?

She sang softly, for his ears alone, an old song her stepfather had told her dated from the time of the first Elizabeth, the baldheaded one, supposedly written by a lady in love with Sir Walter Raleigh—and wasn't it appropriate, because George's last name was Raleigh, too!..

"Ah, the sea is cold
When 'tis dark and stormy
But a young man, passing bold,
Has the pow'r to warm thee."

The second verse she sang more softly still, gazing into the fire, poking it dreamily:

"Though thy shift be red
From the love he show thee,

Iseult, thy tears assault thy bed
Of salt—the deck below thee."

George Raleigh, seeing the girl's breast quicken as she sang the old bawdy words he had known all his life, grinned, recognizing the signs. He had been wielding his own poker since puberty, sparking the fires of second cousins, schoolteachers, wildflower-picking town women who knew just where to go picking and just when to "lose their way" and have to "ask directions." His sexual cynicism was as natural as his politeness but it did not dull the edge of his enjoyment of the fire. He did not know how far this one was willing to go, but there was plenty of time to find out. He stretched his long legs to the hearth and sang her a warning:

"Love's an eager thing
When the thistle new grows
Bide thy time and winter will
find thee
Standing where the rue grows."

"You know," said Tonia, smiling up at Rhoda, "you've got much prettier with the years. It wouldn't surprise me if you outshine Millicent yet. Skin-and-bones women may be what they want in the magazines, but flesh, well placed, equals *real* good looks." She nodded with a veiled look, her lips pursed in secret satisfaction. "Look to the East, my girl, for the truth of *that.*"

"Thanks, Aunt Tonia," Rhoda said brightly. "I haven't put on an ounce in ten years."

"I didn't say you had, girl. I said you'd got prettier." Giving them both the lie, "Fuller in the face." Having won her small round, she looked happy and added, "Murdoch always favored well-fleshed women"—paused, then placed the barb—"before he married."

Rhoda stared at her aunt, whom she saw suddenly as vicious. Her palm itched; she wondered what the general reaction would be if she slapped Tonia's great face. She glanced at her mother, who apparently understood her impulse, for she shook her head at Rhoda, a small ticlike movement but unmistakably a request to forebear. The silent complicity, however, did not ease the rankling set up by what Tonia had said. In spite of the widow's clearly having been the intended victim, Rhoda felt obscurely that it was she who had been somehow hurt by her aunt's nastiness.

She kissed her Aunt Edie with a warmth that startled the sleepy lady, who had been greeted by Rhoda earlier with her accustomed coolness. "How well you look!" Rhoda told her. "Elegant and *trim,* as always." She knew perfectly well that her point had been made and taken—Tonia's wheeze informed her of this—but she was not ready to stop. "Half the women I know, women my age, would give their eyeteeth for your figure. You and I," she confided, pretending that she and Edie were alone together enjoying "girl talk" over a cup of tea—a likely picture—"are fortunate, I hope you know that. *Most* women start spreading as soon as they hit thirty—and spread, and spread—" She illustrated with her hands the awful propensity of most women, winked and shrugged at her aunt, and heard her mother give a high laugh, which told her just how far she had gone. She passed on to her cousins, chatting with infectious, though subdued, jollity, and read their approval of her for taking her mother's side. She felt quite heady with success, out of all proportion to the usual small and bitter satisfaction such occasional bitchery afforded her, when she was driven to it. Her cousins' and her mother's approbation—Edie had withheld hers, though not so obviously as to cramp Rhoda's style, and Andrew was—where else!—in the kitchen with Erin—seemed to provide an echo to some similar experience, though it was probably just the damned recurring sense of *déjà vu* she suffered with family; it was as if, in the first five minutes of their lives together, they had exhausted all possible experience to be shared, and the rest was repetition.

As the case turned out to be with the cousins; after five minutes she could think of nothing more to say to them and found herself rummaging about in the past for some pleasant memory involving herself and them —frugal choice—to bring up and use to close, gracefully, what was beginning to feel like an interview of some sort. She had strolled once with Randolph's new wife through unfamiliar hills, and the girl, appallingly shy, threshing about for something interesting to say, as Rhoda was now doing, had inclined her head toward a cabin peeping like a bashful hillbilly over a rise and said, "Over yandro there dwells a morphydike." The remark had haunted Rhoda for a long time, but it was hardly the memory with which to effect graceful withdrawal.

Andrew came into the room and her need to escape his eyes made her forget her wish to be graceful. She left the room abruptly.

She prowled through the house, feeling the tug of

the past, but uncomfortably sure that it was connected, still, with her exchange of bitcheries with her aunt. In her father's upstairs study, where Christmas ornaments had been laid out for the tree-trimming that would have taken up most of this evening, she became aware of trying to cheat: she found herself trying to summon feelings about him and herself in relation to him that were not there. All that she could find with honesty was a residue of the mutual indifference that had allowed them to be fairly reasonable, unexacting companions when they were thrown together, rather like seatmates on a plane who would have been ill matched for a long flight but who could be convincingly cordial for a short one. She handled his wine decanter hopefully, but could find no genuine poignancy in the fact that it had been washed and polished of any trace of him or of his hunger. She imagined that if it had been sticky with lees and fingerprints, then she might have felt something: annoyance or repugnance.

She gave way to a creeping boredom and with it resentment at this hunt that she saw as enforced—a hunt for emotion, for her husband's sake. He had told her in a dozen ways since the telephone call that he expected something from her that she was not giving, and by deduction—hardly difficult—she had arrived at what it was: a sort of emotional dowry, bound with strings of family. Sentimentality, in other words. Suppose she went to him and said, "Look, I'm a mid-twentieth-century woman; you knew it when you married me, and before that. Why, suddenly, do you want to push me back into the nineteenth century, and tie me up with family until I faint?" Suppose she said to him, "Look, A., count your blessings, for God's sake, and shut the hell up . . . "

In the car Gayle asked Rhoda, "Should we cry, Mother?" and Rhoda said briskly, "Not if you have to ask such a question." Andrew said quietly, "Do you feel like crying?" Gayle thought, then said, "Sort of. I did cry in the bathroom when I thought about Aunt Erin. I ran the water so you couldn't hear me."

Looking straight ahead, Rhoda said, "He's my father, too. Did you think about that—"

"Yes," said Gayle, "but you've got us. Carol, are you going to cry?" Carol considered. "When they put him in the ground, I think. I hate cold dark places. Mother, do worms crawl around in the wintertime?"

Andrew barked "Carol!" Rhoda felt faint and nauseated but she spoke naturally. "I know you're curious about death, Carol, but you mustn't be morbid. Death is as natural as birth. Do you have morbid thoughts about birth?"

"Not morbid, exactly, but I think it's kind of nasty. How can people go koochy-koo and kiss something that's just come out of a lot of blood and stuff? Uaugh! I'd rather *die* than kiss a baby. I don't know why *they're* so hot."

"Enough monologue," Andrew said in such an odd voice that Rhoda looked at him quickly; he had sounded almost tearful. She said to him reasonably, "In some parts of the world birth is mourned and death celebrated. Let her have her opinion."

"I'm going to celebrate death," Marilyn said. "I'll drink and dance and laugh bitterly."

"You'll all shut up," Andrew said, and pulled the car to the side of the road and cut off the motor. The children were silent and a bit scared. Only Rhoda could see that he had stopped because tears were blinding him. No one moved until he took out his handkerchief and blew his nose and started the car.

Rhoda had meant to offer to drive, but as she studied his profile she was warned, as his watchful eyes had warned her, though not emphatically enough last night, not to take the lead. She felt in him a danger that was altogether baffling. She had felt it even as he held her, when she told him about her father's death. At the time she had deciphered it more as some need that could be dispelled by a harmless translation, for him, of the furious pain she felt for herself into reasonable mourning for her father. No, for Erin; she had decided that would be the more politic. Mourning, as it were, at one remove, and for the living—telling him of her sadness for Erin's sake—had been like reading one child a story about another's bereavement. She had kept herself out of it, except as narrator. Could it be, she wondered, simply that she had overdone it, holding forth for too long at breakfast about poor Erin? Even the children had picked up her tactic, which was why she had reminded Gayle that it was *her* father, too; she had really been speaking to Andrew, to tell him that her discretion sprang from consideration and not from coldness. Not really. She had been discreet enough to make those terribly early, apologetic calls of cancellation—no bridge for a week, at least—while Andrew was in the bathroom, or so she had assumed; feeling danger in the room behind her, she had turned and found him hanging there, suspended over her words as if what she was saying into the telephone had robbed him of weight. She had pointed out to him that the hasty calls were economically sensible—calling from the farm would have cost a mint—trusting that she did not need to remind him that the social aspect was equally important, for some of the calls were made to the wives of his superiors at the plant. *Those* obligations, she felt like telling him, outlasted death and taxes, but perhaps only wives knew that, after all.

She laid her hand on his thigh. There, there, she signaled soothingly, it's only your little brown pigeon whom you need and who needs you. However, to make sure that he knew she was with him—wherever he was, or had been, to make him weep—she said, creasing her brow, "I *know* we can't go any faster, but I wish we could, don't you, A.? Erin will have her hands full; Mama will need looking after. They've always depended on me—" He turned his eyes from the treacherous road; at his look something bit at her heart, hard. The look told her that her words were a baseless lie. The lie seemed to be reflected on and on, like mirrors facing each other. She rushed in with what truth she could muster, applying it like a poultice to her pain and to his eyes where the lie was reflected, hoping the sting would burn the lie away—"depended on my cold sort of control—" She bore down on "cold" and "control" but to her dismay they were suddenly descriptive of Andrew and not of herself. His profile promised no more hope of change than a death mask. She held herself with both arms and said, without thinking, words from childhood, "Somebody just walked over my grave," looked at him helplessly and burst into tears.

He drew her to him until her head rested on his shoulder. She stayed there for a while but moved when she became afraid that such close contact might allow him to read her repetitive thought: I'll never forgive you for making me cry. Not really, Andrew. Not completely.

Rhoda wandered down the hall and wound up in the closed-off part of the house, in her old room. There, perching on the edge of the long-unused bed, she found some emotion for Andrew, and one answer for herself.

Her room had been closed off for years, but today she found it an appropriately dusty symbol for a childhood composed mainly of closings-off, and dust, with few open, green memories.

Sitting in the past like a child in a dusty road, muttering of her dislike for Tonia, she found the reason. Her greenest memory—which had looked at the time of its inception like the opening of an undreamed-of door—had been Millicent's twelfth birthday party, when Rhoda had stolen the limelight from her fascinating sister. It had seemed almost beyond belief, then, and had buoyed her up for years—until Tonia's remarks in the morning room, until this ridiculously pathetic moment. Feeling the props being taken out from under her, she viewed the day of her triumph and saw how it had really been: Millicent had shown her most arrogant side, and Rhoda, sensing the mood of the company, had turned herself willfully into a creature of charm and grace, concentrating on Tonia, that arbiter of family fashions. Others had called her a diplomat, a perfect hostess, but Tonia ("pretty is as pretty does" of course!) had declared her pretty—"the prettiest girl in McChesney County, I do declare!" And she had believed—Rhoda the realist!—in some part of herself untouched by the years, that others had seen and remembered her that way, that Tonia had not just been punishing Millicent that day. Over the years, underneath the accurate picture she had of herself, had lain the memory, like a secret powerful strength, which had given her the audacity to attract Bill, to track down Andrew. She told herself that she was more incredulous than sorry to see the truth at last; what on earth did she *need* with such an illusion? She, who had spent her life digging for, and demolishing, such sentimental tripe! But for once the diminishing of a need was not synonymous with relief.

She avoided the cobwebby mirror on the way out of the room; leaning against the closed door she applied her standard test: "Insight? Yes. But progress?" She did not know. She felt tender enough for tears, young and bruised, and she wanted Andrew and his unspoken, undefined reassurances, forgetting, in her real bereavement, that he might refuse them.

She walked down the hallway, disliking Millicent—the strangest of a family of strangers, who had made a success of a slight cast in one eye and a brown mole like a punctuation mark to a message written in invisible ink, or in the secretions of a musk-ox, to judge by male responses to her. She thought, making an effort to be dry and witty: For all her mystery and negotiable flaws, she's had no husbands and I've had two.

She went in to the family, tentatively offering to her husband's eyes the gift of her new sorrow, but it was intercepted by her mother, who beckoned Rhoda to her. She said, chidingly, "Backwards and forwards, backwards and forwards, like a mountain lion upstairs," and touched Rhoda as if she sought information through the touch, and found it. Once again she baffled Rhoda by an awareness of her feelings that was like thought reading. She said, "Andrew, your wife's got too much energy to settle down with us. Take her outside for a good long walk. Don't bring her back till she's plumb wore out, you hear?" She gave Rhoda a look of understanding and pity. It was as if she told her daughter, "I've been through it myself; I know what it's like. Hang on."

Rhoda rejected the look and the comfort with horror. She wanted to tell her mother, "It's not like you and Daddy; it's not, not a bit. I've got nothing in common with you." Instead she touched her mother's gnarled hand, suppressing a shudder, and gave her the smile an adult gives to an overly fanciful child, putting her back in her place.

Out of a long silence, Tonia laughed with the sound of delight.

The day was a river running backward from the sea; the confused people riding it, sometimes half submerged, had, by three-thirty, reached the sluggishness of dog days.

The children were fed, after which they fell into a torpor and lay about their parlors without imagination or desire, with the exceptions of Marilyn and George Raleigh. George, stretching lazily, thought maybe the time had come to do something about this hungry little girl—well, soon.

After Priscilla's denunciation of Spur she had gone and sat for a while with the children in the parlor, knowing they would make no demands upon her, but after a time that very fact made her uncomfortable. Bonny came in to check on her sons, and Priscilla told her that she had fought with Spur and he had run from the house, she did not know where to. She made no effort to keep the children from hearing her, and Tom asked, puzzled, if grown-up brothers and sisters had real fights. Bonny, to forestall Priscilla's answer, which might be too candid, told him quickly that of course they did, that it was also a sign of caring. Buck listened with half-closed, glittering eyes, his mouth quirked, but Tom, after hopeful consideration, said that he understood: you didn't fight with strangers any more than you loved them, so brothers and sisters had to love and fight, too.

Bonny lingered in the room until she felt that her leaving would seem natural and then she left by the front door and went instinctively to the plane. There, in the freezing cold, elevated above the spot where his father had once had sex with a dark child and had been found by his daughter and had grinned, Spur made fierce, despairing love to his wife.

Perhaps because of Bonny's answer to Tom's question, Priscilla felt that something was expected of her, but not here in this room. She could prove nothing here. She went into the morning room and it seemed to be there, whatever it was that was expected. She sat among the family whom she did not know and who did not know her. Ed's presence in the room was sweet to her, like sugar taken for quick energy, and the thought of what lay ahead between them, the necessary bitterness, made it all the sweeter. She sat quietly under the various appraisals: the soft curiosity of the cousins who thought her pretty and wondered how it felt to be what folks called "not quite right"; her Aunt Tonia's sharp looks and, so Tonia imagined, clever questions and remarks; and her mother's silent interest, which Priscilla returned. If she was proving herself by sitting there, she did not know whether to herself or to them.

"How is school, dear?" Edie asked sweetly.

"What?" Priscilla was startled.

"Old fool," Tonia said, not unkindly. "She's been out of school for at least eight years."

Editha had not addressed the question to Priscilla, and she murmured, "Of course. How silly of me," and told herself she must be more careful.

"They tell me you have got married." Tonia felt mysteriously shrewd.

Priscilla laughed, thinking both her aunts were senile, and cast her amused glance toward Ed as she said, "Six years, Aunt Tonia. Haven't you met my husband?"

"Of course she's met Edgar," said her mother with interesting undertones, and to Priscilla's amazement she smiled with pure malice and spoke as though Tonia were not present. "She's old, you know. She can't remember too good," cackled and waited, bright-eyed, for Tonia's reaction.

Tonia reddened and said, "Oh, can't I, Eula Marie Raleigh?" paused to let the use of her adversary's maiden name sink in, and then pointed straight at Randolph. "Yonder he stands, my girl!"

Everyone burst into laughter, including Ed, and after a moment Tonia joined in. When the laughter had died down she said, pretending sheepishness, "Well, I never could remember faces," and added, savoring her touché, "If I met *you* on the street, Eula Marie, I wouldn't know you from Adam."

"I reckon," said the widow amiably, "I wouldn't have much trouble knowing *you,* Antonia."

In the general laughter Priscilla began to giggle and could not stop. Who is this person, she thought, cat-fighting with the best of them? I wish Erin could hear, and without recognizing that wanting to share anything with Erin was also strange, she got up and went back to the kitchen and told her sister. Erin laughed and laughed, shaking her head. Ed came into the kitchen that was filled with gaiety and was put to work peeling potatoes. In their concentration the three of them fell into a warm, companionable silence, but now and then laughter would renew itself and one of them would gesture helplessly, indicating that they were making too much noise. For a while it felt to them like a traditional Christmas Eve, with the cooking smells and laughter and conspiracy.

Priscilla, who was working at the sink, looked out the window and saw Spur and Bonny plowing knee-deep in snow toward the house. "I'm sorry," she said. "I wish I could take it back."

Erin and Ed followed the direction of her gaze. "I know," said Erin shortly, "but only children can do that." Ed, who knew nothing of the fight, misinterpreted their meaning and felt sick to his stomach, thinking: Jesus. Erin knows about it, too. The warmth that had grown in him in the past half-hour rushed out and left him cold. He wanted to fling himself from the door and knock Spur down and tear at his throat like an animal. The women, unaware of him at all, continued to horrify him.

Priscilla said tartly, "It was the time and place that were wrong. I'm sorry for *that*. It had to be done."

"Oh?" Erin bent over, popping pans of biscuits into the oven. "Then why feel guilty, Priscilla? If a thing must be done, the time and place can't matter that much." She straightened up and said, "After all, it can't affect *Daddy* now."

Priscilla turned and the two sisters tried to read each other. Erin continued gently, "I meant the things you said about him, which were undoubtedly true. If it was Jasper you wanted to hurt, then here and now were as good as any."

Ed felt a thaw beginning around his feet; at least he could move them. "I guess I did want to hurt him, or shock him. He's always so damned smug." After a moment, "Were the things I said about *him* true?"

Erin was ironic. "They were certainly harsh enough to be true." She considered for a moment. "I don't know if they were, though. I don't know him." This slipped out and she tried to cover up by adding, "Not as well as you do, apparently."

Priscilla stared at her. "But you're his mother." They stared at each other. Erin's eyes were frightened. Ed watched in confusion. Priscilla made a quick gesture of frustration. "His *sister,*" but the emphasis lacked conviction.

Erin turned away, picked up a fork and tested the potatoes. There was a faint roaring in her ears, too faint to drown our Priscilla's words, or the one word that had crashed so loud.

Priscilla said sullenly, because sullenness follows unwarranted anger, "I would like to lie down."

"There's a fire in your room."

"Aren't you going to tuck me in?"

"You've got a husband for that job, now." Erin smiled, feeling its thinness.

"But it's never been the same." Priscilla turned to Ed: "They used to tuck me in so tight it was like a strait jacket."

"Prissy—" Ed wanted to plead, afraid of his wife's undertones.

"Dearest man, don't you want to hear about my 'formative years'?" Her sarcasm bordered on the savage. "Ask Erin if the other bedrooms have fires in them. Go on—ask her."

"No," said Erin. "No, they haven't."

"You see. She thought I'd have to be put to bed as soon as we got here!" Priscilla glared at Erin, her eyes jumping with anger that she knew was baseless, even before Ed said, "So did I." Roughly he told her, "Shut up, Prissy."

Erin turned. "Oh, let her say it, Edgar." She went to the table and sat heavily, leaning her cheek on her palm. "It's a relief to talk this way. Sit down, Priscilla. Edgar." Priscilla sat but Ed stood guard. Erin looked across the table at her sister. "If I have done you harm, I think you will—forgive me." She wondered if there was a plea in the words, but found that she meant them. "I don't imagine the others will—not easily. I say 'the others' because I don't know which ones. Not yet. I don't think I have touched Millicent, except to bore her, but I can't be sure. I meant well, I think, though I'm not sure of that. The one thing I am sure of is that no one else thinks so. That I meant well."

Priscilla gazed at Erin so intently that Erin felt as though she were being looked through, to someone who stood behind her chair. "Why," she asked, "do you keep saying 'I' when you're really afraid for him?"

"Afraid?" Erin felt the beginning of weightlessness. "For whom?"

"Robin. You're afraid of what we will do to him."

Erin's face began to crumple as though it were the tissue paper that had kept something precious from breaking and was now to be wadded up and thrown away.

Ed could not stand the sight. There was no doubt in his mind about which woman needed him now. "Come on, Prissy, goddamn it. You said you wanted to lay down." He pulled her from the chair, pretending rough playfulness. She did not resist him and he felt it to be a good thing, because he would have hit her without knowing why.

Erin sat at the table, filled with a deadly fear. She would almost have called them back for company, rather than face her thoughts. The button had been pushed, the whirlygig had spun and stopped where she had never allowed it to stop before, at a pendant that had always been there but that she had only glimpsed as a blur, having always sped past it by her will and a sense of mindless necessity.

In less than two hours we will be standing about a coffin and who will believe it is their father lying there, and who will believe it is the wrong man who has died? If you are called in the middle of the night and told that your father is dead, you condition yourself to remorse for past failings, for rebellion against authority, for failure to love enough, for having loved too much. All the way home you think of it, and when you reach home you draw together. But they have done none of these things. They will feel guilty, and guilt must have an outlet. Robin, my dear. Robin, you. You—and me.

She would have given anything to be able to return to the morning of this dead day when her first unquestioned move had been to call Robin.

When I knew so much—when I knew how they have hated us, why couldn't I have put the pieces together? Why did I imagine it was protection, looking at those deliberate gaps?

She answered herself. Because to have faced it

would have been to give you up forever.

She got up and went outside, not knowing that she had wept until she felt the weight of tears frozen on her eyelashes.

It was my selfishness. I wanted him here for my sake. Not to protect me from them. They can't hurt me. Not the way I can still hurt them.

A blast of wind that had been lurking in a tree lunged at her. It was a visible wind and she looked into its white face, as icy as her own, and called it by name. "Truth," she said. "You should always wear a cloak to hide your daggers. Not everyone will stand still for you." She went back into the house and stood holding the door open. "Come in if you must, and let us get acquainted. It's high time." Using all her strength, she slammed the door, so that pots hurtled from walls where they had safely hung for years. Over the din she said, "It's goddamned high time."

Bonny came hurrying in, followed by Spur. Finding Erin retrieving pots from the floor, Bonny helped but Spur stood leaning against the sink, arms folded. "It's a wonder the walls stand up," he said sourly.

Erin turned up to him a bright face. "Yes," she said. "I'll mention it to Robin when he gets here. The house *does* need reinforcing. Or maybe you'll tell him, Jasper, in case I forget."

She was daring Spur to walk down an old, worn path, one whose lashing brambles he had never before been able to resist. She wanted his anger turned against her in fullness, to expend itself against her as the wind had, tearing and biting. One at a time, she thought. Between now and Robin's arrival I must take them on one at a time. She did all the things she knew Spur hated about her, to goad him: she drew her lips into their most prim line; she lifted her eyebrows to the height of their most supercilious arc; she pulled her body up until it resembled a hateful exclamation point, or an insulting tone of voice. But she could do nothing about her eyes. They told him too much.

His voice was maddeningly easy as he said, "O.K., Miss Erin. If you want me to, I'll tell old Rob-boy." He walked over and took the last pot from the floor, found a cloth and polished the pot inside and out, and hung both pot and cloth on their hooks. Then he sauntered from the room.

Erin felt Bonny's hand on her arm and turned her exposed face to her sister-in-law. "Don't, my dear," said Bonny. "He doesn't deserve this much."

"Don't interfere," said Erin, in a voice Bonny had not heard from her before. "Don't interfere, please. Only old maids can do that," and thought to herself, openly smiling under Bonny's concerned eyes: Only old maids can interfere with their children's lives. But because it was necessary, she got herself quickly in hand. She would need all of her reserves, and nothing is so draining, she told herself wryly, as unaccustomed mirth. She apologized to Bonny and accepted her offer to help finish preparing the food for the second shift. Here, she thought, is an ally—no longer unquestioning, as she once was, but an ally to whom I can entrust certain secrets if it becomes necessary.

At four o'clock the cousins went home to tend their own skinny fires and livestock, but at the widow's command they left the children behind. Randolph, after a meaningful glance exchanged with his eldest son, drawled out that he reckoned George could stay, too; he'd do his son's chores this once. Rhoda was sitting in the parlor with the children and saw the glance and knew its meaning and it did not touch her. If George Raleigh had at that moment put her daughter on the floor and taken her, Rhoda would have sat unmoved and unmoving. Her endless search for emotion with which to placate her husband had only led her further into the woods, into a thicket of truth from which she could not extricate herself by wile or will. She had learned that she did not care for her children in any deep sense and never had, any more than she had been cared for—although she did not think her own parents' attitude was the reason for hers. As far as she could tell, her feelings, or lack of them, were responsible only to a lifetime of attempts to see a thing for what it was, rather than what it should be. What she saw concerning parents and children was that they intruded in each other's lives because they had no choice. When the time of choice arrived, they stopped intruding. They paid visits, they wrote letters, they kept up the necessary illusion as prescribed by society, and it was the uncaring that made it possible. A child feeds at the breast because it needs to, to live. When it is given an alternative, it takes it gladly. She had had no trouble weaning her children. As life progresses, more and more of each other, of parent-child, is discarded, until, given the choice of parent or lover, of child or none, both make the inevitable selection, unless there is sickness of the mind, and she did not refer to those aberrations. She had, actually, brought herself up from childhood, caring only for herself, obeying only herself; she had rejected Robin and Erin as surrogate parents—who in hell *needed* them!—and though she might have felt, as a *small* child, her real parents' indifference, and been momentarily affected by it, she had come to be grateful to them in her own way: because of them, and her early rejection of emotion in favor of reason, she was her own woman; could she wish for her children any more than *that?*

Stumbling through the snow with Andrew on their long, silent walk, she had examined husbands and wives, too, sticking herself and Andrew, the specimens, ruthlessly under the microscope. Aside from the complexities of sex, of adult minds working with, or against, each other, of the basis of free choice, of the ideal of marriage as a more or less final act of emotional commitment—preceding and succeeding children—there were symbolical meanings which husband and wife should never divulge, one to the other. Could she say to Andrew: I am a woman who needs certain words, and one of those words is *husband?* I need "married," "husband," "home"; I need "married" to ride like a raft in the sea of women who are, really, what my life is mainly composed of. I need "husband" and "home" as ballast and securing line—as proof, too, that I didn't make "married" up, the way actresses used to, calling themselves Mrs. for a kind of spurious respectability. Could she say to him: A woman, to be successful, must be an actress, because men, who mold the future, behave as if they were molding the past as far as their expectations of wives are concerned, all for reasons that are more symbolical than not? No, she could not say any of it. All she could do, now, was wait, and stay out of the limelight, and hope that Andrew—out of an honesty that was different from hers—could point the way for them to reconcile their differences, hopefully without pain. But she would no longer stand between Marilyn and her nature, nor the other girls' and theirs, for when they were ready to claim their own they would lunge, and grab, and find, and only she, standing in the way, would be crippled by the encounter.

She turned to George and told him, "Why don't you take Marilyn for a walk." She saw their disbelief and felt only the slightest nip at her conscience, like the effort of an old, toothless memory. Marilyn grabbed George by the hand and they flew from the room.

Andrew, Bonny and Spur came into the parlor soon afterward and Rhoda nodded to them—contained, she thought, until only outside forces could shatter her. She told Andrew, "I asked George to take Marilyn for a walk. She looked as if she would faint in another minute." He scanned her face and then rewarded her trust with a smile that nearly blinded her. Not knowing that what she did was a partial refutation of her coldly mid-twentieth-century conclusions about life and love, she turned her head like a sunflower to follow him, the source of a good deal of her light.

In the second parlor the younger children were playing a game of jacks, and through the open doorway the scrabble and thump of hand and ball, the clatter of thrown jacks, the naming of difficult plays—"Over the fence and back," "Twice around the moon"—and the humming of the fires met and mingled in a kind of lullaby, soothing the quiet adults' inner turbulence.

In the morning room the three old ladies dozed. Erin, tiptoeing through, saw her Aunt Editha's hand stroke the air beside her, as though it were the head of someone with long silky hair. Tonia's great galleon sailed the sea of sleep with majesty, taking the swells smoothly. The widow's head rested against the high back of her chair; this drew the line of her throat to tautness, erasing the wrinkles, and in the falling night her face seemed young, pinked by the firelight.

Upstairs Ed and Priscilla lay on the bed, the sides of their hands touching. For the first time in their six stormy years together they were fully at ease with each other.

Nowhere in the house, at this hour of four o'clock, does anyone think of the dead man. Death, like any other music, is most controversial when first heard.

It was Erin's intention to slip upstairs and lie down. Her eyes were as heavy as marbles and her limbs felt as though she had been immersed in water for hours. Stepping from the morning room into the hallway, she walked as quietly as possible, not wishing to draw a glance, friendly or otherwise. When she thought herself safely past the opened parlor doors, Buck, who had been watching for her, ran out and stopped her.

"Aunt Erin," he said, "would you play that song I like so much? It's too darn quiet and it gives me the creeps."

"No—" began Erin, but Spur's voice rode out the door, commanding his son to come back, asking him if he was a damn fool, threatening to tan his hide, big as he was.

"Why, yes, Buck," said Erin. "I can play it softly; music is always appropriate," and she walked into the parlor, smiling, and said apologetically, "If you can call the sounds I make music." She went to the rosewood piano and opened the lid, sat down and began to play.

"Sing it, please, Aunt Erin," said Buck, his eyes on his father's face. The other children crowded into the room, saying, "Please, please."

Erin paused a moment, and in the pause could be heard sounds from the morning room, slightly querulous, and upstairs footsteps and an opening door.

Nobody believes their ears, thought Erin, and played the opening chords again as an introduction.

Her voice was thin, but it carried.

"When the wheel of autumn makes
a turn
Across the fields of summer,
And singing birds
For southern climes depart—

When the scarlet maple branches
burn
Where green boughs once did murmur,
Oh, share with me
The summer in your heart."

PART THREE

The Leavetakings

Notwithstanding the land shall be
desolate because of them that dwell
therein, for the fruit of their doings.
Micah 7:13

The town of Roseville earned its name for six months of the year. Roses of every hue from a dead white to an improbable purple covered the lowliest privies, swept down the courthouse lawn like spilled paint, and drooped heavily along the banks of the Rose River, which bisected the town, as railroads do elsewhere, into classes; in Roseville the depreciatory "wrong side of the tracks" was given as "wrong side of the river," and as happens in so many towns and cities in America because of native idiocy, what had once been the "right" side was now the "wrong," so that the poorer people, without means to keep them up, lived in the more beautiful houses with the best views of the lovely little river. The poorest family, the Vittitoes, with only two monthly pension checks to support eight people, lived in a house said to have been designed by Thomas Jefferson, a marvel of a house even in rack and ruin, while on the other side of the river families with incomes of twenty thousand and up lived in glass-bricked monstrosities called "ranch houses." But there too the roses spilled and burned and partially, thankfully, obscured, from May through October.

The signs bordering the town read: WELCOME TO THE TOWN OF ROSES, *Population 3,000*. This figure had been altered by some new, proud, solemn father to read *3,001*, and so the signs remained with the black clumsily painted *1's* to immortalize his first born, though the census was some time ago, and he, the proud and solemn, has become the disillusioned father of five.

Roseville had, like the two extremes of its climate, two major churches—a Catholic and a Baptist. In the heat of summer religious prejudice ran riot like the roses. In the introspection of its dreadful winter a sort of tolerance prevailed, as under most emergency conditions. In summer, stories of tunnels connecting the monastery with the nunnery, their purpose being traffic of sensual intent, were revived and added to. Tales of pregnant nuns abounded: "Why do you think they wear those long dresses?" and if a child disappeared—rare, but still—it was known to have been spirited away by a nun or monk, to be brought up to worship false idols. On their side, the Catholics deplored the heathen in their midst and the unconsecrated graves marked by headstones with, as they said, no more meaning than laundry frozen on a line. However, the congregations were joined the year around in their dislike and fear of the Negro and the snake-charming hillbilly, whose strange tabernacles of worship hid in hills and on the edges of swamps like outlaws. On still summer Sunday noons, jazzy sounds of Negro worship invaded the more austere temples through open windows: "Hot as hell, and niggers running amuck"—and word of Faith being put to a venomous test on the high bluffs that lay blue and remote as heaven above the town: "Try as I might, I can't see any sense in a snake trying to charm a snake." The hatred and fear, of which such words were a mere token, comprised an inviolable barrier, though in fifty years there had been two breakthroughs: when a Northerner from Ohio had married a black girl and been run out of town in 1938, and when Murdoch McChesney, whose family name adorned the county, had married a hillbilly in 1914 and sired "the damnedest mess of young this side of a salmon hatching catfish." There were those who nodded at the news that he was to be laid out in Owen's Funeral Home—"Time will always tell"—because Owen's was on the wrong side of the river. True, many of their own had gone from there to claim the Last Reward, but that was in a time when Roseville was a one-funeral-parlor town. Now it had two, and nobody but poor whites used Owen's.

"It proves—" said wife to husband, having returned from her duty call on the McChesneys, after she had told with full relish the tales of the spittoon and tin cans and Priscilla's craziness and the old woman's rudeness—"it proves that folks sink instead of rise, by nature," an Article of Faith perhaps more Baptist than Rosevillian, though still not untypical of the region's dolorous outlook, which invaded even its jokes.

One of the standing jokes was built on an arrangement of places of business wherein Owen's was separated from an eatery named Sammy's by a store which sold garden statuary, birdbaths and tombstones: "Eat at Sammy's, go next door and pick out your tombstone, then go lay down in Owen's—it won't be long." These instructions had been painted by a wit (white) on the walls of the Negro waiting room in the depot, because Sammy's was the one colored restaurant in town, but the joke had been spoiled by a scrawled addendum: It beats hell out of LIVING in this town. Two or three times a month, since the coda appeared, the colored porter, Handy, was told by Mr. Logan, the station master, to remove the offending words with soap and water, but they always reappeared. This had been going on for a number of years, and though traps were set to catch the author of the words, which might, in the opinion of several important persons, incite to riot (Handy, a "good nigger," was occasionally put on sentry duty), the culprit was never caught because Mr. Logan, who had worked side by side with Handy for twenty-five years, did not know that Handy could write. Actually, Handy *had* been caught once, by his friend Robin McChesney, so that each time he renewed the editorial comment he thought of Robin and laughed to himself, hearing in his mind the pleasant laughter of his friend.

Robin and Handy did not "grow up together"; Handy belonged to the town—that is, he was its property—and Robin belonged to the county—a part of it being his property—but through the years of growing up they had shared experiences that made them each a part of the other in some way that was indefinable but that each acknowledged to himself, knowing that the feeling of bond was shared. This bit of belonging was apparently undemanding, and again each knew that the very casualness was the strongest thread in the cord.

"Hey," they would say, passing each other on the street after a separation of weeks, and if one or the other looked preoccupied or exclusively purposeful, they let it go at that. Or perhaps Handy would say, impassively, as they met in the square, "Frogs kept me awake last night," and Robin's muttered "O.K." meant lanterns and gigs that night in Frog Bottom, the marshes whose dark waters lapped the doorstep of the shanty where Handy slept literally in the bosom of his family. Alone or in public, there was no glad-handing between them, no inquiries about family, which galled Handy when shouted to him across the street by some politician who wanted to show passers-by that he could recall every last name, down to the new baby, in a nigger family, in case the information should ever be needed as evidence of one kind or another. Because the sole conspiracy in their friendship was of the play-acting kind, for each other's possible amusement, they did not feel called upon to share confidences. Neither brooded privately upon the other's race nor made allowances for it. Neither knew that the oddness of their friendship was not because it was shared by black and white in a southerly place, but because it was true.

They met in Frog Bottom on a night of a dark moon,

when they were fourteen and fifteen, Robin the elder. Lanterns darkened, they converged simultaneously upon the spot where the frogs sang the loudest hallelujah. Both were Indian-footed; their progress through the reeds toward each other was no more telltale than the low-lying dog wind running in circles.

The chorus of frogs open up on a Gloria, the basses tolling like iron bells; two lanterns prove the stunning power of light, two homemade gigs jab for the same fat soloist, two young boys are scared out of a year's growth, thinking themselves literally beside themselves. On second disoriented thought, it is as though they lie horizontally above the water, suspended in the air, looking down at their own reflections: the lantern, the stick, the impaled frog. Each cautiously moves a hand, hands encounter flesh, they breathe again.

Sitting back, not caring about wet behinds, they examined each other by unveiled lanterns. Their eyes met levelly, neither having to look up to the other; Robin took note of the other boy's bulging biceps; Handy saw the breadth of Robin's shoulders. Dollars to doughnuts, a fight would end in a double funeral if they were fool enough to fight over one frog. Handy looked at their catch feebly twitching on the gigs.

"Nasty-looking marshmallow. Got two legs, though. Reckon that's one apiece."

Robin thought a moment. "We can't get fat on that. You giving up?"

"Hell, naw." After a moment, "Not if you ain't."

Robin jumped up. "O.K. Which side of the swamp do you want? We can split fifty-fifty." They chose sides and started off. When they were a few yards apart Handy called softly, "If you figure to back around this way again, whistle or something, for Jesus' sakes."

Robin whistled "whippoorwill" and Handy responded. Through remaining adolescence they used the signal. They dropped it when they entered their twenties, but by that time they weren't seeing much of each other. Handy married at nineteen and went to work as the railroad porter; Robin, too, was increasingly taken up with family matters, but in any case, when they did see each other they did not need a signal to remind them that they had started out by sharing something.

When Robin was twenty-five and Spur was fifteen, they went in to the town one blazing summer day on business for the farm. The country was at war; gasoline was rationed, so that instead of taking a pickup truck they rode in a buggy, which was an oddity even in those days of vehicular curiosities: an English two-wheeler that had belonged to their grandparents. Robin had chosen it over the other buggies and buckboards, which it was his father's fancy to keep stabled like fine horses, because of its rakish impracticality and the brightness of its paint undimmed by the passage of over fifty years. He had the half-hope that it would provide diversion enough to lift, temporarily at least, the spirits of his increasingly morose brother. Robin knew that Spur's moroseness was connected with his own deferment from military service because of the farm, and the gossip, growing more open as

Roseville was emptied of its sons, that laid deferment to the fact that Robin was a McChesney. He and Spur had not talked about it—they seemed to share less and less each day—but Robin knew his brother's feelings and, to an extent, sympathized.

On that particular day Robin and Spur hitched the buggy on Courthouse Square beside the sulphur-water well and jaywalked across the street toward the feed store. They passed a clump of men standing in front of Thompson's Pharmacy, and Robin nodded. This day, however, instead of waiting for him to get almost out of earshot, they began to talk when he and Spur were abreast of them.

"McChesneys too damn good for cannon-fodder."

"Sure enough. But we can't have them gettin killed off. What'ud the county do 'thout *them?*"

"'Agricultural deferment,' my tail. I got another word."

Robin stopped and asked, mildly, "What's your word, Mr. Bell?"

"Ass-lickin in Warshington." It was clearly his intention to punctuate his sentence with a contemptuous stream of tobacco juice; his mouth fixed itself for expectoration, but when Robin did not provide the expected target by moving on, but stood gazing at him, Mr. Bell shifted his dislike to the sidewalk and the pent tobacco juice leaked from his mouth and ran down his chin.

After a time Robin told him, "Mr. Bell, I can lick asses in Roseville, too." He waited politely, feeling Spur seething beside him, and then started on. He felt as pent-up as the juice in Bell's mouth, and when he heard the *splat* behind him, and saw the drops jumping ahead of him on the pavement, and heard the guffaw, he knew that some of the stuff had hit his pants and he wheeled around. He had to work hard to keep his voice down.

"You're all old enough to be my dad, but I reckon the four of you add up to one man—" His shame at having given way in front of Spur stopped him briefly, but the look in his brother's eyes made him complete his threat to the old men, feeling slightly sick at the cowardly swagger of the words; he could quite literally have licked them with one hand tied. But on the other hand—the tied one, he thought—he really would have liked doing it, and not only for Spur's sake. He finished curtly. "If you want me to prove it, there's an empty lot behind Kroger's. I'll wait there." He walked off toward Kroger's and did not turn until he stood in the driveway leading to the lot. When he turned he saw that the men had not moved and that Spur stood with them, his face burning.

At the top of his lungs, Spur said, "I'm gonna enlist next year, so you just wait before you call *all* the McChesneys yellow." He walked slowly toward Robin; when he had gone a few feet he said, "You sonofabitch."

One of the men took a step after him, saying, "Why, you young turd—"

"Aw, come on, Pone," said Mr. Bell. "You touch that young'un the *rest* of the draft-dodgin hillbillies'll be down here."

"With rattlesnakes," another added, and the men moved on, chuckling and vindicated for having been called "sonofabitch." But Robin knew Spur had not been talking to the men.

The two brothers made their rounds of feed, harness and hardware stores in silence, ordering what they could, arranging it so that they could make one trip in to pick it all up at once, and all the while Robin was justifying to himself Spur's feelings. He knew that the boy would like to have a brother in the service of his country to brag about, a volunteer, one of the first, but Robin had not tried to volunteer—had, indeed, sought deferment, and this was well know. He was no coward, and whether this was well known or not did not matter to him; he was needed on the farm badly enough to make the idea of soldiering unimportant—needed for the increasingly heavy work as farm hands were drafted. Most important to him of all the reasons, however, was that he was needed by his sisters and brother, whether or not all of them knew it. Spur, whether he knew it or not, needed him. Robin felt hard and stubborn once more; he could not, aside from his understanding, allow himself to care what Spur thought any more than he could concern himself for long with the town's opinion. And that, he told himself, had to be that.

On the way out of town Robin stopped the buggy at the depot on an impulse and whistled "whippoorwill." Handy came out, disgusing his pleasure behind a look of boredom, and stood with one foot on the spokes of a buggy wheel. He and Robin regarded each other coolly.

"What's all this I hear," drawled Handy, "about you going to Washington and begging the President to make you a 4-F?"

Robin was aware of Spur's tensing. Because of this he answered more quickly than he would have if he and Handy had been alone to share their sense of irony. "At least I wasn't *born* a 4-F. It took some string-pulling to make me one."

They both laughed and Handy took tobacco and papers from his shirt pocket, nodding to Spur, who did not return the nod. Spur had seen Handy around, but he did not know that he existed in his brother's life.

"Want me to roll you one?" Handy asked Robin. "Pardon my spit."

"Thanks, but we've got to get on back. I don't smoke when I'm driving." He clicked his tongue idly to the mare. "I hadn't seen your ugly face in a while. 'Swhy I stopped."

"Well, son, don't you worry none. You're not going to lose me. I just got turned down myself."

"Yeah?"

"Uh huh. Wrong kind of blood, or something."

"Huh." Robin flicked the reins and the buggy moved away. "Be seeing you."

Handy grinned and lifted a hand.

They were beyond the town limits before Spur spoke. "Who the hell was that?" His voice seemed to coat his words with mucus.

"That was Handy Miller," said Robin, "one of our two local characters." He tried humorous pontification, knowing it would not work for either of them but thinking it might stall what he felt to be imminent. "In anticipation of your question, *I* am the other character."

Spur was elaborately, gutturally polite. "I beg your

pardon. I meant to say, *what* was that"—he laughed—"aside from the obvious?"

Robin answered roughly. "It ought to have been plain that he's a friend of mine." He forced Spur to meet his eyes before he told him. "My best friend." He hoped Spur would accept the words, for he knew what he would have to do if the boy spoke slurringly again. As he stalled the event with further words, he wondered if he was reacting to his brother's threatened bigotry or to the open ugliness of the men or to something not yet neatly tagged in his mind. "Old Handy and I ran into each other backwards, frog-hunting one night. That's how we met. I was your age then, fifteen, and I don't think you'll dispute me when I say Frog Bottom is not the most comforting place around here at night."

"Frogs and niggers," said Spur.

Robin had to ignore it. Perhaps his brother had not heard the warning as clearly as he had meant it. "We were backing up, and neither of us heard the other coming. Then—*wham.* We damned near jumped out of our skins."

"And into each other's?" Spur sounded interested.

"Something like that. At least, in ten years we've had a good look inside—several good looks, I guess—" He stopped, thinking: Oh, let it come.

Spur laughed. "I get it. What you saw in there was—" He paused invitingly and Robin obliged him, outlining the warning clearly this time.

"Pretty much the same. Yes. That's right," and he waited, curiously relaxed.

Spur spaced his words for effect. "Even if I was a

draft dodger, I wouldn't own up to looking like a nigger inside."

Robin hit him quite hard across the face, startling the mare with the sound. He soothed her with the reins, then gave her her head and turned sideways on the seat, watching Spur's face where the livid marks of his hand were turning red.

"If you ever use the word 'nigger' to me again, or in my hearing, I'll beat the living hell out of you." He heard himself say the words that that morning would have been unthinkable, and wondered if he really meant them; the voice he heard was casual, even sympathetic, but his hand throbbed from the blow to his brother's face—the unthinkable blow to his own flesh. He felt the anguish of a mourning dream. Which, he asked himself, was worse: the maiming word, subtle and two-edged, which hurt the user as much as the victim, or the blunt crack of flesh against itself? Half hearing what Spur was saying, he told himself that the word was worse because it caused most pain to Spur and someone else, since Robin, in spite of his love for Handy, could not be as hurt by the word as a Negro could; at least he and Spur shared the pain of the blow, and that made it preferable. Someday he would try to explain it to Spur. He put his hand, throbbing palm up, on his knee.

"Nigra," Spur was saying. "Neegro. Na-gra. No-grow." His fists clenched and unclenched, punctuating. "New-grews are well known as draft dodgers. I read it in the Roseville *Favorite*. 'They eat cakes of soap to raise their blood pressure,' wrote our famous local editor, Mr. Hawkins Blake, in last week's *Favor-*

ite. 'They shoot off their big toes and their little toes and their big black mouths,' he wrote. 'In fact,' he continued, 'they will stop at shooting off nothing save their big black dongs. If none of this works, they go cuckoo at the induction center and say they heard those gentle voices calling "Old Black Joe."' "

Robin did not interrupt Spur; he wanted him to vomit it out and be cleansed of it—as he had once cleansed himself of the knowledge of his father's failure as both father and husband by shouting obscenities throughout the night in the deepest part of the woods. For it was immediately plain that Spur's words had nothing to do with Handy, or with any deep feeling against the race he had chosen to illustrate his tirade. His hatred was for draft dodgers, for his brother, as Robin's had been for his father; his disillusion, like Spur's, had come early, but he had had Erin and their shared purpose of compensating for their parents to restore him to at least partial innocence. Spur, for the time, had no one—or thought he had no one. Rhoda, who had always taken his side and to whom he had turned when troubled, was away at school. He shared nothing with fourteen-year-old Millicent or nine-year-old Priscilla. He obeyed—submitted to? respected?—Erin but he did not share his thoughts with her. His father and mother were background figures to him; he addressed them as "sir" and "ma'am" and sat at table with them, but he had never turned to them, not since early childhood. And now, when the head had finally been placed on the statue of disillusion that he had been long constructing—at least since Robin's first deferral, and there had been two—he did not have Robin.

Listening to the spew which eventually tapered off into fatigue and hoarseness over the seven slow miles home, it occurred to Robin that in thinking of Handy, he had provided Spur with a badly needed outlet, and that this put him in Handy's debt, though he could never acknowledge the debt to Handy. He would ride it out with Spur and hope for the best, an old habit. In the meantime, there was work for all of them. He had found work to be indeed a healer.

Within a week or so Spur was himself again, which was not to say that he was easy to get along with; he *was* going on sixteen, there *was* the frustrating call of the war, and nobody's life was any longer without its daily barbs, when there was time for even the sampling of those. But Spur seemed to have worked off his disappointment in Robin on the ride home and in the following days of brutal work. He did not use the words "nigger" or "draft dodger" again. Robin still went into his room at night, hearing him cry out in sleep, and would stand there hoping that somehow the sense of his protectiveness would penetrate the nightmare and give the boy comfort.

In the daytime there was the land—also his flesh and bone and blood. It needed his protectiveness, too, and he gave it as prodigally as he could. Loving, longing, working with his hands that never tired of the feel of the earth, he dared not look toward the harvest until it was upon him and his worst fears were justified.

Grain rotted on the stalk, potatoes in the ground, fruit on the trees. The odor of soft, sweetish rot hung over the countryside and permeated with its smell of death Robin's dreams in the two hours' sleep a night he allowed himself. He tried to convince himself that the spoilage and desecration were owing to a lack of practice at getting along with so little help, because men declared unfit for military service, black and white alike, migrated to the large cities where lucrative work could be found in war plants, rather than—as he had hoped and counted on up until the time of harvest—making themselves available to the needful farmers. But even as he told himself that next year's experience would yield a profitable harvest, in his dreams he saw the death of the land, and then in his waking hours.

The following year, feeling as he had when he struck Spur, and when he had had to shoot a horse, and when he had found out his father's profligacies; feeling the visceral tearing of all the heavy-rooted things by which he had knowingly and unknowingly been violated in his life, he condemned four hundred acres of land to lie fallow. Raging within himself as the plowing and planting began, knowing that in other parts of the country and even of the state, prisoners of war, felons, conscientious objectors were allotted to farms to produce the crops the country needed, to save the land that was the country, he blamed Roseville and his father and himself for being nothings, unworthy of attention and help.

He blamed Roseville for having no historical meaning to the country, to attract patriots to the cause of its salvation. Roseville had sat as smugly uncommitted through the Civil War as Switzerland was now sitting this one out. Its one claim to fame was that Jesse James had robbed its bank.

He blamed his father for his unconcern and, irrational or not, as applied to the case of the dying land, for his increased sexual activity among the bereft ladies of the county. But it was not irrational; it did apply. His father was fucking on the grave of his past, of their collective past, as unconcerned as a wandering mongrel.

He blamed himself most of all and for all of them, for being himself ineffectual. But was he? Let him see before he surrendered.

He found his father in the morning room, sipping wine, gazing into the fire that was not needed against the late spring but upon which he insisted. He lay deep in his chair, his petit-point-shod feet resting on a stool, one hand dangling almost to the floor, where the discarded newspaper with its headlines of world sickness lay like an ailing dog.

"Father," said Robin to the man he had always called Dad.

"Robin," his father said vaguely, recalled from his daydream, and then he smiled and said, jocularly, "I thought the farmer would be in bed by now. Have a glass of wine?"

"I don't want to deprive you, sir." Something in his tone caused his father to sit up straighter, but he spoke crankily enough as he poured himself more wine.

"Well, at least sit down. I'll get a crick in my neck if I have to keep talking to you over my shoulder." Robin sat in the chair opposite him. They found it difficult to meet each other's eyes.

"Sir," said Robin, gazing at the blood-red wine, and then, "Goddamn it." His father looked at him with raised eyebrows. The eyebrows completed the picture of dilettante. Robin hurt all over from working with tools from which vital parts were missing. He was dirty. The lingering smell of manure in his nose did not go with dilettantes in morning rooms. He had no trouble meeting the other man's eyes then. "Your land is dying, sir."

"So is the world." The other man gestured wearily toward the newspaper.

"At least it's putting up a fight."

"Aren't we?"

"We, sir?"

The answering voice was hard. "Could I work those four hundred acres alone, any more than you could?"

"There are two hundred left."

"All turned, I believe?" He had always spoken of "turning" the earth, rather than of plowing it. When Robin was small he had had the image of his father holding the entire earth in his hand, turning it.

"*Plowed,* as of nine o'clock tonight. Yes, sir."

"Good."

"That's about two weeks late."

"What?" He thought, because he was a little drunk, that Robin meant his approval was late.

"Have you ever been a farmer, sir?"

Wine splashed angrily into the glass. "What the hell kind of question is that?"

"I guess it's a leading one, sir."

"Stop 'sir-ring' me every time you open your mouth!"

"I'd like an answer. The plowing is two weeks late. That doesn't seem to mean anything to you. I asked if you've ever been a farmer."

His father's anger was replaced by reflectiveness. He turned the glass in his hand, looking into it as though to find the answer there. "I don't know," he said. "I was brought up to respect the land. We've always been landowners—my father, his father, and so on back. Not always fertile land in the past—Scotland is rocky, I'm told." He thought about the land he had never seen, where the proud and privileged past lay. He would have been a laird there, with the right to sample a young bride's charms before her husband. "I have worked the land, turning it, planting, reaping. I have lived off the land. I have enjoyed its fruits."

His mind strayed as he gazed into the glass, thinking of ripeness: heads of wheat, the perfume of hay, blooming tobacco plants, plump melons, peaches the size of teacups, the breasts of young girls. His mind was cloudy with wine; the images of ripeness were half hidden from him by something soft, as though he gazed through window curtains beyond which a girl undressed. He thought of his wife, flabby as a piece of chewed leather at forty-three, and recalled his father's saying that a man should always have in his castle ripeness—"possible ripeness," he had called it. He had said that a man should never marry a pretty woman, for he would have pretty daughters. "If you have pretty daughters," he had said, "break their spirits, for a spiritless woman is no temptation—"

He reached for the decanter, thinking that he would sleep that night without torment, though more and more wine was required to induce so necessarily deep a sleep. Her beauty was like a thorn . . . He met the waiting unanswered eyes of the son he had forgotten. The question—yes. A good one. Pointed. It deserved a good pointed answer.

"Maybe," he said, "maybe I was a farmer once—" He looked at Robin directly, with smiling enmity. "When the land was mine, when the house that stood on the land was mine, when the children who lived in the house that stood on the land were mine—" He noticed with satisfaction that his son's face had gone white under the tan and the dirt. He said, as Robin got up clumsily, "You said it was a leading question when you asked it. Do you like where it has led?" He got up carefully, feeling the contrast between his grace and his son's clumsiness, and walked to the bookcases and took down a volume. He turned and held the book out to Robin. "If the farmer is not too tired to read, I recommend one of these plays in particular. It is called *King Lear.*"

Robin went to the desk and picked up the *Farmer's Almanac* and held it out to his father. "Thanks. One good recommendation deserves another."

His father gave a mirthless laugh and went to his chair, dropping the volume of Shakespeare on the stool.

Robin spoke to him curtly, without respect. "That wasn't repartee. Starting tomorrow everybody carries his share of work. There'll be no more waste around here." When his father started to speak, Robin said, "Not even words," and left the room.

Through the summer everyone worked the farm, including Priscilla and Millicent. Priscilla made the tobacco her special province, suckering it and squashing the fat green worms with pleasure. Millicent weeded and hoed the kitchen garden; under her impersonal hands it flourished as seldom before. She never seemed to grow tired or to be proud of her accomplishments. Erin cooked for the workers and in between times she and her mother worked in the orchards and berry patches.

In the fields, Robin worked with a feverish masochistic joy that contrasted with Spur's impassivity and the father's silence. Robin did not care that his father never spoke; the only thing that mattered was that he carry his share, and he did. The handful of hired men, though not young, performed as they had throughout their lives: to the full extent of their bodies' capacities. The harvest that year was perfect; smaller than ever before on McChesney land, but each seed sprouted and came to flower and fruit and the harvest was stored or shipped wherever it could do most good.

When winter came Murdoch McChesney began to take his after-dinner wine upstairs in an unused room that was gradually converted into a study for him by his wife. He rewarded her by leaving her to shiver alone in the big canopied bed, himself preferring the sofa in the study. If the wine in the cellar diminished at a more rapid rate, nobody noticed, any more than they noticed the disappearance of the man who drank it.

When Spur was not quite seventeen he quietly presented himself, a perfect physical specimen, hard and brown and sure, to the Air Force. He was turned down on psychiatric grounds. In desperation he tried all the branches of the service, and the answer was the same. After the initial attempt at the Air Force, he lied to the examining officers, not knowing that the tests he took proved the lie and revealed the nightmare. When it was certain that he was not going to be accepted, he told his family that he *had* been, and left. He allowed no one to see him off and stiffly forbade them to make mention of his going to the Roseville *Favorite*. He wanted no drums beaten for his departure.

For five years he did not write because his return address, minus an APO, would have exposed him. He wandered the country, avoiding the feeling of limbo by expressing himself and his inner seething in many ways: in Florida he wrestled alligators for the admiration of old ladies and children; he worked on a ranch in Nevada, where he fiercely broke the spirits of horses and the hearts of not always young women; he learned to fly a plane, and in a brawl he acquired a long scar, resembling a hieroglyphic, on the skin of his chest just below the heart. These last two acquisitions he combined and made of them the story his pride demanded to allow him to live as a man among men: the scar was all that was left of a wound received on a mission over Tokyo.

When he returned to the farm with Bonny as his wife, he returned also as a war veteran. *Now* let them beat the drums in the Roseville *Favorite*. The war was over.

While the war expended itself and the country returned to consciousness to find itself a monster in the world, Robin stayed on at the farm, doing what he could with what he had. Millicent went away to school, forging her own way, as Rhoda had done, out of necessity. Beautiful, bored Millicent, about whom one was never sure whether it was mockery that lay like a secret in her eyes, or a secret that disguised itself as mockery, left, and Robin, Erin and Priscilla—and, of course, the parents—had the place to themselves. But perhaps because of the spacing of the departures of the others, the house did not seem suddenly empty to Robin and Erin, or changed in any way. After all, Rhoda had come home to be married, and there were her letters with the glad news of birth, the sad news of divorce, the reassuring news of remarriage. Millicent wrote brief notes, uninformative, typically, but with love tagged on at the end. Bonny wrote with news of Spur and the birth of their first son. The letters were their voices in the house. Things had not really changed. Even the necessity of Robin's taking a job in another town did not upset the equilibrium of the house. When he had lived at home he and Erin—all the family—had really only had weekends to share with each other, and they still had those. They still had each other. Nothing had changed.

The night in 1959 when Robin looked into the colored waiting room of the depot and found Handy writing on the wall, he laughed because Handy laughed, the response as much a reflection as each had thought the other to be the night of their first meeting in Frog Bottom. The words Handy had written registered, if at all, only subliminally in his mind.

It was that afternoon that the long-teetering world he had helped build came finally crashing down and he knew he would try to cope no longer. When he got to the farm on Saturday morning Erin had given him the mail. Among the useless farm journals and such that continued to come like letters to a person long dead, there was one envelope marked PERSONAL in large letters. It was addressed simply to Mr. McChesney and he left it until last—part premonition and part hope that if it were a dun for some overlooked debt it might in the interim become misplaced, at least until after Christmas; his bank account was shamefully low. He had been racking his brain for something to give Erin that would not reveal how almost nonexistent money was; he had decided that mischief would be his best tack: an openly absurd present, maybe a doll baby that said *Ma-Ma*—then they could laugh together in the face of destitution. But the letter stuck by him, insistently personal. He ran the knife under the flap and unfolded the single sheet. *Murdoch dearest, my darling Murdoch.* He began to fold it, thinking:

No. Erin and he were alone in the kitchen. A cup of coffee steamed before him, placed there by Erin when he was reading the caesural, damning line. Had she seen? He had the feeling that she was waiting, standing at the stove with her back to him. If he read it as though it were his own letter, he would not have to explain the PERSONAL to her; otherwise he would have to account for not having read it. He unfolded it again. The rattling paper seemed to fill the kitchen with warning.

Murdoch dearest, my darling Murdoch,

> I missed two periods and went all the way to Nashville and He said it was so. I am not going to murder that baby Murdoch and I want him to have a name. I'll be a good wife like she never was you said so yourself. It's got to be soon. I don't want any unnecessary talk. I am acquainted with Ward but I don't want to do that. Call me up as soon as you get this.

The letter was signed Very truely yours, Weezie, and underneath, stretching across the bottom, a line of X's.

He went upstairs to his father's study and laid the letter on the desk before him. The old man read the words, leaned back in his chair and said, "This should have happened in the morning room. That's the place for being outraged." Robin started for the door. His father's voice followed him, got in front of him, blocked the way. "You once gave me a little questionaire in there on farming. I don't think I passed that test. If I recall correctly, you also lectured me on the sin of waste. You were curious about my attitude then. Now I'm damn well curious about yours. Where have you planted *your* seed?" His voice was coarse with contempt. "How many bellies have you made ripe in your lifetime?" He slapped the letter in front of him with a sound like a bursting bag. "Do you think *this* is the first letter of this kind I've gotten in fifty years of fucking? I could paper the goddamn house with 'em. But those were the days when I opened my own mail."

Without turning, Robin said, "Don't."

His father waited for a while and then said mildly, "Eunuch." The decanter stopper was a dismissing bell.

That night the father came downstairs to supper, a practice he had long ago abandoned, preferring to have his evening meal served him on a tray in his study. He was like a man rejuvenated. He laughed and joked. He forced his wife to take three glasses of wine, saying wine made a woman fertile. He decried fallow fields and spoke of the need for spreading seed. Erin, ignorant of the reason for his high spirits and missing the malice, found herself laughing at her father's jokes and her mother's tipsiness. She even gave Robin reproachful looks because he did not enter into the unaccustomed but wonderfully welcome festiveness. He had not shared the letter with her, nor had he explained his abrupt actions following the reading of it, despite plentiful opportunities throughout the day. She wondered, in disquiet, if he was involved with a woman.

Later, when they were alone in the front parlor, she played the piano and sang to him "When the wheel of autumn makes a turn across the fields of summer," his favorite song because she had written the words and set them to an old Scottish air. At the words "Oh, share with me the summer in your heart," he made a sound and she turned to find him weeping. She went to him and placed solicitous hands on his shoulders. "Robin, my dear, what is wrong?"

He turned his face up to hers and for a moment was on the verge of telling her, but her eyes were too worried; he could not add to it by saying, "The summer is over. Everybody knows it but you and me." Instead he said it differently. "I was being maudlin, thinking of the days when we wrote poetry and thought of ourselves as the Brontës." They laughed a bit at the foolishness of extreme youth and Robin said he was "whupped" and went to bed.

The following day, Sunday, the father kept to his room and his wife hovered nearby in case he should need anything. The day felt more peaceful. Robin and Erin spoke of homely things, small plans for Christmas, repairs to the house that could, or should not, be put off until spring. His train time drew near before they were aware of it. Erin hurried to call the taxi; Mr. Price was apt to forget to come on his own, though he certainly knew that he was expected every Sunday. Robin went upstairs to say good-by to his parents; routines are not easily broken. Outside his father's door, which stood ajar, he waited, hand raised to knock. They had always, as children and adults, with the exception of Priscilla, knocked before entering their parents' rooms. His father's voice raised a bit, telling Robin plainly that his father knew that he was there: "Why haven't they married, can you tell me that?" He paused and then said slowly, with full effect, "It's damned unnatural."

He had, after all, had the last word.

Robin did not take the train. He remained in the town, walking its streets through dusk and into the night, trying, possibly, to find some one thing of quiet to act as antidote to the noise inside his head. He held himself over the cold as Priscilla had once held her hand over a candle flame, threatening would-be saviors with a kitchen knife, until the flesh of her hand cracked open. At first he confined his walking to the wrong side of the river, feeling that among people as poor and barren as he—the Vittitoes, reading their *Watchtower*'s by yellow kerosene flames—he might find a crumb of comfort-by-contrast in the one thought in which he was more fortunate than they: he did not have God to contend with. But it was the Vittitoes, who believed themselves to have an Ally, who trustingly garnered the night's crumbs and glowed in the yellow circles of lamplight like haloed saints.

He crossed the river, walking and staring at houses festooned for Christmas with sleighs and reindeer riding the rooftrees and Santas emerging from useless chimneys. Some houses were entirely outlined in winking colored lights. It was on the "right" side of town that he found the hate for which he had been searching, hate that was the strut that kept his body unshivering. It was a catholic hate in that it extended upward and outward, including all he knew, even Erin, but it was a vaguely circular hate, beginning and ending with himself. He was forty-two that year; because he had never tasted full, unwatered hatred before, it went violently to his head. He found himself standing in front of a house that seemed to be built of an acre of glass. It was newly finished and sparkling, the cleanliness enhanced by the debris of building materials from which it rose like a lily from cow flop. He handled pieces of concrete block, all but sniffing them for ripeness, as though they were melons in a supermarket, and at last selected one that seemed to have its center of balance precisely placed. He stood holding it, in no hurry, and looked at the enormous wreath which beckoned in holly behind the largest expanse of glass. Behind the wreath the proud family moved, changing positions of chairs, straightening pictures, standing back to admire the whole.

How vulnerable they were, how very trusting to expose so much of themselves, oblivious to the existence of envy and sourness and cynicism beyond the window, as new as their house and the money that built it. Did they, he wondered, like the Vittitoes, find in the thought of an Ally the courage of so much glass? But no—their reward was *now;* the glass house was their reward.

Occasionally one of them would be framed in the wreath, seeming to be posing for a photograph, and Robin would lift the stone and take careful aim as though sighting along a rifle barrel. Once the whole family—Robin named them savagely as they appeared: Mom, Dad, Bud, Sis—stood within the circle of pointy green, looking out with solemn faces. "Poor suckers," Robin said aloud, only then aware, with the exhalation of breath, that he had been standing without breathing. The white air came from his mouth in a gust, obscuring the scene, and he was left lapped by his hate as though it were the abrasive tongue of an animal reminding him that it was *he* who was the sacrificial victim. The weight of the stone in his hand seemed pointlessly heavy, no longer a weapon.

He began to think consciously in symbols, and the meaning of the stone to him presented itself: what he wanted of it was its weight and imperviousness. In some primitive past a newborn child was smeared with the blood of an eagle to make it swift and fearless. Thinking of this, Robin shifted the stone to his left hand and willed its qualities to marry his heart. After a time he told himself that this had been accomplished, that they were one till death.

He walked the length of town to Sammy's Eats and went in, ignoring the disapproval in the eyes of the few patrons and the girl behind the counter. They knew him, and knew that he had a lifetime's awareness of this violation of unwritten laws when he entered the door. They had no power, or inclination, to stop his ordering coffee and drinking it there, but they did not nod or speak as they would have done on the street. The girl served him neatly and carefully, placing the condensed milk and the sugar near at hand, and withdrew to her stool at the cash register. Robin hunched over his cup, shivering at last, so that the cup had to be carried to his mouth with both hands.

Further extravagance on either side was out of the question; the patrons continued eating and talking softly, not allowing themselves the indulgence of silence. Robin wanted and needed another cup of coffee but he did not order it. He paid the girl, taking a dollar bill from his wallet, and saw that he did not have enough money to take a room at the hotel. He had bought, as he always did, a return-trip ticket and had given Erin, against Christmas expenses, all but three dollars of his week's pay. He left the girl a nickel tip, careful that it should be exactly right, and walked the block to the depot.

He passed the colored waiting room and saw Handy inside, writing on the wall. He paused, his foot crunching on cinders, and Handy turned with a look of furtiveness, a touch of fear. Robin did not notice that Handy's body slackened with relief at the sound of their old greeting, "whippoorwill." He echoed Robin's call and walked to the window, and the two men, separated by the dirty glass, stood looking at each other.

When Robin made no move to come in, Handy strode to the door and flung it wide, beginning to laugh. "Hell, so I'm safe for a while yet." Robin laughed with him and came into the room, saying, "Good," both because of the warmth and because he liked to think of Handy safe. "Am I?" he asked, looking at, but not seeing, the writing on the wall.

"Son," said Handy, "you better be." They sat down side by side near the stove. Robin's "good" sounded like approval of his literary efforts to Handy; Handy's "you better be" sounded protective to Robin, who needed it. So for a while the two men continued their vertical conversation. They were forty-one and forty-two, both big men, neither of them gone to fat of body or head, but for a while they spoke as children speak, without mutual comprehension. Only when Robin asked if he could sleep in the waiting room did they make connection. Handy brought in an extra scuttle of coal for the round stove, said, "See you in the morning. I come to work long about daylight," and whistled off.

Robin turned off the lights and lay on a bench. Looking at the glow from the stove's window, thinking of the scuttle of coal Handy had provided for his comfort, he began to think of the coal as Handy himself. It was old comfort, dark comfort; like Handy, it had been formed by centuries of fallen matter that had been submerged and hardened, had been sought out and hacked at, scarred and sold and burned. Addressing Handy in the coal, he said, "You know more about betrayal than I'll ever know." He got up and went to the wall and struck a match and read what Handy had written there. He read it over and over and the match burned his fingers and he struck another and went on reading. It seemed to him that no volume ever contained so much; he felt that however long he went on reading, he would never reach the end. He lay back on the bench and thought at length what Handy had been in his life, and he wondered about Handy, the man, and then about Handy, the "nigger." As he thought, Handy receded to some point in the far, safe distance, out of range of his circle of hate, and consequently, permanently, unreachable.

He slept with caution. He awoke before dawn and left before Handy came to work. He walked until a restaurant (*No Dogs and Coloreds Allowed*) opened, and ordered and ate breakfast without tasting it, keeping an eye on the clock. Five minutes before train time he went back to the depot, approaching it from the windowless side. He waited, concealed, at the far end of the platform. From the corner of his eye, as he made a dash for the train, he saw Handy watching him, trying to get his attention by waving. He flung his hand backward in a gesture which Handy could read, if he was able to, as a final farewell to him. Actually, it was, because Handy and the town belonged to each other to the extent that they wrote to each other on the walls of public rooms, and so it was to Handy as well as to the town that Robin gave the back of his hand, the left one that had absorbed the stone, in an imperious, if heavy, good-by.

Owen's Funeral Parlor has two public rooms. There is a sitting room with a carpet the color green of fading grass, furnished, since a modernizing effort a year ago, with chairs made of varnished plywood and leatherette seats, like the chairs to a breakfast set; some heavy-based floor-model ashtrays; and because some things are slow to change, no matter how forward-looking the proprietors, there are four brass spittoons. The walls of the sitting room are a dryer green, with three pictures of a comforting nature: a dog guarding a sleeping (or dead) child, a child vigilant beside a dead (or sleeping) dog, and a Christ with eyes that look at you, no matter where in the room you sit or stand. There have been those who have found this latter work of art unnerving, but only once has it led to an actual incident: the time Mrs. O.K. Shoulders bore it dramatically into the "chapel" where her daughter reclined, innocently pink and white and dead as the result of birthing a fatherless baby, and placed it at the foot of the coffin, facing the girl, and called upon her daughter, throughout the eulogy and hymn singing, to look Him in the eye if she dared.

The other room—the "chapel"—is austerely gray: carpet, walls, drapes and ceiling. Its only permanent furniture is a Hammond organ, which during the modernizing replaced the old pump organ that accompanied "We Shall Gather At the River," the most popular funeral hymn due to the optimistic nature of most of those who have lost a dear one, or "Lead Kindly Light" for those who are not too convinced. These hymns are sung by a quartet of men who shuttle between funeral parlors and the Grand Old Opry in Nashville. As a consequence of this double life, nobody is ever given the Final Send-Off on Saturdays, when the quartet are in Nashville singing "Wabash Cannon Ball." Not to have the quartet would be like only half burying the body; it has become a superstition to have them, and because the four men are getting along in years, more than one person, with parents also getting along, has been heard to remark that they hoped Mama or Papa would die while the quartet was still around to plead for their salvation. They were like a direct pipeline to God; their harmonies alone were enough to guarantee gushets of tears in the most thankful or bored bereaved.

Mr. Patrick Owen, the fourth Owen to operate the business (he also painted the faces of the corpses, which led Millicent, years ago, to dub him Princess Pat), upon receiving Erin McChesney's call, had placed a hurried summons to the quartet, nervous as a cat that they, like him, had not anticipated a death at Christmas and had made plans impossible to cancel. As a matter of fact, even he, because he kept necessary tabs on the state of health of everyone in the county who could be counted upon to use his establishment, had almost gone off to Louisville to spend the holidays with a married sister. He trembled at the thought that he might have missed the opportunity to bury a McChesney. The spokesman for the quartet, knowing the importance of the family, had demanded a higher fee for working on Christmas Day, and Mr. Owen had agreed, certain that there would be no question of opposition from the McChesneys when the bill was presented. When they arrived at five-thirty, after he had murmured his words of comfort to each and everyone, including a total stranger who had followed the crowd in the belief that the blue neon sign with the one word "Owen's" indicated a bar, Mr. Patrick Owen drew Erin aside and told her with pride that he had been able to obtain the services of the quartet. He said it reverently —The Quartet—just as he said The Body. He was shocked and clutched at the lapel nearest his heart when Erin asked, "The quartet of what, Mr. Owen?"

"Th-th-the s-s-singers." He could not believe that she had heard him. "The famous—"

She did not let him finish. She was kindly, but abstracted. "We will not have hymns, Mr. Owen. My father was not a religious man."

"Bubu-but—"

Again she interrupted, appearing not to hear the twin moans from the next room as Antonia and Editha, the only ones to have left the sitting room, looked upon their brother. "You have an organist, I believe?"

"Yes, Miss Erin, but—"

"That will be all that is required." She looked at her mother, who had sat down in one of the slippery chairs without aid, and noticed in a bemused way that the chairs all had arms. Where would Tonia sit, on the floor? Mr. Owen was tugging at her sleeve and she turned her calm face to him, her eyes inquiring what else he had to say.

"Miss Erin—" The enormity of what she was doing had knocked the breath out of him, so that his words rode the intaken air with a ghostly sound. "Miss Erin, The Quartet has brought peace to every soul that ever lost a loved one in Owen's." It sounded wrong, even to him, but he *had* to make her understand. "Miss Erin, without The Quartet we can't guarantee—" He stopped, caught in the myth. Everyone was looking at him. He began to sweat. He had guaranteed the quartet money that he would have to make good whether they sang or not; he had never lost money on a funeral before.

Erin's reply sent his heart to his shoes. "My father disliked group singing, religious or secular."

Priscilla, from across the narrow room, said, "He despised the Andrews Sisters." To Mr. Owen that was an odd enough remark, but he had at least heard of the Andrews Sisters; Erin threw him completely when she said, with finality, "We will only require the organist to play "Greensleeves." She walked away, leaving him dizzy. He knew every song in the Baptist Hymnal, but he had never heard of that one. He followed Erin and stopped her at the doorway to the chapel. "Miss Erin, I don't know that hymn."

She told him, without looking at him, "It is not a hymn, Mr. Owen. It is a love song," and she walked away, in to the sisters whose moaning rose like fog.

Mr. Owen looked about him at the remaining people: the old woman sitting impassively, the girl whom he had finally placed as the crazy one, the man he did not know who was walking backwards and forwards watching Jesus' eyes follow him, causing the crazy girl to smile and say, "Ed, you fool." His skin crawled the way it never did with the dead. He left the room hurriedly.

Rhoda, Andrew, Spur, Bonny and the children had stayed behind. The children were not to see their grandfather until the funeral. None of them had been exposed to death before and nighttime—Spur had made the point—was not considered a sensible time to initiate them; it could result in damaging nightmares. It had been Rhoda's suggestion that the four of them should take the shift from eleven o'clock onward; thus the older people could sleep at their regular hours. Erin had smiled at Rhoda when she stressed slightly the word older, which of course included Erin. It was an arrangement typical of Rhoda's thinking: kind, and, except for the stressed word, unemphatic; it told them plainly that it was only a suggestion and alternatives were welcome. She did grow a bit assertive in her statement that she thought Priscilla should be on the first shift, and was trying to extricate herself from the apparent illogic of this when Priscilla came to her rescue by saying that she had no intention of waiting until eleven o'clock to see her father. Her point did not escape Rhoda. Erin had kept silent, to everyone's relief. Since she had played the piano and sung, so out of keeping with the occasion and what they expected of her, they had watched her for signs of further eccentricity. When the hours of watch were divided up she did not let anyone know that she had no intention of going to bed at all.

Just before they left for town, Erin asked to speak to Bonny in private. When they were alone, she said, "Listen carefully for automobiles. Go to the door yourself. If it is Robin, don't let him come in the house at all. Send him back to town in the taxi. Promise me."

Bonny looked at her, puzzled, wanting to ask her to explain, but all she said was, "What if the taxi leaves him here, Erin?"

Erin's answer gave her a chill alien to any she had known. "Run down the road after it. Scream 'Mr. Price.' He'll hear you." She left Bonny and went back to the front hall, where the others were waiting.

Ed carefully did not look at Tonia when he said, "The six of us can't get in my car."

Andrew said, "Take mine, too."

"Who," said Tonia, getting back at Ed for not looking at her, "who will drive it?"

"Priscilla, of course," said Andrew, handing her the keys.

"Come on, Aunt Tonia," Priscilla said casually. "You can sit beside me in the front seat. It'll be warmer there."

Tonia's eyes walled as she thought that a heater would hardly be necessary to raise her temperature with Priscilla at the wheel. Even Erin could hardly keep from smiling at the old woman's predicament. Rhoda and Spur were openly grinning; they knew that one lame word from Tonia would probably lead Priscilla on to bait her aunt unmercifully. But time was running out. Erin brought the moment to an end by saying, "I'll ride with Priscilla. We have things to talk about. The rest of you go with Edgar." Tonia's breath popped out of her with relief.

The rest of the arrangements were simple. At ten-fifteen Ed would drive the widow and the aunts back to the house; Priscilla and Erin would wait at the funeral parlor until the other four arrived and then Priscilla could drive herself and Erin home. Thus the vigil would be unbroken.

Marilyn, who had resisted George at the final moment and was living to regret it, gave, out of her bewildered and possibly angry frustration, a grisly note to the outwardly reasonable arrangements of fetch-and-carry being agreed upon in the hall. The word "vigil" was used by someone, and she, leaning against the doorjamb leading to the parlor, said, "I read somewhere that the real reason for sitting with a dead body was so something wouldn't carry it off and eat it."

Not one of the adults felt equipped to cope with such a remark. Even Editha, who moaned softly at any infraction of good taste, lost the power to that most primitive articulation. In silence the departers filed to the cars and in similar silence the remainers drew near the fire, thinking similarly of cruelty so basic or deep-rooted that it was no longer cruelty. Some of them considered the perilous thinness of the veneer called civilization by its manufacturers, and the many patented substitutes for even that thin covering of the "something" that would rob a cave or house or funeral parlor of a dead body, or a live one, to "carry it off and eat it." An angry child's frustrated fear that she might be a "good girl," and the consequent need to disprove it by saying something ugly, came closer than anything had to revealing the family to itself in a way that they had never, collectively, faced. But despite their daylong crying at the locks that kept them apart, they were unable, still, to make a concerted effort to draw together, even long enough to reprimand a child for insensitivity, or to laugh her out of the fear that prompted the remark. They each had had reason to believe, during the course of the long day, that the past had placed them in one of two groups: the destroyed and the destroyers. They were kept apart by the belief that two such disparate groups could never commonly meet; they could not see how deeply synonymous they were.

Erin walked to her father's coffin and looked upon the face of the stranger lying there, disliking the amount of color in his cheeks and lips.

"He looks," said Edie tremulously, "like he was asleep."

"Yes, dear," said Erin. "Now go out and help Mother find the strength to come and look at him. You've been very brave," she added, feeling like the basest hypocrite.

Edie patted Erin's arm gratefully and took one last look at her brother, this time suppressing the moan that came to her lips, and left. Tonia was immovable—or looked to be—but Erin did not try to move her because she had done nothing about rounding up a seat for her aunt.

Priscilla came in with Ed. When she got to the coffin she said, furiously, "What have they done—*tattooed* his cheeks!" She took the handkerchief from Ed's pocket and rubbed at her father's face. The red did not come off and she wet the handkerchief with her mouth and tried again. She was totally preoccupied with her task. Tonia did not see what was going on because she was bent over the foot of the coffin as far as she could bend, as though trying to kiss her brother's feet.

Neither Erin nor Ed tried to stop Priscilla, but Mr. Owen, entering obsequiously in case they should have changed their minds about the quartet, stopped dead in the doorway, his hand going to his madly thumping heart. When he could draw in enough air for navigation, he turned and ran like an old crooked-legged rabbit back to his formaldehyde-smelling sanctuary, where he fell onto a slab and took long, shuddering pulls at his brandy bottle. He would go to Louisville. He would leave his assistants in charge. To stay here would mean a heart attack. He had already called up the organist about playing that song. He had had trouble remembering the name and at first had told the man that it was called "Clean Sheets," and then "Green Sheaves," and the organist had decided that they meant "Bringing in the Sheaves," a queer choice, he said laughing, but still, it was their funeral. He and Mr. Owen settled on its having something to do with their being farmers—and, too, it was just as well not to check again in case the McChesneys wanted a song he could not play. He was a self-taught musician: he did not read notes, nor use his feet on the Hammond, except sometimes by accident. Too bad about The Quartet, though; in addition to being near-sacrilege not to use them, they helped to cover up his mistakes. But God moves in mysterious ways His wonders to perform; he could charge extra for playing a song he wasn't used to playing.

At ten that evening a 1935 Hispano-Suiza drove up Courthouse Lane and turned onto the Square. Except for swags of colored bulbs outlining the north arcade, and the twelve street lamps, three to a side, and the star that was the terminus of the courthouse spire, all was dark. Christmas Eve in Roseville was a time of family gatherings—not, as the citizens were fond of saying, a merchants' field day, as elsewhere.

Millicent drove around the square (*No Parking Except on Saturdays*), and parked, unable to think beyond the event of her arrival. Despite the boring drive with its enforced "long thoughts," which should have led her to a state of, at least, inner compromise, she was still plagued by an atypical sense of uncertainty, of something unfulfilled; and though the eerie joke should have expended itself, she found herself still thinking that she was here to attend a wedding.

She had driven from Louisville, where she and her current lover were to have spent Christmas with friends. When her answering service tracked her down at close to noon, and gave her Erin's message, she had turned to her lover—who was beginning to bore her to death—and told her that she had been summoned to her father's wedding. Cecile had laughed uproariously (another thing: she was showing too much heartiness in her complacency, lulled into revealing her butchness) and had found it just as funny when the mistake was explained.

Millicent lit a cigarette, a black, gold-tipped Sobranie, the only kind she could find in the car. They were usually reserved for public appearances, one of a hundred private gestures—another was the inconvenient, beautiful automobile—by which she indulged her self-satire. The fact that she was out of plain cigarettes in a closed-up town and, alone and unobserved, was forced to pretentiousness out of need, sent her into a spasm of laughter: the game had beaten her. It was as if she had come back to her roots to find that her distant misbehavior had deformed the poor simple things into the shape she affected for them when abroad in the world.

She hunched down in her sable coat, laughing and smoking, keeping decision at a distance. A tap close to her cheek sent her head jerking back and sideways in surprise, causing the abnormally fine copper hair to lift and float as though she were in free fall.

"Sorry, ma'am, no parking," the man, a policeman, said, or started saying; she saw his lips puffing at the "p," trying to inflate the word into being, and watched the dissipation of his breath around the letter on an ineffectual cloud of white. When he leaned one hand for support on the spare tire riding the fender, Millicent was released from enthrallment.

She flung her hair forward to cloak her face as she bent to the ignition, feeling perfectly frantic. His hand tap-tapped on the window, faint and terrible as a dream, without the energy of volition, as though it worked and thumped there with no connection to the mind which had been artificially put to sleep.

"Millicent—" he called in a thickened voice.

"No!" she yelled. "No!" her hands scrabbling among the instruments, and then she sat back and opened the window to him and said, "Hello, Luke."

His only comment on her behavior was, "Scared you."

"No." She shook her head, hair flying like spray. She felt that she was being truthful, though she did not know why. Her underlying thought was: Not you.

"Sure I did," he said, sounding weirdly pleased. "I know what I look like," and she saw only then what he meant.

"What happened to you, Luke?"

"War," he told her, grinning with lips that were already set in a perpetual grin of scar tissue. His face was a patchwork of hues and textures. As though he were compulsively taking her on a tour, he laid a gloved finger on a cheek: "That's a piece of my back—" He moved the finger downward: "That's the inside of my arm," indicating which arm, and where. "There's thigh meat there, and even a piece of the pope's nose somewheres."

She heard in silence his masochism underneath the practiced humorous spiel, like that of someone who spent his life steering people through a cave. He waited but she did not comment at all. He asked her, "Can I get in and set a spell?" She felt franticness beat like birds at her wrists and throat: the two of them together in a car— "Ah," she said. "Ah—yes, Luke. All right."

He walked around the front of the automobile to the left side, watching her warily through the windshield. He ducked in beside her, splaying his thighs and twisting his legs, seeking accommodation for their length. "I can keep an eye out from here," he said, "good as any place," though he had not yet looked away from her; his eyes seemed, over and over, to be laying out her face for a game of tic-tac-toe: two horizontal lines, two vertical.

"You and me," he said, "the two best-looking kids in school. Remember, Milly?" She regarded him in silence. She remembered nothing of the sort, but his memory was apparently equipped to do service for both of them—"Milly," for instance; she had never been called anything except Millicent. "Now—my face—" he said, and she thought that if he wanted sympathy there was an easier way to gain it, equally as cheap, and she gave him the opening.

"Were you a hero?"

"Whut's *that?*" She heard it as an old response, the nuances frozen dead by time, though she could imagine that once the joshing question had served him as an affirmative. She thought that now he would change the subject, and he did.

"Sorry about your dad, Milly. Heard about it on the radio this morning."

Enough was quite enough; she told him, "You had it right the first time—Millicent is my name." His only response was a quivering about the nostrils as though he could smell the cold burning that prompted her words. Relaxing her voice, she said, "People and names—fascinating, sometimes ludicrous as couples.

I'm simply not a 'Milly,' any more than you're a—Cyril."

"Cyril is a good-looking name, huh?"

"No. I've always thought it was a fat name."

"A fat name." He laughed, slapping the seat. "Effie—that's a fat name, too." He looked at her and guffawed. "So's *Milly*. That's your objection, huh?"

"Uh huh."

He jiggled on the seat as though to some erratic tempo unheard by her, slapping the leather again with his hand, asking, "What'll she do?"

"A hundred—in 1935. I touch seventy now and then."

"Whew. Not bad for an old girl. No wonder she's got a bird on her belly."

The inaptness of the comparison of a radiator to a belly told her the direction of his thoughts. "It's a stork," she said. "The perfect emblem for a belly," and smiled coolly, but found that she had not called his bluff.

"Whata you do for parts for her? You can't graft them off of *her* ass." The inner lining of his lips shone at her, pink and blistered as a wad of bubble gum.

"She's made to last. Perfectly indestructible."

"Like you?"

"Yes."

"Not a goddamn line in your face." He bent forward to peer closely.

She relaxed to keep from moving away. Then, for an odd moment, it was as if she had stepped onto another plane of time and she had the perfectly clear thought that it was strange to be expected to have lines in your face at the age of fourteen. Following that, she thought: Why, he has a peculiar power, and her impression of it was of a thing both fanged and clawed, and she felt it was what had destroyed his face. As though she were able to hide her face by the suggestive word, she said, "My forte is shadows."

"Huh? Well, you sure've kept up the old school rep. That face of yours been just about every place by now, I reckon."

She was able to laugh then. She offered him a Sobranie. "I'll swap one of these for a Chesterfield, or a plain cigar."

He searched the pockets of his overcoat with one hand and held the exotic cigarette with the other, turning it before his eyes, sniffing and looking at it with the wide, half-crazy stare that had been set on her—the result, she wondered, of the surface or the interior wound? He gave her a cigarette and lit his, then brought the match, shielded like a candle, to the tip of hers as if he were Prometheus, bringing his bulk along with it until they were as close as possible without embracing. She nodded her thanks and moved back a little, a suggestion that he do the same, but he stayed hunched over her.

"A lot of water under the bridge, Milly. Twenty years' worth . . . Milly." She had had experience of being baited by strangers—which was what he practically was—though her antagonists were commonly women; still, the trick learned was that one did not give the expected replies, and what he was openly asking for was correction. Flatly, she said, "Hurray for bridges."

Like a strip of film, she ran the panorama of the Square through her mind as it had looked when she drove around it, hoping this time to discover some lighted window by-passed a few minutes earlier, behind which clerks bent reassuringly over merchandise or counted the day's till. As if he viewed the deserted Square on the screen of her eyes and found it pleasing, he laid his lips back in the double grin, then withdrew into a state of cigarette puffing and thought, the effort tugging at his rigid eyelids; she imagined him sleeping with his eyes wide open, sightlessly staring.

"Not all of it goes under, though," he said after a while. "Some of it gets caught in rocks and whirls around there, digging a big hole." His tone, gloomily portentous, was the last ridiculous straw.

"Look. Luke. I'm sure that's perfectly true, but I can't think what in hell it's got to do with anything—with me, anyway. It's been nice seeing you, but I've got to get—" His tongue lapped the remaining words from her tongue. The ridges of his face, like bared muscles, raped her cheeks as he rolled his face upon hers, side to side. Except for the reaching, straining tongue, and the touching of facial bones and muscles, and one hand clamped behind her head, he did not touch her body at all, but seemed to be avoiding her breasts and legs with great care. During one of his rolling movements that left a gap for its insinuation, she brought her cigarette up and held it between their eyes in a vertical position, so close that her shrinking eyeball could feel the heat. If he was without fear, or crazy, she would soon be as maimed as he.

His eye, centered by the reflected coal, glared into

hers. He drew back an inch or two. "You think you can hurt *this* with *that?* My face's got no more feeling than an elephant hide. On a floor, not on the elephant." But he released her roughly and moved away. Feeling like a melted watch in a Dali—time out of sequence, function impaired if not destroyed—she felt also like the intrigued observer. He sat back, folding his arms, telling her, "Go on—call the cops." He taunted her: "I'm the only one there is. I'm *it* around here, in the nighttime." Coyly he said, "Bet you can't guess why I picked out the night beat for myself."

"So you can attempt rape?"

He looked as if he would attack her again, this time with a blunter instrument. "Because of *this,* you damn fool," and he wiped his face savagely with his hand as if he might be able to erase the lumpiness and reveal again the firm even hide of youth before war's indelible kiss taught it all about love.

Listening to the sleety snow hushing on the ambient glass like slippered feet on a carpet, feeling the—at least—double surrealism of her position, Millicent tried to think back to high school days, when she might, however inadvertently, have hurt him enough to make him want to hurt her. He had been one of the ones she had thought of as the "mooners"—boys who mooned at her always from a distance, separated from her by desks, basketball courts, other people; not just at her but at all the girls not cross-eyed or noticeably knock-kneed. Even then she had found males who were shyly idealistic about females to be foolish but not sad; determined stupidity hardly deserved sympathy. As if he were silently giving her clues, she glimpsed an area of herself that was not so much closed off as shunned.

When she was young she had lived for a time with a woman analyst whose compulsion it had been to put her through the intricacies of her childhood and adolescence as though she were pacing a horse. Because of this, Millicent doubted if there were any classic "blocks" left unturned, though she had kept things back from Joan, meaning to look at them in perverse privacy. When she and Joan broke up she found that she had been forevermore rid of the impulse to excavate her own ruins because she had learned that the idea in back of sifting all the debris was never the hope of turning up a lost pearl; the starting assumption was that the pearls had been eaten, so that what was looked for, and in most cases, paid for, was swine droppings. Millicent found the thought of new unearthed tragedies that might help "explain" her as boring as hell; the only things for which she was willing to dig, now or ever, were absurdities. But Luke was the one who needed explaining, and surely whatever it was that had made him lunge at her could not possibly be boring. From her radar equipment that could signal *bore* across great distances she received not a peep—though if she had, following the Ears, Eyes, Nose and Throat bit, she would have trotted back to Joan, ego and id in hand, pleading for more of The Word. And, strangest of all, though tonight was the first time a man's tongue had been in her mouth, she had no feeling of violation. What she felt—though it was too elusive to catch and hold and examine closely—was something like . . . vindication . . .

"What did you mean about the water caught in the rocks?"

Her mild tone, her interest, did not seem to surprise him. If anything, he assumed the role of the violated and spoke sullenly. "What I said. It stagnates."

"You said it dug a deep hole."

"Rot digs holes, too. Eats away. Disintegrates."

"Distintegrates *what?*"

"Don't you *know?* For God's sake, Millicent, don't you?" He seemed to be on the edge of tears.

She shook her head, fascinated. "Tell me. May as well." She tried not to sound too eager, but he heard the effort.

"Uh uh. I'm afraid you can use it."

"For what?"

"To feed your goddamned face. Keep it young and smooth till you're a hundred. Like that jelly they take from insects that you advertised all over—billboards, everywhere—" Slowly he said, "To look up and see you—" He shook his head. "Once I counted your face ten times between here and Louisville. I tried to find out where I could buy one of those posters. One of the big ones. I was meaning to cut it up and paste it around the room . . . an eye here, nose there, lips . . ."

Her face seemed to freeze, seemed to try to become of a material impervious to his shears.

"Kinda grabs you, don't it? That's what was done to me." He took a deep breath. "I've waited twenty years to blame you, Milly. Now, that's a long time." His tone insisted on an answer; she nodded: a long time. "What'd *you* do if you'd waited twenty years for something?"

"I'd spit it out."

"Yes'm, I bet you just would. Skin soft as a baby's ass, but *I* know how hard you are. You're like a keg of nails. Always were, too."

"You can't know that much about *me*."

"What?"

"The person you know—this 'Milly'—is a stranger to me. You've made her up."

"Would anybody make up such a devil?"

"You have, Luke."

"Tell me, then: you're not as hard as nails at all—is that it?"

"That's not the point, is it? Whether *I* am or not. I said that we—or you—were not talking about *me*. I may even be a devil, but I am not a devil named Milly, nor am I somebody you knew well enough to call *anything* except Millicent."

"Well, now, I just did. Called you hard as a keg of nails—"

"No. You called Milly that."

"—and called you a devil—" She was silent. "Giving up?" he said. "Or bored? I remember that about you, too. Or"—he was sly—"is that Milly I'm talking about? Are you bored, Millicent? Does my"—he snickered—"pain bore you? Suppose I told you to lay down and take your medicine."

"You won't," she said with total conviction, and the flicker in his eyes confirmed her assurance.

He looked away from her then as if to find needed strength. Doggedly he said, "When I heard about your dad dying, I started waiting for you. I knew you had to come back for a funeral. I've met every bus and was going to meet the late train. I knew it was my one chance . . . and, by God, and now . . ."

"Oh, Luke," she said with a certain feeling of compassion, "you're hurting yourself, you know, and—" she had almost said "boring me," but still it was not true—"and baffling hell out of me—" She put her hand on his arm, not knowing until after she had done it that what she was interested in was his reaction to her voluntary touch.

He stared at the hand as though it might be a night creature, a winter moth, a snow insect—a thing entirely unexpected between them. Sounding hypnotized, he said, "I was going to put the hand . . . the one your face leaned on in that picture . . . I was going to put it"—he lowered his hand to his crotch—"here."

On its own, laughter came and sat in Millicent's throat. Her brain, astonished, asked it why it was there. Wait, said the laughter, wait . . . All at once Luke seemed to explode all over her. "I wanted to lock you in the room and stand on the outside and talk to you, through the door. I wanted to tell you what all I've thought over these twenty goddamn years—the way I've wanted to go back to that night and either have it my way, or your way; either have you somebody like I thought you were—innocent, somebody that didn't go around *grabbing,* somebody I could think about overseas, and maybe come home and—or have it your way: take it out, skin it back, stick it in— That's what you wanted, it sure as hell was. But I didn't have it anybody's way. Nobody's way at all. Well, I can sure as hell give a whore a hot time. Guess they need it, too." Opening the door he said to her, "They all thank you, ma'am. All the good old whores I've stuck." He looked at her, waiting. At her blank stillness he said, astounded, "Well, by Jesus." And she knew . . . even before he came at her, almost climbing on her, and put one big hand in her trousered lap, palm down, and said, "Remember now?" and squeezed. When she still did not move he said, "You owed me a feel," and it sounded like the voice of a young boy after punishment. Tears dripped from his eyes and slid from patch to patch as though irrigating a field . . .

Once, toward the end of the affair, Joan, half drunk and mocking, said to Millicent: Deny a memory of all the pleasure I have given you and I will not mind, but remember oh remember the pain you caused me. Say that I gave you pain commensurate with yours to me and I will pluck one by one the jewels from my bleeding crown and stick them on yours with Duco, blood and jism . . .

Millicent was flooded by melancholy, the one cardinal humor that most emphatically did not contribute to her disposition. She watched Luke wipe his eyes on his coat sleeve; darkly she wished that for once she possessed in abundance one of the two qualities—ruthlessness and hypocrisy, at least to males—that she had found to be the cornerstones of lesbian natures. Then she could either pretend that she did not understand what Luke meant, or could order him out of the car, refusing to discuss further what had obviously been the trauma of his life, for he could joke, however masochistically, about his face, but he could only weep about what she had done to him—the night of their only date, forgotten by her, the night of his graduation from high school, the eve of his induction into the Army. Bright and clear she saw them, the fourteen-year-old sophomore, the big quiet senior who had mooned at her for two years. She saw them at the graduation ball, saw him dancing about her like a celebrant in a religious ritual, dancing about the foot of her pedestal, touching her only when liturgy demanded it. When he drove her home he sat staring over the wheel—how clear the picture, how damned bright his clean face—illuminated by an entirely private ectasy that she knew had no more to do with her, as a flesh and blood creature, then her father's tireless attempts at seduction had to do with permissible reality. A reversal of roles would at least have made some kind of sense, though she did not want to be worshipped as a goddess by her father any more than she wanted Luke to come tapping at her door night after night, when wine had put his conscience to sleep and left only the mindless instinct to rut. She was a controlled girl who honored the power of thought above instinct, and so it was with thoughtful control that she put her hand between Luke's legs and found the symbol of her father's menace; the symbol, like as Eleusinian mystery, of Luke's religious use of her—one use as bad as the other because Luke's erection had shown her the paucity of choices offered by men, whatever the outward pose. Satyr or mystic—the mystery, revealed, was the same: a damned ear of corn. And she? A hill of dirt that they hoped would be fertile.

She came from the memory to find Luke quietly looking at her. It seemed to her that she had been away for only a moment, but something between them—a peculiar kind of ease—informed her time-sense, acutely developed for living a life on schedule, the schedule meaning money or livelihood, that they had been together for some time. Then she noticed that the snow had covered the windshield and clung stickily to the side windows, so that they were enclosed as though in an alabaster box. The satin lining of her coat was, too, a reminder of death, and Luke, whom she had once used, she now saw, with both hypocrisy and ruthlessness, was bound up with her father in her mind and memory to the extent that she felt herself buried with him and sought some means of extrication—of herself from deathless involvement with her father, of Luke from the identification with her father that she had imposed on him twenty years ago. All things were now explained, apparently, including her initial reaction of panic when she saw Luke; it was as if he were her father redivivus. But somehow, in the passing violence and quiet of their time together, she had come to have an unexpected feeling of genuine compassion for him, so that she did not see how she could extricate him by explaining. She felt that to untangle him from the skein of her father and herself and turn him loose unfettered was to push him until he fell. The binding threads, dense and tight as a shroud, were what kept him, in all senses, erect. Unbind him—she felt—and what would he blame his wounds on, excusing, explaining? For he had told her that he blamed his shot-to-hell face on his disillusion with her—so much simpler than indicting a country, a world. Easier to get satisfaction from. How can you get back from a world what it has taken, in insanity, from you? She knew what she would do: she would send him stacks of photographs of herself that he could cut and reshape and paste, like a map of the world. She was not superstitious; she did not believe that she would be, in time, what he made of her with shears and frustration . . .

She thought: O.K. That takes care of Luke, I guess. Now what about me? And the waiting laughter said *now*. True . . . she had that. She always had that. Especially now, she saw, for what she had found was truly absurd and truly deserving, as few things actually were, of gales and screams of mad mirth: a perfect Freudian gem, flawlessly faceted, marvelously mounted, beautifully boxed—and blocked. A classic castration attempt that succeeded: poor Father-Luke, impotent with "good" women. And, by the by, her own "castration"—*because that night, students—an dieser besonderen Nacht*—there was formed from the events thrown into the air like a handful of ='s a . . . lesbian.

"Go!" she said to Luke, covering her rising laughter with simulated fury, and seeing his fright, she pushed him toward the door lest the laughter burst its bounds and drown him and stick her with his corpse. He bent at the door, peering in at her, his expression intentionally comical. She did not want to leave *him* laughing, because the poor idiot, whether or not he knew it, would literally laugh until he fell down. Oh, noble Millicent, to save the good man from such a fate. You're quite a girl, Milly. But that's what a fast twenty-five minutes of group therapy does to a girl. But just at that moment electronic trumpets sounded a fanfare from the courthouse tower, Roseville's traditional greeting to the Christ Child, and she knew that somehow or other she and Luke had attained midnight together.

"Good-by, you motherfucker," she told him, and after a moment of still shock he slammed the door almost hard enough to crack the glass. The engine caught on first try and she slued from the curb amidst spume of flying snow. She drove toward Owen's, but when she reached the cross street she paused as if hanging on the edge of an abyss. Mama? . . . and then decided: No. I'll call her later. And she turned around the Square and opened the throttle and sailed onto Courthouse Lane and onward toward the turnpike. Laughing loudly, even painfully, she asked herself if it was the laughter of bravado? Perversion she had never thought to be remotely tragic, unless it involved systematic blood-letting, and yet—laughing madly—she wondered if a few tears for herself as she had once been might not be in order? And a few for Luke—and, yes, a few for her father's anguish or whatever in hell it had been to make him breach laws of taste and common sense, among others. But she felt with somehow unshakable certainty that she would go on laughing. And on laughing. And on laughing.

Ed stood in Owen's parking lot, cursing; he could not get either one of the cars to start. He checked every connection while Priscilla held the flashlight for him. All was in order, every part in place; the buggies just would not go. Priscilla aimlessly swung the arc of light around the ground and caught the glitter of a metallic response. It was the cap to the gas tank of the Pontiac. Needless investigation proved what they knew: some charitable soul had drained the tanks of both cars. Priscilla went inside and told Erin what had happened, and that she and Ed were going to walk to the gas station on the other side of town because the one across the street was closed. It would take a while, so maybe Erin should call the house and tell the others not to worry.

"I know," said Priscilla sweetly, "that they *will* worry, don't you? I can imagine how anxious they are to get here. Rhoda will probably start out on all fours. Spur," she said, going out the door, "has learned to get along on just *three* legs." Erin missed the sexual allusion; she thought that Priscilla meant he used Bonny as a crutch, or third leg.

Erin had functioned well enough throughout the evening, in face of her frustration. On the way in she had asked Priscilla point-blank what she intended to do to hurt Robin. She timed the question to fit squarely in the middle of a five-mile silence, giving Priscilla plenty of time to place her thoughts elsewhere, hoping thereby to catch her completely off guard.

"What on earth do you mean?" Priscilla asked her, maneuvering the car expertly over the frightening roads. "What could possibly make me want to hurt Robin?" She patted Erin's knee. "Poor Erin, you must be tired beyond belief."

And there it was, thought Erin, the lifelong fluctuation between remembering and not remembering. Her tone had been genuinely filled with concern; Erin had to believe in it. She thought of the power of mental blocks and told herself that once Priscilla had said the terrible words—"You're afraid of what we will do to him"—her mind had encased itself in protective forgetfulness. Chilly comfort, indeed. If the block was suddenly removed by the sight of Robin in the living flesh near the dead father—that was the moment to beware, to set up guards against. Not only against Priscilla's reaction. All of theirs together—the transmission of impulse leaping from person to person that could forge creativity or destruction. Robin had become an abstraction to them in the past three years, or a rumor, like a planet that could only be seen through the largest telescope. She was the telescope. If they, or she, could destroy *that*—unfocus the thing, break the lens, smash the mirrors! She shoved the thought away into the mass of her brain that was, in fatigue, like limp, bitter sauerkraut. She no longer knew what she expected; she half suspected herself of dramatizing a situation dramatic enough without her help; then words would come back to her, inflections, looks—she could not rest.

After Priscilla and Ed set out for the gas station with two five-gallon cans, heading into the thickening snow like children diving into feathers, Erin pulled all of her will into one great round cannon-ball shape and projected it with ballistic force—she hoped it was so—through the telephone when she told Mr. Price, who was argumentative in tiredness, to go instantly to the farm and bring back the people there. Whoever it was who had drained the gas tanks had given her a gift beyond Price. The pun amused her a great deal; she chuckled and grimaced into the office telephone to the terror of Mr. Owen, who was watching her. Now she would have them all together when Robin arrived. She called the bus station and got no answer; she called the depot and commanded the voice lurking in the receiver to identify itself.

"This is Handy Miller."

The Lord, thought Erin, tickled pink, was on her side whether or not he knew it. "Handy," she said warmly, "this is Erin McChesney," waited until he said what he had to say and then told him, "Robin will be coming on the late train. Send him to Owen's. Tell him—" Tell him they are waiting for him, armed to the teeth? "Tell him we are waiting for him. Tell him to hurry." She waited a moment then said, "Bless you," abruptly and hung up. In the sitting room she found the three old ladies asleep. Only Tonia rested in comfort on the cot Mr. Owen had furnished and hurriedly set up, scabbling sideways like a crab when one of the family got near him.

Erin leaned against the door, equidistant from the sleeping mother and the dead father: I am the product of the distance between them and their strength or lack of it; I am a magnetic moment. But there is no pull. Neither of them draws nor repels me. I could stand here between them forever—as I have done forever?—if I depended on either of them to move me. I thought this morning that she was strong, but it was only relief she felt at suddenly being freed from the terrible pulling of that opposite pole; a part of herself of which she had never been part died and the pulling that had bent her double stopped and she could straighten up. It must have felt like strength to her, just being able to stand up straight. But she has begun to bend again in the direction from which the pulling once came. People who lose limbs are said to feel itching in the space where the limb was, and try to scratch the air. We are all scratching the air and some of us are clawing holes in it. The air is filled with ragged holes; I wonder who has had the nerve to look through to the other side of the air? Jasper and Rhoda can't have been left alone together. They would not need much time to formulate some terrible plan. They were always close, too close. I thought that I trusted Andrew and Bonny but I was wrong. I will trust no one except Robin tonight. Tomorrow when he is safely covered over with earth we will blockade ourself in one room, we will pile the furniture against the door, we will read poetry and listen to them blither as they run from room to room looking for us. Tomorrow I will trust ourself not to care. Tomorrow we will not know fear. If we grow hungry we will eat the bindings of books and the pages of books and we will at last know everything. The world will crumble and the ashes settle and we will sit in our room and eat knowledge and there will be no one left to take it from us and we will be free.

One of the sleeping people stirred and Erin rushed to the embalming room and went in without knocking. There was no one there, but if there had been they could not have kept her from taking the thing she sought, that she knew was there because she had found Mr. Owen drinking from it when she went to ask for the cot. She found the bottle and drank until she felt herself reviving, until her mind could reject her thoughts of a while before, until she knew that she was sane with an undreamt-of clarity.

On the way to the gas station Priscilla took Ed's arm with both her hands, causing him to have to carry the ungainly cans with one hand, which he did awkwardly but gladly because she leaned her head on his shoulder.

"Do you want me, Ed?"

"I always have."

"Is that the same thing?"

"It couldn't never change."

"Ever."

"Never."

"Don't you want somebody who can cook and likes it?"

"I wouldn't know what the hell to do with her."

"Somebody who wanted children?"

"Yes."

"Who could have them?"

He was silent. "I've lied to you."

"I know it."

"When have I lied to you?"

"What's the use in answering that?"

"Answer it."

"When you said somebody called up about Nonie and me."

"Why did you cry, then?"

"Because."

"Because what?"

"Because somebody'd hurt you enough to make you do it."

"When else did I lie?"

"When you said 'I do.' " He was hardly audible.

"If I said it now would you believe me?"

"I don't want to take no chance."

"Any chance."

"No chance."

"If I looked you in the eye and said 'I do' would you feel happy?"

"I did once. That'll have to do me. I don't regret nothing."

"Anything."

"Nothing."

"Is my head here a lie?"

"I don't know what that means."

"Answer it anyway."

"I can feel it there."

She pulled his head down and they kissed. "Was that a lie?"

"I could feel that too."

"Was there love in it?"

"It was different."

"You could tell!" She began to cry, holding his arm and sobbing with her face pressed into his sleeve.

He stopped and let the cans drop into the snow and took her in his arms. "Honey baby, what's the matter? Oh Lord, honey baby—" His skin broke out in goose-flesh that had nothing to do with the cold. It was more as if lightning played around them. He understood nothing except that there was this feeling between them.

She lifted eyes blinded by silver. "Ed, I thought it was going to be so godawful being that other woman—" He had no notion of what she meant but he found himself hanging onto her words while the lightning played. "It always *seemed* to be godawful, for other women who didn't have the choice of being somebody else. Think of all the people in those houses rolling down the turnpike with no way to get off, except stingy little places where they can pull over to one side long enough to fix a flat and then go on until the next accident. At least that's the way I thought it was. I didn't see the green fields on each side. I didn't know that you could drive slowly and enjoy the scenery." She kissed him again and then picked up one of the cans and started walking. He picked up the other can and followed her, puzzled and waiting, but thrilled. After a while she said, "I've got so goddamn much to tell you. I was going to wait but I can't. He gave me a present, Ed. Tonight, from wherever he is— If you still want me after I've finished, I'll give the present to you." Ed shook his head at her: I don't understand; don't stop. "First things first, then." She took a deep breath. "To begin with, you married yourself a virgin."

The air was so still Ed could hear the hissing of the snowflakes. And then the lost Roman candles began to go off. He thought he spoke but he couldn't hear his voice over the loud colored balls of fire. He tried again, shouting this time, though he didn't know what it was he said. But he could hear Prissy. She said, "Shhhhh, honey. You'll wake up the children and they'll find out who Santa Claus really is."

"But why on earth didn't you have Mr. Price bring *them* when he came for us? Look at Mother—she's practically drawn up in a knot."

"It didn't cross my mind."

"Really, dear—" Rhoda tried to soften her indignation.

"Ed and Priscilla will be back any minute—" Bonny's tone was faintly warning. She had smelled Erin's breath; her eye told her things more disquieting than that Erin had been drinking.

"What if the gas station is closed?" Spur asked them all. The door to the other room yawned ominously.

"It is. They close at nine o'clock." Erin was factual. "It is now past eleven."

"You knew that all along?" Rhoda heard her voice as Portia's, warning Shylock that death was the penalty for taking more than his pound of flesh.

"It didn't cross my mind."

Rhoda and Spur exchanged looks; Andrew and Bonny exchanged looks.

"Why," asked Erin mildly, "are you staring at each other? You must have known."

"Know what?" Spur's voice was pitying.

Erin clasped her hands and waited a moment to answer. "Why, that the gas stations close at nine. They always have." She looked from one to the other, asking corroboration. "Nothing changes in Roseville."

"What good would that have done us? *We* didn't know the cars were out of gas."

"We do now, Rhoda," said Andrew, "so we'll just call the taxi back."

"No," said Erin inaudibly.

"Sure. He can let us have some gas," said Spur. "Mr. Price has his own pump."

"No," Erin said again, loudly. They looked at her, two of them in fear. "I want them here when he comes. They can go then." No one asked whom she meant. They knew. The four of them gazed at the tall woman clasping and unclasping her hands, her color high and feverish. She was bringing them close to the edge of something they all feared, without knowing what it was. Her voice was thick with fatigue as she continued, "It is late for them, I know, but it can't be long before he comes. We should all be together this once." *This once.* What could she mean? She told them. "Tomorrow there will be people watching us for signs of morbidity. We cannot—we must not—gratify them with any sort of display."

All at once the four of them could find nothing in themselves but concern for her. She had been through a lot and none of them had done anything to help. That she had never before required their help did not seem to them excuse enough; in their contrition and relief at her considerate, eminently sensible words, Rhoda and Spur effected a change in the current of air between themselves and Erin, and she felt it as soothing; they were mutually soothed.

"Of course we won't," said Spur with conviction.

"Of course not, darling," Rhoda assured her, the endearment springing gladly from her lips.

Their assurances confused Andrew, who had mourned his parents openly without thinking of who might be watching, but they were in answer to Erin's request and he trusted her. Bonny, though she did not recognize it as such at the moment, felt defeat. She found herself thinking, out of the blue, that she could go back to her study of medicine; the boys were growing up— Erin walked to one of the chairs and sat, folding her hands in her lap. Because neither Spur nor Rhoda made a move to go into the other room, and took chairs themselves, Andrew and Bonny sat also. Tonia's snore was the only sound in the room.

After a time voices from the street were heard and Erin's hands flew like birds from her lap and gripped the arms of her chair. Priscilla's words became distinguishable and the hands returned again to each other. The door opened and Priscilla and Ed came in with glistening eyes. Rhoda, seeing the tears on her sister's face, felt revulsion. Priscilla gazed about her, seeing the people there for the first time. She wondered if the beating of her heart could be heard by them. Ed rushed across the room to Spur. Spur flung his hand up to his face protectively, as he would do in dreams of his plane crashing. Ed grabbed the hand and wrung it. Spur, shocked, got up, thinking the man had gone crazy. Ed left and went around the room, kissing the women with loud smacks, bestowing on the mouths of the sleeping old ladies gifts that curved their lips with reminiscence. Finding the circuit completed and himself not satisfied, Ed started toward Spur again. In trying to avoid the second onslaught,

Spur stumbled back against his chair. The chair fell over with a thud and Spur lost his balance and sprawled on the floor, causing the room to shake and the pictures to rattle.

Tonia woke up with a snort and rose ponderously to a sitting position. "Fighting," she keened, "in the house of the dead!"

The widow and Editha were awakened by the wail and sat blinking in the light, making half-articulated sounds of question and protest.

"Ed," said Priscilla, "you fool."

Everybody spoke at once although no one could hear what anyone else said. It didn't matter. Once again they had been saved from thoughts that burned. Robin walked into the cocktail-party hum of voices and stood weaving in the doorway, holding his bottle of liquor by the neck. Handy stood in back of him, and only his eyes, for a moment, were not impassive, but no one was looking at Handy.

"Mer' Chris'mas," said Robin, and spit ran from the corner of his mouth and hung thickly from his chin, lengthening and stretching and finally separating from the stubble of his beard to fall onto the dark of his coat, where it quivered like a salted snail.

Erin walked toward him, a reflection of a reflection, a thin faint shadow, a bird wing passing before a candle. "You've hurt your hand." She knelt at his feet and took the hand gently between her two hands that had waited so long, counting the hours upon themselves, and kissed it. The hand slipped from hers as her head fell lower until it was bowed at the height of his knee. His slack fingers grazed the crown of her hair and then lost touch as the head dropped lower and lower toward his feet. "Let us be together in our loss," said Erin, her mouth against his shoes.

"Mer' Chris'mas," said Robin, and heaved and the vomit splattered her with bits of old food, and of Scotland.

Bonny went back to the kitchen and found Priscilla alone.

She had been for fifteen or twenty minutes in the bathroom, alternately crying and laving her face and eyes with snow gathered by the handfuls from the roof that slanted outside the small window. The nightmare, which she thought had reached its culmination in the funeral parlor with Robin's return and the subsequent, disjointed incidents that followed, had gone on growing until she had given way to her terror and fled to the bathroom.

On the way from town the widow sat between Priscilla and Bonny, babbling incessantly and incoherently, but now and then Millicent's name emerged with clarity; she seemed to be invoking her missing daughter with puzzling fervor. In the back seat, Robin sat, by his insistence, holding his unconscious sister's head in his lap. He was as quiet as if his mind had joined Erin's in some comatose communion, but when Bonny turned around she saw that he was staring straight ahead at the white road that lit the interior of the car eerily. He cried out just once, just before they turned off the main road into the avenue of trees leading to the house, as the lights of an oncoming car, feeble as they were, scorched his eyes. The car was an ancient Model-T with flapping side curtains, jammed to its roof, and Bonny heard Priscilla draw in her breath as she recognized it.

"Mama," Priscilla said, "there go Randolph and his family to stay with Daddy. Isn't it thoughtful of them, Mama!" The words were like witchcraft; in a moment the widow was sitting erect, her pride mysteriously returned. "My folks," she said, and sat the rest of the way looking sternly in front of her like an old Indian chief.

When they got out of the car, Robin stumbling and cursing, his mother gave him no more attention than she would have given a clumsy stranger, except to say, at the door, "Scrape your feet good. We don't want to track up the carpets." The two of them started inside, useless to help the two women struggling with Erin's body, but the widow remained in the doorway, propping the door open for them, saying in a detached voice. "Keerful. You don't want to hit her head."

Bonny and Priscilla carried Erin up the stairs to her room. As frail as the body was, it was a struggle for them, but they read each other's minds and silently agreed that to place her on the bed where her father had died, though convenient, would be too macabre. Robin had disappeared.

While Priscilla helped her mother undress and get into bed, Bonny worked over Erin with the despairing feeling that what they all had assumed was a prolonged faint was really a state of shock, just how profound she could not tell. Respiration, pulse, skin temperature—all shouted danger to her, and she, who had never gotten her wires crossed, found herself struggling to remember all the steps in the emergency treatment of shock while the images of the events in the funeral parlor kept superimposing themselves over her once-controllable brain. WARMTH jumped from the textbook page in her mind. While she piled blankets on Erin's clammy body she saw all of them frozen in time and space while Robin drank noisily over his sister's body until the Negro man took the bottle from him and cracked it on the railing outside, and then, as if no one else was in the room, he—IMMOBILITY—took Erin up into his arms and carried her to the cot where Antonia sagged and said to her, "Get up. Make haste." He placed Erin on the cot, then took a handkerchief from his pants pocket and wiped at the vomit on her dress and hair, turning her from side to side like an infant. His dark hands were the only moving things in the room. Bonny remembered saying to herself, "In a minute—soon," but unable to move. Robin walked among the still figures, white vertical counterpoint to the dark horizontal hands, offering to one and all mock holiday greetings. His utter contempt could not have been achieved through any degree of drunkenness. His contempt, she thought, was stone-cold sober.

Bonny saw him standing in front of Rhoda, the courtly incline of his head. His bulk blocked her view of the other woman's face, so that it seemed like ventriloquism when the high, childish voice, nothing like Rhoda's pleasantly reedy way of speaking, said, "Please," drawing the word out until emotion was achieved by the length, rather than the content, of the sound: "Pleeeease"—high, flat, like a note drawn from a piece of wood. Robin wavered, his inclined head taking on the set look of deep attention as though it would remain bent before Rhoda, listening, while his body moved away. When he did move on, Bonny could see that Andrew had gone to his wife and was standing behind her, his face wearing a wholly inappropriate look of joy.

Bonny made a great effort to banish what followed from her mind, but it was not banishable; she and all the people present were branded with it like cattle, except that the brand of Robin's words was as cold as the flesh of the man to whom it was applied. He stood in the doorway between the two rooms and looked toward his father's coffin and said, "I condemn you to lie fallow without seed and the rain to fall on you and erode you and carry you away grain by grain."

The widow gave one piercing cry. Simultaneously the Negro man got up from his knees and hit Robin twice with the back of his hand, one blow for each cheek. Robin's eyes focused under the blows; with a loose-lipped smile he said, "I hit somebody I loved for you once."

Bonny heard again the small sound of Spur's breath from where he lay on the floor, before he turned face downward and wept. She felt again her impersonality at the sound of Spur's crying, the crying for which she had come close to praying, and then the snap of the cords that had bound her. She heard her voice issuing orders about gasoline, a car, who should go to the farm, demanding that Priscilla come with her. When the orders had been carried out by Andrew, Ed and the Negro man, and Erin was in the back seat with her head on Robin's lap, with Priscilla at the wheel and her mother next to her, Bonny, about to get in the car, saw that the Negro man was leaving. She called to him, "Thank you. Thank you for all your help, Mr.—" He turned and looked at all of them, and when his eyes met Robin's he spat deliberately in the snow, then walked away, neither hurrying nor lagging. It was Bonny's clear impression that he forgot them completely as soon as he turned away.

Antonia had put up a fight for a place in the car, saying that she was too tired to take the taxi all the way out to her own house.

"That's too goddamned bad, Fatso," said Priscilla, starting the car with a furious grinding of gears, and the last sound they heard as they left was Tonia's uplifted voice, piteously asking comfort like a baby's.

FLUIDS. Bonny had no way to give Erin fluids intravenously; she was, in fact, helpless to do any more than she had done. She would have to call a doctor—Erin made a small movement and Bonny's heart leaped with hope. She took Erin's wrist and joyfully felt the steadier pulse and warmer flesh. She bent over and kissed Erin's brow and murmured, "Thank you, darling." Hot-water bottles, coffee in case it was needed, brandy—she hurried down the stairs and into the kitchen. There she found Robin seated at the table, a bottle of whiskey in front of him, a brimming glass in his hand. The look he gave her of cunning was all the more unbearable for being surrounded by, or composed of, flecks of blood. Bonny wanted to snatch the bottle the way the Negro had done and smash it over Robin's skull. In the middle of the air between them her hate met something as unfamiliar and turned back toward its source. She stepped lightly around it and into Robin's dimension like a bullfighter. "May I have a drink?" She sounded as if she wanted and needed one. Something in his eyes altered at the request. He wore now a wary look of hospitality.

He spoke slowly, his words barely slurred. "If you can't lick 'em, join 'em?"

Bonny gave him a calculated stare of noncomprehension, got herself a glass and sat opposite him. She reached casually for the bottle but he withdrew it, resting it on the edge of his shoulder at such an angle that if it had been fuller, it would have spilled.

"I'll pour," he said, and laughed. She pushed her glass to the center of the table and he poured a generous amount in the glass and some on the table because he did not take his eyes from her. It was only then she noticed that he had turned off the overhead light, and by that and his presence had created for himself, and for her, the atmosphere of a bar. Or perhaps she had created it by walking into the dim room filled with anger and asking for a drink. Perhaps she was obeying his will. He was broken and disgusting and frightening, but she felt from him the flow of power that only such people can emanate: the total lack of ruth that comes from knowing one has nothing left to lose.

"Drink up," he said, and she drank, choking a little; she had never liked it straight. He told her, "There's plenty more where this came from. Don't be afraid we'll run out." His reassurance was quite real; he meant her to take nothing but comfort from the words. She wanted badly to cry at what he had told her about himself so simply, but she could not afford time out for tears.

"Oh?" she said. "Oh, of course. In the cellar." As soon as she could she would go down and break every bottle.

"Wine," he said with distaste. "That's for dead men." He watched her, his suspicion returned, waiting for her to ask where the whiskey was. She read his mind easily and kept silence on her side. But she was caught with him in the silence, which was broken from time to time by his orders to drink up. Her head began to spin. Suppose, she thought, Priscilla had gone to bed, or had forgotten her, or simply did not care that she was trapped here, or—because anything was possible —*wished* her sister-in-law to suffer. They had, all of them, always spoken of her as cruel. Suppose— "Paranoia," Bonny told herself. "You can't afford that either. It's a dangerous game." Then it occurred to her to use what weapon she had to save herself, for she did have one. With boldness she told him, "This is a dangerous game we're playing."

"You mean who goes under the table first? We know who, don't we?"

"No, I didn't mean that exactly. But if I get drunk"—she took careful aim with her voice—"if I get drunk, who will look after Erin?" She watched the cloudy emotion crossing his face.

"Bull. Erin looks after people. You've got it ass-backwards." He poured for both of them although she still had half a glassful. "If she needed looking after, I'd do it. The way I've always done."

"Always?" she said, telling herself the game was indeed dangerous. She bent across the table, fixing him with her eyes. "Erin is in severe shock. Can you handle that?" She waited for the flicker and when it came she said, *"She may never recover,"* and crossed her fingers under the table, barely restraining her tears.

He half rose, clutching the bottle, and Bonny acknowledged her full terror with the corner of her mind that could still observe. There was no way for her to measure the length of the moment before he sank slowly back. He drank, and if his hand trembled when he raised the glass, it was steady when he lowered it. He told her quietly, "I've always admired you, Bonny, but you're a goddamned liar."

The words set her free. She left him without a word and met Priscilla coming down the stairs. Trying to keep hysteria at a distance for yet a moment, she asked Priscilla if she knew where the whiskey was kept, telling her why she asked.

"I saw several bottles in the pantry. Three or four."

"Please—we've got to get him out of the kitchen and break—" Bonny's voice gave way and she fled up the stairs and into the bathroom, where she cried and bathed her face with snow and cried some more.

The bathroom was at the back of the house, directly over the pantry where Robin's "unlimited" supply of whiskey waited for him like soiled wings to carry him out of himself. Each time Bonny gathered handfuls of snow from the roof she looked at her husband's plane glinting in the light of a pallid moon. Down the hall, in Erin's room, unknown furies had gathered whose identities she dared not guess at. She was all at once overwhelmed by things with wings which chattered to her. Erin's words "Let us be together in our loss" were explained to her: the rest of them had been shocked by Robin's drunkenness and contempt at such a time, but by the surface fact; Erin had seen through to, and been plunged into shock by, the soul-deep self-condemnation of her brother. Her attempts at recovery were as soul-deep and for his sake alone. When Bonny looked at the plane, the furies parroted her own words to Robin about Erin—"may never recover"—and she wondered if her husband was also self-condemned, and if so, what were the reasons, and what method had he chosen to stop his brain, which she would never know about? It would have to be something hideous to be effective against the weapon of his beauty. Her hands covered her eyes at the thought of Spur gone, Spur made hideous, Spur condemned, as though blinding herself could change that, as though sight were the only sense. She lost control again and cried aloud, "Oh, my love!" and pushed her fists to her mouth as her words seemed to have found an echo down the hall. Suppose she had awakened her sons? She listened carefully, and in thinking of her sons she felt the return of her strength, and with it a resolution: as inadequate as she now knew herself to be to the task, as impossible as impersonality had grown to be, she had somehow to see it through. She could not indulge herself in their games of pass-the-buck and change-personality. Whatever her idea of ministering to the sick had once been, it must be again. Yet to make it possible, she would *have* to play a game: she would have to pretend (or was it pretending?) that whatever she did for any of them would be in the cause of her sons' future and sanity, for she felt that if she thought of the rest of them, including Spur, as themselves, she would not lift a finger. She thought that people composed of hate should not be allowed to live. Her mind, tremulous and afraid, told her that she had gone too far. It told her: Spur. She answered it positively: He loves. He loves me. He loves us. The reiteration recalled to her the word she had directed toward her husband so much of the day—feel feel feel.

"Oh, God," she said, angrily helpless, and closed the furies in the bathroom. Her resolve stood: she would do what she could, what she had to do as the only person medically proficient in that house of sickness, and it would be in the name of her sons. She felt instantly refreshed and strong. She would begin with Robin and the whiskey. This time she would not pussyfoot. But when she got to the kitchen Priscilla was alone.

"Where is he?" Bonny asked, feeling deflated.

"Upstairs," said Priscilla. She did not look up from the coffee cup into which she gazed with creased brow.

Bonny acknowledged a prickle of fear. "But I just came from there."

"He's with Erin."

Bonny turned and headed for the door.

Priscilla stopped her. "Leave them alone. All they can do is help each other."

"She's very sick, Priscilla—" but her instincts understood Priscilla and she came back to the table.

"So is he. That's what I meant." Bonny wavered uneasily; Priscilla looked at her and smiled faintly. "Don't worry. I've hidden the whiskey."

"Only hidden it—" Bonny perched on a chair, prepared to argue.

"I couldn't *break* the bottles. They *did* cost money. I buried them in the snow. Next year there'll be a whiskey tree by the smoke house." Bonny got up and poured a cup of coffee. Turning back from the stove, she saw on Priscilla's face once again the creased look of puzzlement, or enlightenment, or something inbetween. Bonny gave her an open look, inviting confidence if she wished to give it.

"Did you wonder," said Priscilla, "why Mama kept saying Millicent's name over and over in the car?" Bonny nodded. "She's Mama's love child. Mama had a lover." She seemed to be listening for an acceptable reality in her words. "A redheaded hired man who came and went." She looked at Bonny, startled, as though the crudity had come from her. "Robin told me everybody knew it except Millicent and me. He asked me to tell Millicent."

"Why?" Bonny meant "Why you?" but Priscilla said, "He said it might save her to know she had *another* father. *Save* her, he said." She shook her head. "He said it would explain certain things to her. I don't know what."

Bonny recalled that no one but Priscilla and the widow had mentioned Millicent all day, not even to remark upon her absence. She wondered why Spur had never told her. She wondered what else Spur had not told her about his life. She stemmed the thoughts with the picture of her sons' faces.

"The strangest thing—" Priscilla was saying. "He was quite lucid. Really lucid. He didn't seem drunk at all. He told me things—how he started drinking in Bowling Green, before he went to New York and—he said—'made a career of this drinking.' In New York he worked in a stable where rich people kept their horses. After he was fired for being drunk all the time, some of the people he'd met there, looking after their horses—I mean, *he* looked after *their* horses—" Bonny nodded encouragement to the woman who was struggling with precision, a consideration that had never engaged her before when relating stories about others, and Priscilla went on— "they gave him money. For almost two years he has lived on the money they gave him. He told me the supply had run out. He said, 'The old man got me my last handout.' He didn't say, but I know he meant Daddy."

"He talked to you so simply." Bonny meant to sound warm and approving but thc words were curiously flat.

"Yes. People tell the truth to loonies. He thought I was still—" She stopped.

"Still—?"

"Still crazy. I may be. The only—one reason I think I might not be is that today and tonight all of us have seemed—monstrous. Perfectly monstrous. Yesterday—if I had noticed at all—yesterday it would have been goddamned funny."

Bonny, with the acceptance given to miracles in the small hours when the life force is too low for incredulity, said, "Accept my condolences." Both women sighed and were silent. After a while Priscilla said, out of nowhere as Robin had said it to her, "He never got over what he called 'condemning the land.' He talked about it the way a murderer would. I didn't understand him at all. I mean, the land is still there. I told him that, but he didn't listen. Do you know—?"

"No. I'm afraid I don't know much of anything."

Erin sat up urgently. What—what? One of the children was crying. She listened carefully to see if she could find the direction of the sound before she put her feet onto the cold floor; it was her habit to go to them in the dark, without lighting a light, in case they should be having a nightmare. A sudden light bringing them out of sleep could do them serious injury. Better a soothing voice to penetrate sleep gently, bringing sleep and wakefulness together with the thinnest of dividing lines. So much crying in the house lately, so many to look after and reassure in the night; the crying was almost an epidemic, striking them all at once like measles. *Why?* The wind had something to do with it—at the back of everything, all trouble and woefulness, was the wind. It was in the house now, wandering from room to room, drinking out of the pitchers and stealing pennies from mackintosh pockets —*slurpp waaa.* Of course, it was the wind crying in the midnight-black room. There it was again, *sniffle boo hoo sniffle.* Who has seen the wind? I have, when it sits in my room sniffling with the white sheep tails running down its chin. Oh, for heaven's sake, go back to sleep. I am not the mother of the wind.

She fell back on the pillow but the sound hurt her. She wondered if she should sing quietly. She crooned a note or two, testing the response. "Erin—" "My goodness, you know my name! Though I don't know why that should surprise me—you've been in this house often enough, and you are—" She was delicate, not wanting to offend, but truth is important when you sit talking with the wind, otherwise it will spread it abroad that you are a dissembler. She said, kind but strong, "You are something of a snoop, aren't you? Many a morning I have woken to find that you had rearranged the papers on my desk, or forgotten to close doors behind you, so that I could easily tell which room you'd been in. I must say I don't care for that kind of thing—" She waited, giving him a chance to defend himself. It seemed to her that he did say something about only wanting to hurt himself, odd though it was. "Why on earth would you try to hurt yourself, and how would you go about it? I've seen you hurl yourself against buildings and trees all my life, and come away unscathed!" It seemed to ask her how she knew—if she had dreamed it! "Really, sir, I'll have to ask you to recognize that I *am* a gentlewoman. I do not dream of anything masculine whatsoever. Especially a thing so—prodigal with its seed. There. At least I am not so old-hat that I can't talk about such things." She giggled self-consciously. The wind said her name again and she told him, with pleasure, "May I say that I *do* like the way you pronounce my name? I have seldom heard it said so softly—well, of course, my brother, who is away, always says it thus: *Ear*-in. Hereabouts, people say 'Urn,' which, aside from the receptacle aspect, has an unpleasantly abbreviated sound, as though they were trying to get it over with: 'Miz-urn,' they call me. 'Miz-urn.' It has almost a—or is it an?—Hungarian feeling." She peered through the darkness. "Now." Her tone was, she imagined, brisk and businesslike. "Since we are sitting here, both of us awake and inclined to be truthful, tell me why you are crying. Perhaps I can help. You see, I never knew before that you were vulnerable. I've heard you crying all my life, but I thought you did it to get attention." When he was silent she said primly, "I'm sorry. I didn't mean to pry. But you *did* wake me up—" She lay back, staring up to where the ceiling must be, doubting peculiarly if it was really there. Familiar barriers seemed to have gone, like the casting away of restraints. She felt open herself, like a tube through which the wind could travel. It was far from unpleasant, the wondrous lightness, the way a straw must feel. "Willy-nil, willy-nil!" she said, laughing, imagining herself bounding about on the wind, sustained and filled by the wind. What measureless comfort! She was not averse to comfort, with Robin away. She told the wind, "My brother Robin is away on a little trip for the farm. Do you know him, too? We work against you, sometimes—against your devastation. Have you come back to reclaim your own?" She thought: Come back? and had the distinct impression that the wind had died, that that was what she meant. Then she entertained a ghost. She said rapidly, "We write poetry, like the Brontës. Poems of exorcism. You never left them alone either, if one can believe their accounts of your interminable visits." Her words rushed out to meet and conquer fear. "I have written a poem for my brother's return. You shall be the first to hear it. If it seems cryptic or somber, I give you advance warning that it is only a poem, if that, and there is no need to cry over it. For we have wounds, as who has not?" She said, because of the nagging, "He—hurt his hand—" She could not remember how; she did not want to. But desolation and fear had caught up with her, with intimations that he had hurt his hand and somehow it had made her sick—they had been sick together. Her head pounded. Her hands grasped the pillow behind her head as though she were holding on while someone cut into her deeply. She cried out. Whoever was wielding the scalpel was clumsy and ruthless. She began to chant the words of her poem as she might have said a childhood rhyme, to soothe her brother's wound and to send her own pain out the window. She forgot the presence of the wind and talked aloud the fears which she had tried to force into the shape of a poem for her brother, to let him know—to let him know—

"Let us hoard our wounds
(I told him)
Life is astringent
And Death's last guise antiseptic
by decree.
Let us suffer beauty secretly,
If need be.
But let us, you and me, just us two,
Knowing the beauty of rue
Running wild,
Hoard our wounds.

Thinking of our riches,
He smiled."

The magic worked. Through descending sleep she heard the wind stumbling against furniture and she told him, barely audible, "Be careful. Some things in this room have great sentimental value."

Priscilla and Bonny heard the heavy footsteps coming through the morning room and the dining room and then he was in the kitchen, shadowed within the doorway. They had not turned on the overhead light and could not see his eyes, but each woman felt herself to be the recipient of his hooded gaze; both women were also sick to death of fear and frightened to death of any more sickness. They spoke at the same time.

"How is she?" said Priscilla. "Did she move?" said Bonny.

"We talked." Robin started past them, toward the pantry.

"Oh, Rob—how wonderful! Did you hear, Bonny? Robin helped Erin—" Priscilla knew her words to be all wrong as soon as she heard them: "See what baby's done!" But it was at Bonny that Robin looked.

"Bonny heard," he said, and went into the pantry.

The women sat still, listening to him rummage. When the rummaging became scrabbling, Priscilla got up and went to the doorway and said to his bent-over back, "You won't find what you're looking for. I got rid of it." His slow straightening-up and the heaviness she sensed in the movement brought Nonie clearly into Priscilla's mind, as the woman had looked and felt to her the night she stood surveying her wrecked belongings. Priscilla wondered if she and Nonie were to become inseparable, for always, the murderer and the albatross. Behind her she heard the scrape of Bonny's chair and quick footsteps toward the woodbox and then the clink of metal, and she knew that Bonny had armed herself with the poker. I was hasty, she thought. I'm still crazy. Robin came toward her and she stood her ground, only turning sideways to allow him to pass.

"Whiskey costs money, Prissy," he said, merely reprimanding. "You shouldn't have poured it out," but beneath the words she heard a tiny pleading, especially compelling for its faintness. It sounded to her like a dying call issuing from a deep dark hole. It was to that fainting creature that she said, "I didn't pour it out." Her profile was to the room; the corner of her eye caught Bonny's signals to her—to shut up, or lie. She believed that she should obey—Bonny surely stood for wisdom, sanity, certainty—and in her mind she rehearsed words of compliance, of feeble recovery: I *broke* the bottles. But something not yet fledged enough for identity cheeped inside her the word "brother," and a grain of sweetness fell from its beak onto her tongue.

"I hid it," she said, gazing at him concentratedly. The changes were barely perceptible, like those wrought by a skimming eraser in the hand of a larking student who pantomimes, behind teacher's back, the obliteration of tomorrow's assignments: Robin's face knew the lessons still had to be learned, but the game, to both slate and pupil, brought a sense of temporary dispensation. These things Priscilla saw with her brand-new eyes.

"Then," he said reasonably, "I'll find it." He walked past Priscilla and saw Bonny holding the poker. He spoke pleasantly. "Our family doctor, prepared to operate." His eyes turned about the kitchen, speculating on and rejecting hiding places. When they encountered Bonny's in their search she was amazed by the sharp intelligence in them and wondered if it were a trick of the room's dimness; it was as if she looked into human eyes set above the snout of a beast. Even as she thought it, the idea tried to become a fairy tale—men into swine, et cetera—as if her tired brain demanded the reassurance of childish things, familiar horrors, but she could not help a further thought, one she had had before but had not fathomed, she now saw, in the least: that his intelligence was to him the disease, as terrible as cancer, and the whiskey was the only sedative. Why, then, did she not run from the room to the snowbank and bring him the sedation his pain demanded—quick, efficient, objective Bonny? She did not move.

The eyes left Bonny's and went on with their search like two swift animals whose only connection with the hulking, motionless body was that they nested or burrowed in it between foragings.

When Robin once more looked directly at Bonny she saw with relief that the eyes were blurred and weak. To kill shame at her relief, she thought about her sons.

Far back in the caverns to which they had retreated in temporal defeat, the two animals turned their heads around and looked over their shoulders and snarled at Bonny. "What a hell of a fake you are," Robin said, as if he were spitting. "Pretending to know about people." His eyes went out of focus, his forehead wrinkled, and when he spoke it was with the humbleness of a person truly in need of advice. "Does a person in shock talk, and say poems?"

Bonny answered him the only way she could by putting the poker back in the woodbox and sitting in the chair nearest him, as though offering herself for the punishment that she half wished he could inflict. Above her he made a contemptuous sound of dismissal, a blubbery expellent noise with his lips. He addressed his sister. "Prissy."

Priscilla went to his side and waited, serious and attentive, unmournful and uncommitted. He turned so that they stood face to face. He swallowed audibly. "I need that whiskey." He touched her arm, then withdrew his hand. "Look. Let me tell you about drunks. You don't threaten them, you don't reason with them. You give them. Give *to* them. And they give you—the story of their lives. Sometimes it's even true." She looked receptive, no more than that. He thought about Erin—the vomit on her, her shock. No, not shock; his brother's wife had as much as admitted her lie about that.

"She talked to me. She thought I was the wind, but she talked to me." Shouldn't have said that about that wind. His brother's wife had stirred. He did not function well here, with all his past looking on. Something of that past made him smile at Priscilla with one corner of his mouth, his old rueful grin. Enough to rue,

God knew. Erin knew. Writing poems in a coma. Functioning on and on, unimpeded by wounds. Prissy was strange, strangely unwounded. He had felt the strangeness in her earlier, midway in their talk. His talk. She hadn't said much. If anything. Her half-strangeness brought a remembrance of honor. A reminder: among strangers and thieves. Honesty, then, for a while, for as long as he could. He had been honest with the kid on the train. His hatred had been real; his payment had been real. He owed Prissy that much, but no more. In the past they both had extracted and paid. Now they were equals: two strangers.

"Sit, Prissy." Save breath. He sat, too. Weak. Couldn't she *feel?* However, he didn't want that advantage. Her pity. Yes, he did, if it would get him the whiskey. But he wouldn't use that card yet. Honor first. A try, anyhow. "I—uh—I told you about New York." She nodded. "All you wanted to know?" She shook her head. That was more like the old Prissy. "Ask me, then. Go on." She thought, then shook her head. "Go ahead. I'll tell you the truth . . . won't I?" Bad. Be firm.

"I—don't think so. I—" At least she was rattled.

"Why?" He listened for her answer with eagerness, bending to her.

"It's yours. I mean—like my looniness was mine. Is. Oh, *was,* I guess."

Priscilla wished that Bonny would understand the moment and leave. Bargaining with one's blood was not something she really knew about, but she believed it should be done in privacy.

Robin nodded, pleased. She had found it exactly. He had always thought that she was clever, more than clever. If she hadn't been born with the handicap . . . "Was," she had said. "*Was.*" And had struggled with honor before him. That was the strangeness. Her wounds had been healed. Nobody had told him. He felt a weight of what seemed to be dry salt rimming and burning his lids. He wanted to release it. To let it scald him blind. But with his luck the salt would clear his eyes, clear the remaining scales away, subject him to more light.

He did not know how to handle the idea of Priscilla's wholeness. He felt that he should do something, call the family together. He was on two planes, "then" and "now"; after a brief moment of willful subjectivity "now" won. But in passing he noted that he had had to will himself to think of himself, and the danger brought him to attention. He looked at her coldly. "One day in New York I rented a car. A big car. A Cadillac. I drove—"

He felt the wheel, slippery with his excited sweat, heard the air whistle in his ears because of the lowered top, and the clamor of horns that was the afternoon's signature because of him. He had taken the car and broken every rule, every official "don't" that he could find. No parking; no standing; no U-turn; one way; no passing; no littering; speed checked by radar; entrance and exit speed 25; private road keep out; no crossing white line in tunnel; for official use only. He had gotten out of the car and overturned wastebaskets, spat on sidewalks. And more. There must have been more. It had taken an entire afternoon. He had returned the car to the agency, exhausted and dry and with no feeling that he had vindicated anything.

Priscilla was staring, waiting. He became aware that he had not spoken, had not told her anything. If he had, what would she have heard—the story or the truth under it? He knew what he had done and why. He had rejected society's authority, but the point was that it was his own authority, back there in the past, that he had been trying to get at and negate. And its objects, one of which she was. Rejection extended to its furthermost point was, of course, murder. Would she reward him with whiskey for wanting, for trying, to murder her? He told her. "I tried to kill myself in that car, and all of you with me." He grimaced at her with malice. "You were still with me, then."

Inside Priscilla there was the cheep again, louder: "Brother." She nodded. She understood perfectly. She saw the hatred flare in Robin's eyes. I am still with you, she thought, with a certain malice of her own.

"Time," he told her with difficulty, feeling her unchanged, searching for something that might strike a different chord in her, "was something that gave me trouble, in New York. Time, and money. Time, mostly. Keeping track of it."

He had tried using Christmases as the end points of a measuring device but they somehow melted together in his mind, a pool of waxy red studded with bits of glitter, some of which he recognized as remnants of summer days, for under scrutiny they would turn into sparks struck by the sun from the sea, or beer cans half buried in sand. He tried to sneak up on himself by measuring from summer to summer, but the portable radios aslant the beach bags poured carols over the sunbathers, coating them with the smell of pine in a Christmas room. He became obsessed with trying to make stationary some date to serve as the hub from which his days or months or years in the city could be *seen* radiating to the rim that he believed himself, out of his great need, to have reached at last. When the device of the dates failed him he had tried to find some repeated action of his or others that would serve. This had led him to the shirt boards.

"I saved shirt boards from the laundry—" And made lists. He had saved them for a long time without asking himself why, and then one night he saw that *that* was why: a continuing catalog by which he might measure his time spent, his time still to go—catalogued items in one place, those unaccounted for in another. He began with the things in his room, not worrying about the time when its meager contents had been exhausted. He marked off a space on one side of his room to receive the inventory. He allowed himself one drink for each article listed and transported.

FIGURE, he wrote, or printed, beginning randomly, then changed the "e" to an "i" and added "ne." FIGURINE. He had never had to be precise about it before; it was one of the objects merely there, a glazed thing, lumpish, which occupied a crocheted island in the dusty sea of the bureau top, but feeling himself challenged he put a dash after FIGURINE—and wrote ANDROGYNE, thinking the two could be made to rhyme if one employed his mother's way of pronouncing (it had been called "Elizabethan" by the knowing), which gave long "i's" to the heavy airs which blew from heaven's corners. The wind is rising she would say when he was a boy, and he would see tides of wine, blood-red, filling the barrel of the horizons.

BOX he wrote, and having committed himself to description, after it he wrote EMPTY. It was so forlorn, as a word and as a state, that he sought to change it. In the wastebasket beside the bureau (WATEBASKET he wrote in haste) he found a cork, placed it in the box, wrote CORK beside EMPTY, and was moved to compassion for the word EMPTY, which was no longer descriptive but which surely had earned its right to the space it occupied on the shirt board. It was a loathsome word, but the more he loathed it the more compassion he felt compelled to give it. He hated the cork for hurting empty, despised the box for bringing the situation about. Sitting on the floor, sobbing a little because his thoughtless exercise of power had hurt helpless things, he drank until he was restored enough to resume.

GLASS—CLEAR; BOOK (it was the Bible; he controlled himself with effort)—BEST-SELLER; DOILY (he carefully avoided looking at the Bible)—DIRTY.

BUREAU-DRAWER he wrote, moved it across the room, balanced on one hip like a baby, and described it on his list as SOCKS, HANDKERCHIEFS. But they were different—each pair of socks, each handkerchief; they were quite individual in their degrees of holiness, color, the initials some wore; some were handstitched, some snitched, some ditched and found by him in alleys, trashcans, lying in gutters. One bright sock in particular came to mind, banded with colors like Joseph's coat. They would all have to be listed and described, accounted for, or he was no kind of God at all. Handkerchiefs that had been made for him by his sister, the careful stitches cramping her hands! The individual threads—they should all be counted and numbered, listed and described! And the shapes they had had before—the cotton boll, the pod, the plant, the shoot, the seed; the silkworm, the cocoon, the larva, the egg. And the desire. And the idea. And the man. And the brain. All should be disassembled and listed and described and placed in the bare corner of his room. And the dust. GOD he wrote, and after it D-A, and forming the crossbar of the A he fell asleep.

The following day he finished the word by adding M-N, since it seemed the most apt coupling with God, but he could go no further. His room was a mess, which he had to undo, and anyway the game, or whatever it had turned out to be, had palled. The rest of the day was taken up in the usual fashion: cadging drinks in bars, visiting what friends he had once had who would still admit him to their apartments, where he could pour whiskey from their full bottles into his flask. But, surprisingly, the day differed from all the others like it that he could recall in that he looked forward to his hours of aloneness, when bars and apartments were closed, with something akin to pleasure. He was intrigued enough to track down the reason, and mystified when all he could come up with was the pile of unused shirt boards.

When at last he was alone he took them from the drawer and gazed at them for hours, waiting for them to speak—or so it seemed. Finally, tentatively, he began. He made lists of all the things needed to keep a farm going. Seed and feed and fertilizer. Harness and rope. Grease and soap. Buckets. Wire. The time between list-makings grew longer, more intolerable, and he found a way to shorten his necessary foragings into the outer world, a mental shortening, so that he wandered the streets when he had to in a zombie-like state. He wrote down the thousand spare parts to be kept on hand for machinery, from the creamery to the sheds and barns and stables, mentally taking apart and reassembling with loving care each machine on the farm. Things of leather, metal, fabric, composition, each of special odor and texture and taste, each with personal responses to stress and ease and weather changes—all of them, as he set their names in block letters big enough to see through the booze, calling out to him in their own voices like friends acknowledging his greeting. List upon list, dresser drawers full of them. Sometimes he dreamed that they were real and would stumble out of the dream and open the drawers, his joy at hand to make a great noise, expecting to find them there in rows and heaps to be fondled and used. It was after just such a dream, one too real to let him bear the sentimentality of the lists, that he had taken the shirt boards in armfuls to the furnace in the basement and burned them.

Priscilla watched him brooding before her, herself and the dozing Bonny forgotten, only his body available for her to touch if she felt the need, and she saw how it ran on sluggishly with twitches and starts and piston-like bobbing of Adam's apple like a machine continuing on stored-up momentum after the switch has been turned off. She saw quite clearly that he was running down. More than that, she felt it, in her own body, and it was her body as well as her brain that pronounced, no longer cheeping, the word "Brother."

As if he had heard her call, he came back lumberingly, shifting in the chair until his questioning face was at her service. She had a sense of the times he had come to her, whether or not she had called him, and the sense was large and dark above her like the unknown, guessed-at object in a game of Forfeits.

The question faded from Robin's face when Priscilla did not speak. The call he thought he had heard was probably hope, frozen to death in the room by the two women, one sleeping indifferently, the other impassive as a snow figure, and by his failure to find anything in his life worth a drink of whiskey. He felt like hope's coffin, with his frozen extremities. Experimentally, he placed his cold wounded hand on Priscilla's and savored the bitterness of her expected recoil following shock at the coldness. She got up without a word and left.

Robin thought of the wine in the cellar, his father's wine, and clinched his teeth against his thirst, the tearing in his guts, the wanting. "Not blood," he said to them, "not his blood," and shuddered when they punished him. THEY had come to be too close to him, he thought; close enough to be finally destroyed, too, because the paradox of his life seemed to be that the closer a thing got to him, the more embedded in his flesh and brain, the more individuality it assumed. It did not become part of him in the process; if there was a transmutation, it was he who became part of it, more and more a cipher, a blob, a nameless food for IT to fatten and expand upon and, final paradox, to keep him somehow alive on. The parasite become the tree. But he could, in the end, take it off guard, because of its ego, which gave it pretensions of immortality; he, who had none, could destroy it by destroying himself. In the one way he had been too cowardly to take before. Abrupt death. Its means were all around in fire, water, air, earth; death by life. He had always found the idea appealing; only cowardice had kept him from it until now.

Bonny struggled when the reptilian cold twined her legs, and was immediately awake, aware of the source of the cold and Priscilla's absence and its probable meaning. Once again she was relieved—of responsibility, and because it was being done. She did not know if her gladness that it was Priscilla whom Robin had moved was hypocritical or not; she did know that she could not have surmounted the hurdle of her sons' innocence and contributed to a fraction of its dissipation by administering to Robin, however appalling his need, without becoming something else with heart and brain permanently unconnected. But she was glad, and she observed Robin stealthily, wanting his next words to be to Priscilla.

Priscilla came in with one of the bottles and placed it on the table in front of Robin. "I'm sorry," she said, "I tried like hell not to." She waited until he lifted swimming, half-comprehending eyes to hers, then deliberately bent to kiss him. He wove and twisted to avoid the kiss but it fell relentlessly on his forehead. "Damn you, Robin," Priscilla said as though it were a benediction, and left the room. When she could, Bonny followed her, weak in the legs at what the three of them had enacted, for she had been needed, too, as witness to the betrayal: somehow he had made Priscilla condemn him, and he was as the land again.

The dawn came hard and clear, prepared to judge as pitilessly, now that its chance had come, as a jury that has sat bored and obscured by witness after witness, examining its nails, brooding on time and money lost, counting mental laundry, resenting the slow, always ugly processes of democracy when it makes demands. The dawn representing this specific, possibly special, jury did not care for the defense testimony. Its path had been clearly indicated in the preliminary briefing —"Foul weather ahead," which was easily interpreted to mean "Stick it out; you'll get *your* opportunity when the crap is dispensed with." It was the desires of "the people" beneath the austere and archaic ritual for which a jury listened, testimony be damned—and, after all, just what was testimony except an admission of bias? "The people" would get the justice for which they clamored; justice is frequently bloody; always one must be impersonal—cold-blooded.

The dawn, in the figurative sense of self-knowledge, came infrequently to Roseville, which liked to refer to itself as the "typ'cul suthun *taown*," and the inverse circumflexion that made of the would-be declarative sentence a question revealed the insecurity, and proved the truth, of the statement. It was through such convolutions that self-knowledge was kept at bay and the town "typ'cul"—not merely "suthun" typical but "Umuricun" typical as well.

Hollis Ward, practicing member of the Bar, retired County Judge, embodied the town's image of itself: he was substantial in person and property, was a law-enforcer and abider; his contempts were the proper ones, as were his deceits, and he cried a lot. He cried publicly at a baby's fat hand, beautiful sermons, the plight of the poor—though they were not part of the town he embodied—and the fall of a sparrow, upon which *his* eye was set, too; when he shot it down in the privacy of his own woods he cried at its fall. Because he was an embodiment, symbol, pace-setter, the town followed suit: it was a very crying town. Some cynic minus tear ducts remarked that they need have no fear of a drought in Roseville; Hollis Ward and his rain-makers would keep the valley green and the roses red.

Almost three years before, at the age of sixty-five, he startled and, for a minute, appalled the town by marrying twenty-four-year-old Louise (Weezie) Taylor. The difference in ages did not bother the town, but the floating rumor that Weezie was pregnant did. Nor would that have bothered them if the rumor had named their embodiment as the impregnator; it would have been, actually, understandable, because Weezie was pretty and sexy, and though her immediate family was nothing much, she had some passable connections. But this rumor was specific in naming Murdoch McChesney as the expectant father, and the specific rang too authentically to be ignored. When the engagement was announced, the idol tottered; when the marriage took place precipitately under the eyes of the town, the suspiciously fat bride almost succeeded in bringing the idol crashing down then and there to the cadences of "Lohengrin." But before Ward and his pale bride were whisked away for an extended honeymoon, he gave the town a gift that was also a directive.

When Weezie came to him for advice he had not at first been able to believe that the singular object of his lust, for the past twelve years at least (she had developed early and Ward, as the town knew, loved children), was within his reach. He had begun with a hardly more than conventional description of how self-maiming a paternity suit against his old friend would be, citing one or two similar cases—though not against Murdoch—to make his point. Weezie had been so easily horrified that the rest was comparatively easy. Ward gave a mighty performance, weeping and quivering about his office, and before she knew it, Weezie, who was more than a little stupid about many things, found herself betrothed. Ward swore her to secrecy concerning the engagement until he could figure out how to handle "the problem," the only way he could find to refer to the embryo that was his ally, without having to admit that the solution he meant to propose, when he had hiked up his courage, could be called murder. When he finally brought up the subject of abortion he found himself head to bricks with an uncollapsible wall, and the alternative, as painful as it was to his greed, to giving up what he thought of, in his babyish way, as Weezie's "balloons" and "whistle," was The Gift. Balancing money against toys in daily and nightly weighing sessions that circled his eyes and blocked his colon, he had at last opted for the toys. He recalled with satisfaction that toys could be misused, even broken a little, and still belong to a person, but that money could not.

Following the marriage ceremony, standing on the church steps and calling with uplifted hand for a suspension in the shower of rice (some of it was falling too hard to be nourishing), he told the town that as a wedding gift to his wife he was causing to be built an addition to the library.

The structure was already as labyrinthine as the palace of Knossos. The contents of shelves and stacks were random and indifferent, but the building contained a ballroom, a tennis court, a squash court (never used), a museum that was also a community project—its treasures were composed entirely of objects brought back by the citizens from trips around, and sometimes out of, the state: pretty rocks, embroidered pillows, pennants, whittled things, carved things, things chloroformed and pinned to bits of cork, odd fleshy things in jars of alcohol among which there may have been a fetus or two. There were also kitchens and dining rooms and sitting rooms on whose couches privileged key-carriers had brought to culmination more than one illicit arrangement.

Ward's gift was—as he put it, and the town saw it was so immediately he told them—the *sine qua non* that would put them smack in the middle of The Times They Lived In: a theatre. A theatre where—he told them jovially—bands of strolling players could display their wares; where—he told them with fitting sternness—television shows might originate, beaming to the ill-informed nation the True Nature, High Spirits, and Bountiful Talent of this typ'cul GRASS ROOTS state. Et cetera.

By the time a thinner Judge and a thin Mrs. Judge returned, the Hollis Ward Theatre was forming before the town's eyes, and the rumors that had preceded the marriage had been transformed without too much effort into rumors that the Perry Como Show was to be the inaugural presentation. An illegitimately conceived baby or the town flooded with famous Wops was about equal in rumor-weight to Roseville; the important thing, really, was that they have *something* to talk about. If there were those who wondered about the baby—if there had been a pregnancy at all, which was increasingly doubtful even before the Judge and Weezie had left town for the honeymoon—they wondered it in the dark privacy of boudoir and bathtub and back seat, where speculations of a sexual nature could either add to the proceedings at hand or detract from them through the chill of warning.

Thus Weezie, the new Mrs. First Citizen, was assimiliated by the town and nearly, literally, by the Judge: she was the one dish at an interminable feast, a thing she had not dreamed would be so when she agreed to marry the old man. She had imagined, then, because of his famed religious bent, that they would live side by side though never touching; that they would read the Bible and pray together on weekdays and praise the Lord in company on Sundays. She had seen herself in soft grays and blacks, the colors of her secret, perpetual mourning for Murdoch, whom she loved and would always love, and would love the more when he came to his senses and rescued her, and for their baby, because it was part of Murdoch; she had hardly foreseen that the mourning colors would be on her flesh, the results of Ward's greed and ("Just playing," he would say when she occasionally yelled) roughness. Hearing him slobbering away at the parts of her he called by weird names, but feeling next to nothing ("I'm getting callouses on my titties," she confided to her mother) she would imagine that the sound was made by bloodhounds devouring *him.* And she certainly prayed, on weekdays and in company on Sundays, for some sign to tell her how she could get even with the old bastard for doing such nasty things to her, for she had not told her mother all that went on, by a long shot.

When the call came from Erin on Christmas Eve morning asking if the Judge would say a few simple words at the service, Weezie, in the darkness of her loss and knowledge that she now would never be freed by her repentant lover, found the answer to her prayers. It was simple, it was entirely fitting, and it might —just might—kill the old man dead.

Ward turned away from the telephone, and Weezie hid her feelings from him for one reason that she was sure of: she did not want her grief to be soiled by his rooting at it like the old pig he was.

"Well," he said, and in spite of the tears he had turned on for Erin still muddying his eyes, Weezie saw and heard, from a distance, his satisfaction. *"Murdoch's had it."* He walked around the breakfast room, his fingers automatically testing the furniture for dust. "Brain just split wide op'n during the night." He held up a fingertip corrugated by his eternal hand-washing and turned it in the light. Finding nothing, disappointed, he flicked his fingers, saying, "Ce-ree-bee-ral hem-o-ridge." He looked at her thoughtfully. "I don't imagine you know what that means." Weezie made a faint movement with her head.

"Blood. All the blood in the body goes to the head, like flood waters. A man, I imagine, could feel it rising in him, the lower parts of the body getting cold and empty as it rises up, up. That old heart's a-going like ninety, naturally. BOOM BOOM BOOM. If there'd a-been anybody in the next room, they'd a-heard Murdoch's heart. BOOM—BOOM. I imagine—although I could be wrong—that the neck would swell out something awful when all that blood went a-rushing through it, heading for the brain. Big old veins a-standing out—" He shook his head mournfully, clucking his tongue. "That old head, I've heard, plumb fills up with blood." Weezie gazed at him, shaking her head and clucking. "Mercy," she said. That seemed to mollify her husband. He grew brisk.

"Naturally, you will attend the funeral." Weezie lowered her eyes to the table. She thought as hard as she ever had while he spoke further. "*Not* going would bring up—certain matters—best buried with the dead man." He waited. "You are in agreement with me," he told her. She was not ready or able to answer him. A picture was trying to take shape in her head but she could see only the outline. Ward lowered his voice in case the maid was nearby. He spoke earnestly. "Sometimes, as they get on in life, men will do strange things. Such as asking the whereabouts of their bastards.

Murdoch was mighty peculiar even before he got on in life, and I can tell you now that I was oftentimes afraid—and *you*"—she heard, distinctly, the instant apoplexy in his voice—"*you made it easy for him to blackmail me, didn't you?*"

The picture in her head came on in color and Cinemascope. She raised her head and looked at her husband. She told him, "Judge, the man's dead now." She watched the swelling begin to go down. "Dead," she said, seeing behind the throbbing veins in his neck a little pillow of satin. Watching his clenched hands loosen she told him soothingly, "Dead."

As soon as he had left the house for his half-day at the office, she called her mother on the telephone and told her what she wanted her to do, giving in exchange the promise of a larger-than-usual check for her stocking on the morrow. Within the hour Mrs. Taylor, in the automobile Weezie had blackmailed the Judge into buying for her, picked her daughter up at the corner of Frances Perkins and American Beauty. Their meeting place was in that part of a new development that had no completed houses and therefore no prying eyes.

"Why *jeopardize—?*" Mrs. Taylor started in, as soon as Weezie was in the car.

"Just shut up, Mama. I know what I'm doing and that's good enough for me."

"Now, young madam, you listen to me—" Mrs. Taylor's temper was not always in her best interests, as she immediately saw.

"Shut up," said Weezie murderously. "Just drive the car I gave you, wearing the Persian lamb I gave you, and start spending that money I *may* be giving you tomorrow. And shut up." Mrs. Taylor was silent. After a time, speaking to herself, Weezie said, "That old baby's never even seen its daddy."

Mrs. Taylor ventured a question. "Is that the reason you're—?"

"Not by a coon's pecker, it's not."

They headed on into the snow, northward.

When the windless dawn broke, Andrew, Spur, Ed and Rhoda returned to the farm to make themselves ready for the funeral, leaving Randolph and his brood to keep the vigil. The cousins were apparently incapable of fatigue, and Randolph's quiet sense of duty had impressed all those of the family able to think at all. It was he who had driven Antonia back to her house, and his solicitude for her comfort had radically changed the unbearably tired old tyrant's attitude toward him. She had insisted that he come into the house and have a drop of brandy; over the "drop" Tonia got a sudden hunger, fiercer than hunger for food or drink, to feel the man's hard hands on her flesh. The need was not sexual in any sense that she could remember from her youth, nor was it related to the odoriferous responses engendered in her by the conquests of Mike Hammer. It was vaguely identifiable as something akin to her desire sometimes to touch the earth, to plunge her hands into it (a thing she had not been able to accomplish for many years) and so to be touched by it. It had to do with clean and safe things, and sex had never been for her any of those. Her servant-companion was long since in bed and asleep. She was also deaf as a post, and Tonia often wondered what earthly good she would be if Tonia needed her in the night to fetch a doctor; that double-deafness could never be penetrated. But her speculations had been generally theoretical, because she had believed, until yesterday, that she would never die. Perhaps it was the unfamiliar certainty of mortality that made her hunger for the touch of something strong and living to reassure her flesh. Abruptly but with a touch of real shyness, she said, "Randolph, my companion is asleep. Besides, she's old and I don't want to wake her . . ." He waited, interested. "I—it ought to be plain that I can't undress myself. Would you be so very kind as to help me?"

He was courteous and understanding. His hands, unaccustomed to their work, were too forceful and a button flew across the bedroom and struck a windowpane. He was apologetic, red-faced with shame, but she told him gaily that that old button was trying to get outside the window to the buttonwood tree, had been trying to for years, and she had to keep an eye on that button. When she was down to her slip they were both embarrassed—Tonia for him, knowing how he must be viewing her unbelievable flesh, and Randolph for her, for being so godawful fat. Her nightgown lay on the foot of the bed like a discarded parachute, and Randolph picked it up, trying to figure out which end was which.

"Randolph," she said, her voice strange with the hunger of old age, "Randolph, please put your two hands on my shoulders for just a minute." He put down the nightgown and took her flesh in his hands. Neither of them was embarrassed any longer. With something of the abstracted rightness of knowing what is expected when a dog puts its head against your knee, Randolph rubbed and kneaded her shoulders and upper arms until she said, "Thank you, son." He helped her on with the nightgown and into bed, drew the curtains for her and turned out the light and left, both of them silent throughout, understanding each other, and their kinship, for once.

Editha, who had a small apartment in town, refused with surprising firmness to go home to it. Erin's words of praise to her by the coffin of her brother had given her a feeling of pride, of having something to offer by her presence, and if her continued presence could help in any way to alleviate the effects of the night's dreadful happenings, then she would stay. She was somewhat confused by the idea that after all these years she might have something to offer to others, but Erin had said it was so and she wanted to believe Erin. It would be so lovely to be needed; to be able, by saying just exactly the right words at the right time, or even by being silent in a comforting way, to give something to others. The thought was brand-new strength to her and she believed; in believing, she worked a little miracle, and the others did feel from the gentle, gently eccentric lady a small current of saneness and light by which, though the wattage was necessarily low, they could see past barbarity to a world where old ladies could effect little miracles by their presences, and through their connections with a past that must, after all, have had some meaning.

As the first morning light, deceptively soft and nacreous because of dirty windows, seeped into the sitting room of the funeral parlor, Edie asked if one of the men would walk her home. It was only a few blocks, she said, and she would enjoy the exercise. Ed, feeling that walking in the snow was his rabbit's foot, bundled Edie up like a baby bunting in coats and sweaters and scarves collected from one and all, and they left.

When Edie made her request, Rhoda could see in Andrew's eyes how much he wanted for her to suggest the two of them as Edie's escort—the final surrender. Since she had exposed the terror that had been her submerged secret—secret even to herself—he had hovered around her as if he expected her at any moment to expel from her body a tangible shape, like an egg, that would be the sum and total of their differences, so that then they could merge into each other and become as one. Pleading with Robin to spare her, she had also pled with her father and with Bill—and, yes, with Andrew too—rapists, all, for between them they had used up almost all her strength and she had not known it until Robin stood before her, proposing yet another violation—of her privacy, her independence, her indifference that was hardest won of all, requiring most strength. Three of them had left her, fattened with her indifference—Robin had reeked of it tonight, had visibly expanded when she broke and cried out—but Andrew still clung about, demanding that the final crumbs be handed over to him. He should not have them; that was final. She would gamble him for them, but that was an exercise which involved no risk for her. She was a gambler to her marrow, and knew how to cheat. At last—*at last—she* occupied the winning seat and nothing this side of death could budge her. What was left, crumbs or not, was hers, and poverty had never frightened her; only depletion could do that. She smiled at Andrew, silently refusing his request that they walk Edie home. She felt the mystery of sexuality in her refusal and thought: At least it won't be boring, this brave new life.

Andrew was confused by the deliberate, patently artificial brightness Rhoda put into her expression, a puzzling combination of purpose and vacancy. He found himself thinking that it was a familiar look, though not from her, and then he placed it: it was the look a woman on the make gives to a strange man at a party before she asks to be introduced to him. I'm tired, he thought, excusing himself, and then: She's tired, but, touching her in tenderness, he felt the radiation of energy that pulsed in machines at the plant: tireless, endless, mechanical.

When the others returned to the farm they found the children washed, fed, dressed and placed like wax figurines about their parlors, so that the bathroom and kitchen were free for the adults. Priscilla and Bonny had accomplished this with expediency, neither woman seeming to the other the least bit the worse for wear, each seeming to the other a kind of wonder, a gem to be worn on the breast of womankind. Bonny was amazed at how well Priscilla handled sleepy, recalcitrant children, and assured herself that the ability was part of woman's instinctive equipment. She was ashamed of thinking that Priscilla's case history—a schizophrenic made apparently whole by the death of her father—would be a fascinating subject for a paper. She felt a bit like a case history herself, with the new, comparatively late insight she had gained into her relations with her sons. She told herself that insight was growth no matter when it occurred, and that that was what had happened to Priscilla—so to hell with case histories.

Both women had spent their three hours of "rest" thinking about Robin and their husbands, sometimes interchangeably. Priscilla saw that the discovery of her husband was the terminal point of the long line begun with news of her father's death, but that it had been hurried along by Erin's fear of what they might do to Robin. Therefore, her father was the gift-box (the gruesomeness of the thought was the measure of its accuracy) but Robin was the key.

She got up from bed and went to her closet, where, in an old hatbox on the top shelf, she found it wrapped in a chiffon handkerchief. She unwrapped it, the key to her box of effects, an old tool box which she had painted bright blue, and as she did so she said the words with which she had laid it to rest:

"I shall lie folded like
a saint
Lapped in a scented linen sheet
On a bedstead striped with
bright blue paint,
Narrow and cold and neat."

The box itself, never opened since the day she had symbolically buried the key to her past, stood on the floor of the closet, its bright blue unchipped, ugly only where the paint had run in thick welts from her inexperienced brush. She took the box to the window, opened the window and, amid the billowing curtains and blowing snow, unlocked it. She took from it the package of letters that she had written to herself, as though from a jealous lover, and had thrown (taking the harder, more satisfying way) through her window wrapped around rocks. They were, all ten of them, in rhyme. She opened one:

If you keep seeing you-know-who
I'll poison him and strangle you.

The crudeness of it and the others was the most artful part, meant to chill Robin and Erin by conjuring something that hulked with poison in one pocket and a coiled rope in the other, and an accurate, lethal hand with a rock. Priscilla found it difficult to imagine the girl who had invented such a "lover," but on second thought that very difficulty was also difficult, perhaps most of all: that girl was the only past she had, just as these letters were its only tangible documents. Not to recognize either was like waking up to find your skin beside you on the bed, rubbery and misshapen with dented features, and to rise and walk (invisibly?) away, unmoved. She wished she could ask her father how it felt to leave one's skin—if he was regretful or unmoved; she wished that she had been able to be close to him so that if he chose to come back for a last look around he would come to her.

The seemingly eternal wind blew the curtains about her, until she was wrapped in them, hidden by them, facing outward into the stark night. Beneath her window a figure stood unmoving. She knew with every nerve that it was a shade, a shell. The life, so new in her, felt the figure's lack of it and rose up in her, howling and arching like a cat. It was not fear she knew, but a profound distrust of a thing so unlike herself. "Go" her will called to it. The figure raised a hand, tilting it toward its face, and she saw that it was her brother Robin who stood, his back to the house, facing the orchard. She saw the moonlight glitter in the bottle; she saw that he was coatless. With these impressions there came to her entire one incident out of the mists of her indistinct past of autumn moods, solitary wanderings and flashes of cruelty: A fall when the harvest was full and heavy, when the trees in the orchard cracked their branches with the weight of fruit. Robin, Erin and Priscilla stood in the midst of the trees, and Robin, jubilant, shouted, "Look, friends and neighbors, elephants and babies—look! *They* know there's a war on, these trees!" He encircled the trunk of an apple tree, pressing his body to it until it seemed that he would enter and merge with the wood, and shook the tree with all his strength. In the rain of fruit he stood with his bright laughing face turned up, taking the heavy blows of apples on his head and face. "Go on, kill me, you first weapons of Eden! It's the only way you'll ever get me to leave this place—" He became quiet, smiling at the ground where apples lay like red cobblestones. After a while he said, "I won't leave even then. I'll be buried here." He looked at his sisters. "See to it," he said, and Priscilla laughed at the crack in his voice, which didn't go at all with his smiling face.

Priscilla pressed a fold of curtain to her mouth, muffling words that came unbidden, unconnected with the memory, returning, rather, to the letters and the Elinor Wylie poem:

The midnight will be glassy
black
Behind the pane, with wind about
To set his mouth against a crack
And blow the candle out.

She closed the window quietly and ran across the room and jumped under the feather comforter, refusing to think any more morbid thoughts, rhymed or not.

Bonny lay on the bed in Spur's old room and thought of words: cowardice, pride, weakness, strength, success, failure, whole, maimed. She thought of the words as they applied to any creature, as well as to the two brothers who had used, but not used up, her emotions. The words were as much a part of the nomenclature of the animal as were sinew and tissue, bone and blood: they were natural provisions. They were shadows of each other, antonymous twins—Dionysus to Apollo, discriminated against for darkness or worshipped for light, depending upon one's position. Tonight she had seen that "success" to Robin would be "failure" to her, and vice versa. But without knowing what it was that drove him toward a goal that was at least apparent by the night's end, how could she assume (what a swaggering braggart of a word that was!) that she could know better than he what was "good" for him? And yet she did think so. Because of a word that had been used to excess: condemn. The word had no actual meaning used against his father; it was said ritualistically and had only an effect; in time (she was aware of juggling words as if they were hollow balls) the people who had been affected by it would manage to alter that effect until it would no longer be effective in the same way. If words had unalterable meanings, this could not be so. Therefore words depended upon people, not people upon words. Consider the way Priscilla had said to Robin "Damn you—" the way he must have said it to the land, and yet, not, for she had used it as a benediction because she did not believe—as Bonny did not—that condemnation—to condemn—was either an inalienable right or even possible in a provable way. It was possible to condemn *to* death, or condemn *to* be torn down, but it was conditional, limited to a specified act. Beyond the act lay something, the essence, and nobody, at any time in past or imaginable future, had, or could offer, proof that that essence had been in any way altered by "condemn" as word or act. Robin had condemned the land; the land could surge again with green life. Priscilla had condemned Robin; but he was as the land itself. So to hell with her cowardice and Robin's pride; down with Spur's weakness for by-passing his family responsibilities; she would, and her money should, be the countering strength. Robin and her money should take the maimed land (the maimed man), and make it whole, and failure should be success, and success, as Robin was seeking it, should be the failure she sought for him.

As she was drifting to sleep she had one last thought about a word, which had eluded her conscious mind but which was the reason for her courage in believing that she could effect a real change: Tears. Spur cried. Tears can tear. Can tear down walls. The tear that tears is not destructive. Such tears are the very, very extremist opposite of condemn.

The funeral service was to be at ten o'clock and the body returned to the clay by eleven. Some would leave the graveyard for the church and the act of adoration of a baby most of them could not visualize as a baby at all, but only as a sad-faced man wearing thorns in his hair, or, thinking of Christmas dinners to follow, as a sad-faced man turning out bread and fishes by the basketful. But they would sing rousing hallelujahs, stand up, sit, kneel at the proper times, and the women would take note of who wore what, whose neck and hair were dirty, who sported new hair-dos and whether they had been designed by Miss Edythe and Which Twin Had the Toni. It would be cathartic, emetic and emptying in general, which was usual, but this Christmas service would be tied up with the scarlet twine of scandal, and if there is anything better than a good emetic hallelujah it is a good cathartic scandal. Hallelujahs, no matter how violently retched, do float away on the air like belches and farts, but scandal has body and meat and, above all, it is almost impossible to dissipate. It is cathartic only in the sense that it gives one a feeling of cleanliness alongside of it, but this leads to self-righteousness, which also has body and meat and is difficult to dissipate. So perhaps scandal is not cathartic after all.

Spur and Bonny held each other in the hallway. The embrace was close and long, until it seemed that their nerve ends were spliced and they flowed in and out of each other on a continuous current. Their closeness, their rhythm, their oneness had never in sex approached this, and neither wanted to let go. And yet when they did part, the current continued between them under their words and it imparted to them the knowledge that they had somehow stumbled onto a secret too good to be spoken of.

"How are the boys?"

"Clean—full—"

"Erin?"

"Sleeping. We won't wake her until we have to."

"Do you think she can make it?"

"She shouldn't, but she'll insist. You know that."

He hesitated, then asked, "Robin?"

"With her."

Spur started to take her in his arms but instead took her two hands with his and looked at her direct with bloodshot eyes. "That—what happened tonight—last night—I'm partly to blame. A damn big partly."

"We all are."

He did not look at her then, but gathered his courage in silence. "Bonny. When he came in—drunk, dirty—even when he puked on her—" He looked at her. "Even then I was glad. I wanted to yell out—"

And he did, the way he once had, busting broncs: "YIPEEEEEEEEE." The tears spilled down his face. The children rushed to the door, and Tom, seeing his father crying, began to sniffle. Spur dug his fingers into his son's carefully combed hair and roughly shook his head from side to side.

"*Stop* that," said Marilyn, who had decided that she detested all parents. "You'll hate him." When they all looked at her she said sullenly, "Hurt him," and went back into the parlor.

"Shut up," said Tom. "He won't neither," and he threw his arms around Spur's middle and hung on for dear life. Over Tom's head Spur looked at his other son, the dangerous one, himself, and saw that Buck looked as scared as he was—had been—was. No longer enigmatic. Scared.

"You look spruce," said Spur. "Your grandfather would have liked that."

"Ewe look lyke holy hay-ul," said Buck in his flattest Texas accent, and it was as near an endearment as he had uttered to his father in years. He turned back to the parlor, saying toughly, "Come on, Tom, for Christ's sake. Act your age." None of the children asked why Spur had yelled and why he cried.

Spur and Bonny were left alone.

"I said I was glad," he told her.

"I heard you," she said, starting for the stairs. "Come on, for Christ's sake. Act your age."

She waited for him and they climbed the stairs together. Ed and Priscilla stood on the landing. Ed was holding a blue-painted tool box and his expression was aghast and bewildered.

"First dibs," said Bonny, "on the bathroom. My husband's back needs scrubbing."

"Go ahead," said Priscilla. "Ed's still getting dirty."

At eight-thirty the black-clad family had gathered in the morning room, with the exception of Robin and Erin. The widow sat in her high-backed chair and her children and grandchildren stood about her, unconsciously arranging themselves in tiers—tallest in back, smallest in front—as though waiting for the photographer to come and record the moment and allow them to get back to their normal lives, dressed in normal clothes, apprehensive no longer of the eye that does not lie.

The door to Erin's room was locked. Priscilla had tapped on it at fifteen-minute intervals, getting no answer, until eight o'clock, when, hand raised, she had heard her brother and sister talking inside—almost gaily, it seemed. Robin called out in a clear voice that they would be down soon; Erin was dressing. Priscilla had kept the fact of the door's being locked from the rest of the family, she wasn't certain why, and so she felt intense relief at the sound of Robin's voice. She turned away from the door and as she did so she heard, or thought she heard, Erin say, "Where are we going, Robin?" and disquiet replaced relief. She pondered the wisdom of insisting admittance so that she might trust her eyes because she could not trust her ears, but then she told herself that the important thing was that Erin's voice had sounded well and even young, and it was the effect and not the word that counted, as she knew so well from her own experience. Once again Robin had somehow or other, by presence, word, or deed, brought about a welcome change in one of them.

But now, thirty minutes later, they waited silently in the morning room, hearing in the distance the approaching snort and chug of Owen's battered old limousines. With their usual funeral pace slowed down further by the snow, it would be well after nine when they arrived at the funeral parlor. Relatives—her father's side, the ones who had founded the county and had been referred to as "estranged" through most of her lifetime, but who might show up now that he was dead—and friends not yet seen must be given their moment. It had to be endured, she thought, because it was tradition and the family had flaunted enough tradition.

Spur, Priscilla and Bonny all made little starts forward when they heard the door open upstairs and footsteps travel the hall and down to them. Robin stood alone in the doorway.

"Erin won't be ready in time to go with you all," he told them. "I'll have to call for somebody to come for us." He spoke with the soft slurred voice of long ago, of his brother's and sisters' childhood. Rhoda heard it as a ruse to disarm her, without hearing the words, and gave him a knowing, bitter look. Spur thought about second chances and knew that he had been given one, but felt somehow certain that it was exclusive of his brother. Priscilla, who had heard many voices from him throughout the night, thought how complicated was a person, how faceted; and thought further, vague as to reason, that the probable difference between a crazy person and a sane one was in the amount of horror that could be taken for granted by each.

The limousines had made the incline and were drawing up to the door. Robin said, "Don't you all worry. We will be there. Erin said don't anybody come up and waste any more time."

There was a discreet tap at the door.

"Go on, now," he told them. "I'll call a taxicab for Erin and me."

They obeyed him as they once had, filing past him, only Rhoda averting her head as she went by. Bonny said in a whisper, "Robin, *is* she all right?" and he nodded, his eyes clear. Spur and his mother passed, and the old lady looked at Robin searchingly, shook her head, walked to the door and turned, shook her head again, and gave her hand to the driver who helped her over the slippery ground to the car. Spur had stopped, watching his mother's cryptic behavior, and when she was gone he said, "I'm going to wait and drive you and Erin in myself. I'm going to wait."

"The taxicab will be better," Robin told him. "You want to be with your wife and sons." When Spur waited still, Robin said, "They need you with them." Spur left, walking rapidly.

Ed, because he felt like it, shook Robin's hand. Only Priscilla was left, standing just inside the morning room. Robin lowered his eyes when he passed by her, heading for the kitchen.

"I'm going upstairs," Priscilla said.

"No, Prissy," and he went on through the room where his father had died.

She called again, "I am. I'm going up to Erin's room." He did not answer. She waited, unable to tell what to do.

Ed stuck his head in the door and said, "Come on, honey. Everybody's waiting." A draft blew through the rooms, which meant that the back door was open.

"Ask them to wait," she told him, starting for the kitchen, hurrying only inside herself. She wanted to ask Robin something but she was not sure what it was. By the time she got to the kitchen and saw him standing on the back step gazing toward the orchard, she knew. "You aren't coming, are you?" She was certain of it, as she was certain he would tell her the truth because he thought she was still a loony.

"We will be with you," he said. "Erin and I will be with you, Prissy."

"Who's coming for you? Mr. Price won't be at the taxi company. He'll be at the funeral. Who's coming, Robin?"

"My best friend. Handy Miller."

Priscilla recalled the man's contemptuous spitting in the snow, the way he had looked at Robin when he spat. "Have you called him?"

"No. But I will as soon as you go." He looked her in the eyes. "We will be with you."

The reiteration bothered her. She said, "The way you've always been?"

"Yes." Someone was coming through the house. Hurriedly she said, not knowing where the question had lain until now, "What was it really like for you in New York?"

He waited long enough to make her nervous before he answered. He told her slowly and concisely and rather mildly, "I didn't like New York. New York is a place where they put poison on the streets to kill animals."

As clear as a photograph she saw herself giving Robin the bottle of whiskey. It was as if he had taken it from an album and handed it to her. She said in a rush, "When we get to town I'm going to call Handy Miller and make sure he's coming for you."

"Yes," he said. "If that will make you feel better."

She rushed from the kitchen and took Spur's arm with both hands, tugging him the other way. "Come on," she said, "we're going to be late. Hurry. Hurry." Spur pulled a wry face at her.

Robin stood in the opened door until he heard the limousines leave, then he walked slowly through the house, facing the fact that he was afraid of going upstairs. In the last hour and a half his sister had jumped precariously around in the past, thinking one moment that they were all children again, unable to recall that they had never all been children together, the next moment giving him the news of the birth of a niece or nephew. His last act of protectiveness to the family had been to lock Erin in her room and lie about her condition. They would have to know that she was mad, but it could not all come at once. Fumbling in his pocket for the key to her door, he wondered if he could somehow get her to the burial and help her to sit quietly through the ceremony at the graveside without her family knowing that she was unaware of who was being put in the ground. He knew that he would not try, but the speculation kept at bay for a while yet the thing that would be done, that had seemed, when glimpsed by a corner of his mind, like a half-materialized ghost of an animal killed, or thought to have been killed, long ago. Inserting the key in the lock he spoke God's name within himself. Breaking the long silence, he wondered if God was as surprised as he. Foxholes and deathbeds, he thought, and went in.

Erin was sitting before the mirror, wearing a soft colored robe and brushing her long hair. She turned bright eyes to him; fever lay in her cheeks like the hands of summer. "I'm up!" she said, triumphant. "Old lazybones is up! Are they waiting for us?"

"No. They've gone on."

She looked chagrined. "They'll have picked all the dewberries before we get there. I *hate* myself for oversleeping. You shouldn't have allowed it—"

"You needed your rest." Her eyes became cloudy with trying to think of why she needed her rest. He said, because he did not know how old she was at the moment, "Every—woman—needs her beauty rest."

"Gallant," she said, smiling. "What carthly good does beauty rest do a woman of—over twenty-one," and she mocked the evasive tone of women concealing their ages.

He laughed with her while inside he cried out to know where she was. He was fearful of saying the wrong thing, of jarring her from whatever moment of security she was the precarious center of. So many anxieties waited to grab her. "Mama still talks about *her* beauty sleep—" he said, though in actuality he could not recall ever having heard his mother use the words; his assumption was that all women did, and as lame as the assumption was, it was all he had at the moment. He was rewarded for his poverty.

"At forty-two," said Erin, "Mama is developing a sense of humor."

He now had some facts. Erin was twenty-six and it was early summer, because of the berries they were going to pick. He was twenty-four; Rhoda was away at school; "the others" who had gone ahead would include Millicent, Spur and Priscilla. Was her mother picking berries? Her father? She had never overslept except on weekends. It must be some lost Saturday of sun and dewberries. "Priscilla," he told her, "said for us to hurry or she was going to check on us."

"Oh, what a good sign! Then she wasn't indifferent—?"

"No, not indifferent at all—"

"I'll hurry," she said, rising. She was made dizzy by the sudden movement and had to put out a hand for support. "Goodness, I'll be giddy and fall in the briars, and what kind of example will that be—" She sat down slowly and looked at him meaningfully. "Daddy fell again last night. I heard him in the hall. I didn't know whether to go out or not—" All at once the implication was unbearable to her. She covered her eyes with her hands, crying, "Ohhhhhhhh."

He tried to comfort her with his hands but she was unaware of him. She was giving articulation for the first time, in her reliving, to the inner cries with which she had lived the greater part of her life. He could not stand the thought or the sound. Before he could try to help her—and then how?—he would have to help himself. He turned and rushed from the room and down to the kitchen. He found the quarter-bottle of whiskey that he had hidden—the remains of a lifeline gone terribly meager. He opened the back door and stood in the icy air, gulping the whiskey. Before he could stop himself or consider what he was doing, the bottle was empty. Erin's moaning had risen until he heard it as wind in the house. Desperately looking at the empty bottle he recalled the early morning struggle in the kitchen and Priscilla's act of charity and destructiveness when she gave him the whiskey. She had come in the back door— It had not snowed for hours, so that her footprints, going to the smokehouse, were only partly filled in. He followed them to the snowbank that contained his bottled fate and his plunging fingers found a bottle. He did not look for more than one; he did not wish to know how much of courage was left beneath the snow. He reentered the house and started to Erin; then, recalling an important point of etiquette, he got two glasses and with the bottle tucked under his arm he climbed the stairs once more.

The rows of chairs faced the coffin bare of obscuring flowers. Relatives had been instructed not to send wreaths because this had been the dead man's wish—this and "Greensleeves" for his funeral music had been his sole instructions, meant to enhance the bleakness of leaving life, which he had loved, which he had planned to leave with the plaint: "Alas, my love, you do me wrong, to cast me off discourteously—" But when they were all seated and waiting for Judge Hollis Ward to come and talk to them, every eye found the unadorned coffin too stark. Those of the uninstructed who had sent flowers wondered where their offerings were; surely, they might have thought, truth-dealing death deserved the harmless obscuring lie of flowers?

Ward, whose presence had been noted but who had kept away from the family, made his entrance. To the people who saw him almost daily, he did not seem to be himself. He walked to the front of the room with the gait of an old man, quite unlike his usual rubber-ball bounce. He looked as if his back might be giving him trouble. When he faced them they saw no evidence in his eyes that he had been crying, and when one looked closely, finding this very odd, one noticed a thing entirely uncharacteristic: he was afraid. He stood in silence before the family and friends, who numbered perhaps three dozen. When the silence stretched out, the organist, made nervous at such unorthodoxy and wondering if he had missed a cue, began to play "Bringing in the Sheaves." At first the song was not recognizable because his hands were playing in two different keys, but when he had corrected the atonal beginning, people began to shift in their seats. Even those who did not know of the requested song found this one singularly inappropriate, and glances were exchanged by all but the immediate family, who sat looking straight ahead.

Ward's tongue flicked at his lips, and he began to speak. "My wife has asked me to express her condolences to the family. She is unable to be with us today as she is attending the bedside of a sick mother. Though absent in body, her sorrow is joined to ours on this most sorrowful day." The widow nodded her thanks for all of them although he did not look in their direction; his eyes roamed the part of the room where the knowing sat, trying to assess their knowledge. He paused for such a long time that the organist got through a chorus of the hymn.

"My wife was fortunate in the relationship she enjoyed with my old and very dear friend, Murdoch McChesney. She has told me so many a time. 'Hollis,' she would say, 'he was like my own daddy.' Together they knew that purity of regard and mutual consideration which exists only between a father and his beloved daughter. Ask any of these bereft girls here today" —he told the people of the town—"ask these children of Murdoch McChesney, and they will attest to my words and to those of my absent wife when she would say—and many's the time—'Hollis, he was like my own daddy.' "

It was plain that he was compelled by some private force and was unable to stop. The knowing began to look at the family surreptitiously for signs of enlightenment; Ward was spelling it out for them, but except for Spur's ears looking unnaturally red there were no signs. Eventually, as the voice went on and on in the same vein, a feeling of unbreakable eternity seemed to envelop the room and the words grew to have less and less meaning.

"—as most of you here know; this is not meant in any way to discredit the influence and wisdom and selflessness of the mother, who did what she could with what she had. It is meant only to remind you that a girl growing up without a father's steadying hand is a pitiable object, given to irrational behavior, and my wife never knew her father—" But at last, miraculously, he seemed to have found his way. It was as if he had waited for a moment in time to come and go, and it had come and gone, restoring him in its passage. His voice began to swell in its old way, matching the tremolo of the organ, which played on.

"Ask these girls here today, grieving for their father, if they would exchange the safety and honor of their years with him for all the gold and fame in the entire world, and they would tell you, simply, 'No.' They were made to grow, and to flourish, and to come to radiant flower, by that father's unfaltering hand, which tended them with a boundless affection. And the sons, who have followed in his footsteps, planting and reaping the fruits of their concerned love. For Murdoch McChesney was a farmer. He belonged to the land to which he is being returned today—and how fittingly! Not for him the consuming flames of cremation; not for him the alienness of a burial at sea. To the land he belonged and to the land he shall go. Rejoice with me that a man of the earth may have the security of knowing that he will be returned to its bosom—"

He turned his head and saw Weezie at the door, holding a small boy by the hand. Caught in his own words, he smiled, his automatic, public response to children, before he saw and understood. By the time he knew that he had been overtaken, most of his audience had turned, too, following the direction of his strange smile so removed from the occasion. "Go back," he said, but Weezie made no move to enter the room. She merely picked the child up, putting it astride her hip, and stood in the doorway. Mother and child were attentive and discreet.

"—go back to the earth," Ward said, "from which he came. The fields will know him no more—and again I say to you, rejoice. The earth has reclaimed its own, the earth whose secrets he knew so well: its prodigality, its cruel demands, its perfidy." He grew dizzy at the back-and-forth motions of the heads below him, and the sibilance which sounded to him as if a fly had got in the room. He lifted his face to the ceiling; his hands held each other tightly. The tears broke and poured down his face in a sheet. It was to be remembered that he had outdone himself in tears that day. His voice, an organ capable of many sounds, almost sang to them.

"As for a man, his days are as grass; as a flower of the field, so he flourisheth. For the wind passeth over it, and it is gone; and the place thereof shall know it no more." He was convinced that there was a fly buzzing and knocking about the walls; he felt that he should stop and request that it be caught and killed before it could get in the coffin and crawl into the dead man's eye. But when he lowered his face and looked for it he saw the working mouths that were making the sound and he saw the beginnings of outrage on the faces of some members of the dead man's family. To those who were still puzzled, he said: "If any of you lack wisdom, let him ask, but ask in faith, for he that wavereth is like a wave of the sea; a double-minded person is unstable in all his ways. Let the brother of low degree rejoice in that he is exalted; but the rich"— He closed his eyes to all of them and looked in darkness at his possessions, watching as they slipped away one by one, leaving him as blithesomely as untrained birds—"but the rich in that he is made low; because as the flower of the grass, he shall pass away. For the sun no sooner rises with a burning heat but it withereth the grass, and the flower thereof falleth, and the grace and the fashion of it shall perish; so also"—he mourned—"shall the rich man fade away in his ways."

He lifted his wide-open eyes to heaven, pleading the defense with all of his persuasiveness. "But every man is tempted, when he is drawn away of his lust, and enticed!" Somberly, in God's voice, the prosecution replied: "Then, when lust hath conceived, it bringeth forth sin; and sin, when it is finished, bringeth forth death—" Slowly he lowered his heavy eyes and looked about the room. The organist made one of his mistakes with his feet, one foot pushing the swell pedal forward, the other slipping its mooring to land on the lowest note of the pedal keyboard. The bass C thundered in the room. As if that were the true voice of judgment for which he had listened, Ward walked from the room. He passed his wife in the doorway, pushing by her and the youngest McChesney without a glance, and left the building.

One by one the family and friends filed by the coffin, and when they had done so, Weezie brought Murdoch's son to his side and together they looked at him. Weezie held the boy tightly in case he should be scared, but he was not.

Bringing the boy back, Weezie had discovered a weakness in herself that she would never have suspected on the long drive to her mother's cousins' house, where she was known to her son as "Cousin Weezie." She had gone on the journey, brimming with hate and vindictiveness, her thoughts and plans exclusively for her husband and his undoing, but on the return trip, with the boy nestling warmly at her side, she found that her concern for him grew until it was almost overpowering, and, most peculiar of all, that she also felt concern for Murdoch's other children, because they were her son's brothers and sisters even if they might never know it. She had planned to sit with the family and make some kind of commotion—she had not planned the commotion, thinking that spontaneity would serve her best—but she viewed the plan now, with her son in her arms, as incredibly childish and pointless. The fact that the town *had* seen and the story *would* be spread and her husband undone, while irreversible, was of very little interest to her now. The most important thing was that she had to tell her son something, something he would remember in the distant future when she told him it was his own father he had seen that day. She whispered to the boy, "What that man said about the grass dying was a plain old lie. He just said it because he was upset about something. Why, it doesn't die at all! It just sleeps through the winter and comes back up in the springtime. You know that; you've seen it happen, haven't you?" The boy nodded. "All right, now. You remember that, and remember it good, 'cause someday when you're big I'm going to tell you a secret. A big old secret for my big old boy."

"Who was that man?" said the boy as they left the room, after he and Weezie had made the rounds of the family and been detained by the widow long enough to make Weezie wonder. Weezie smiled at those around her, considerate of their acute attentiveness. "A dear, dear friend of Mama's," she said, knowing the child would believe that she meant her mother and not caring what the others believed.

When all the family had gone from the place, Priscilla shooed the organist off the bench and sat down at the organ and played "Greensleeves" for her father, impatiently turning off the tremolo and giving to the song its bone-clean modalities. She thought that if Erin had been here she would have been the one to do so, because kept promises was Erin's way of life. She remembered that she had not telephoned Handy Miller, but remembered it with thanksgiving. She was as suspicious as the rest of the family (with the exception of the widow, who was not suspicious at all; she had seen Murdoch plainly in the boy's eyes and understood that her husband's blood was endless and indestructible), and as outraged, by the interminable seeming irrelevance of Ward's words and the whispering and buzzing that had gone on, but she told herself that it was almost over and let it end, please, as quickly and uncomplicatedly as possible. Soon they would leave for the graveyard, and she expected that Robin, knowing the service was over, would ask Handy to drive him and Erin directly there. She made the thought resolute.

He set the glasses and whiskey down with a series of bangs on the table. She lifted her face from her hands and in a moment she smiled.

"The 'medicinal,' " she said uncertainly. "But a water glass, Robin? *Two?*"

"Whither thou goest—" he said, pouring two half-glasses of whiskey.

She was scandalized. "Robin! Did any of the children see you?"

"Priscilla," he said, handing her a glass.

She took it, worried. "Did she say anything?"

He drank the half-glass in a gulp. "She said something about calling Handy Miller."

"Handy Miller?" It did not make sense to her. She was getting lost.

He said rapidly, "She asked if we were coming." That was better. She looked happy. But "Christ" he said inwardly when she said, "Oh, that's a good sign. Did she sound as if she wanted us to come? Or was she indifferent as usual?"

"She wasn't indifferent." He could hardly say the words.

"She missed you, then. That's a *very* good sign." She took a sip of whiskey. "Worse than black draught—a fitting penalty for a cold. I'm so ashamed I could die—"

"Drink up," he said harshly.

She continued inexorably, "—getting a cold the minute you turned your back. Leaving the fort untended—"

"Your health's more important than any old fort—" He poured whiskey and drank as her words continued as if by rote, a formula to conjure the devil.

"—I wanted to get up when I heard him fall last night, to make sure none of the children went out and saw him lying in the hall, but I was too dizzy—"

He waited for the moaning to begin, but she continued staunchly for his benefit, "I'm sure they didn't, though. I listened carefully for doors opening. Someone cried out, but that was later. I suppose it was poor Jasper again. He needed you—"

On an impulse—he was reaching the stage of drunkenness when considered words were getting beyond reach—he said, "Are you sure it wasn't his father, or his mother, or even Rhoda he needed—needs?" He turned so that she could not see his face in the mirror.

"You sound strange, my dear. Poor boy, you probably haven't had enough sleep—"

"Why is that a strange question, my dear?"

"From *you*—to *me?* Of course he misses Rhoda, but she will be home soon." She said gently, "He has the nightmares when she is here, you know."

"He has them when I'm here, too." He drank.

There was silence and when Erin spoke she sounded endangered. "Don't—twist my meaning that way. You know—*we* know—that we're needed more than—that we're needed—"

"Yes," he said. "Of course we know it. Of course we know it." He turned to her suddenly with the brightest smile he could manage. "When were you happiest in all your life?" She looked startled but there was also anticipation on her face. He played to the anticipation. "It's a game. When were you happiest in your life?"

"It's silly—" she said finally, with some reluctance.

Because he did not want to force her, he said, "Of course—happiness is—I remember my first pair of school shoes—" He was making it up, saying anything, punctuating with drinks.

"I remember, too! I was there with you—I wanted a pair of boy's shoes like yours—"

"Yes," he said. "Yes, I remember—" thinking: Did we go barefoot until memory set in like a siege of bad weather?

"We went in to the Dry Goods Store and they put us on high chairs and brought out stacks of boxes—Oh, it was like a dream—" There was silence and then her voice saying, "Jasper cried out last night—Daddy fell again—"

He shouted at her, "When you were happiest—*that's* the game. *When?*"

"—I wanted to get up but I was too dizzy—Oh, I'm so ashamed of catching a cold and leaving the fort untended—" Her eyes were glazed, their pain exaggerated by their muteness like an animal's; they were trying to tell him so much more than her words could manage. He was very drunk, but he would never be drunk enough to listen to what her eyes were trying to say. He spoke in despair. "While I was away this time I thought a lot about our decision. I think we made a mistake. We can't shield them from life. It was a mistake—"

She tried to rise. His words pushed her back. "It was a lie, all we told them. We've never told them the truth. We've never told it to ourselves."

He turned his back on her and waited. He heard the loose bedpost rattle as she reached it and clung to it. His mind cleared and he could see where they were: he was in the future, she in the past. The strip of room between them was a void which he must fill in with obstacles to keep her from coming to him and sharing his fate. The present, which she could not reach, was in Roseville with their dead father and the children they had maimed in unimaginable ways because he had maimed them first, his two oldest children, handing on to them blindly the blind traditions and myths and distortions of the country he had never understood, had never tried to understand. No more did they, or they never would have made mistakes more terrible than his because they affected more lives. If only they had known, before they took their vows. But hadn't knowing preceded the vows? His had, but he wanted to believe in her innocence, he needed her innocence as a final gift. He must somehow, through shock, grief or disbelief, push her further back to a safe place in her mind, to their pre-vow days. He had pushed her to where she now was, which was an anxiety-filled madness. Let him at least leave her in a madness that had tenderness and trust. The South was filled with such trustingly mad women. They were, in a way, its shield. He was aware of Time—his own; it was closing like a great book; he could hear the rustle of its leaves. He talked to her, stumbling over the words, slurring, hurrying.

"We couldn't take the truth about ourselves—couldn't look at it through our own eyes—so we took theirs—the eyes of the children. We have given ourselves false innocence, and nightmares to them. We have robbed them, pretending to be protective—and they cry in the night—and when they wake up from our nightmares they find the givers hunching over them—" If she dies now, he thought, I will have killed her with euphemisms. Even to save her I couldn't say the truth . . . Because I don't know what it is, after all. After all.

There was silence. The bedpost did not rattle. She was either standing alone or grasping the post so tightly it could not rattle. He was afraid to turn, afraid of where he might find her, but he had to . . . She was standing with one hand lightly resting on the foot of the high bed.

"Robin—" Her eyes wandered uncertainly around the room. She saw the bottle of whiskey and the glass on her dressing table. "My goodness, I hope none of the children saw you—"

"Priscilla—"

"Well, don't be too sure—that *that* means we're safe. "She has said her first word, after all, at the age of one—" He relaxed and joined her on that happy day when Priscilla had said, "Da-da."

The funeral procession left Owen's for the graveyard, and when they passed the depot Priscilla saw Handy shoveling snow from the platform. She asked the driver to stop, and got out. The line of twenty cars behind them lay trembling on the snowy hill like a pied, nervous beast. She ran to Handy and took his arm. Watching family and friends saw the Negro turn from her, heard her, through rolled-down windows, say, "Please." They saw the Negro drop his shovel and leave. Priscilla returned to the car and the cavalcade moved on.

. . .

They were walking arm in arm around their grounds. Occasionally Robin stumbled and Erin laughingly helped him to his feet, calling him "clumsy colt" and other pet names. Periodically, feeling her shiver, he would tell her to go back to the house; he would be in soon. But she refused.

"I can't recall snow this late in the year, can you? Some say the Gulf Stream is changing its course. Will that make us an arctic state, do you think? Oh, Robin, we should cover the canna beds with tow sacks. Just yesterday one red bloom peeped out—And the trees! Every leaf is covered—"

"Don' wor'," he said.

"January in June, practically," she said. "Imagine such a thing, outside of a song. It's like red rain, or falling stars. Let's grow a crop of stars next year and water it with red rain!" She threw her head back and laughed, hooting satirically at herself. "I hope to God I don't grow up to be one of those 'lyrical' old maids!"

He didn't know if they were reliving some actual incident of the past, or if they were inventing a new past for themselves. She was twenty and he was eighteen; had she planned even then to be an old maid? He asked her if she did not plan to marry. Her answer was mockingly stern.

"I have duties, my good, good man. 'To cook and sew and tend the fires—suppress desires—' " She looked at him mischievously. "You are forbidden me by the law of the land, but you are the law, you are the land, so I will marry the land. A sheaf of wheat shall be my bridal bouquet and my marriage bed"—she looked around, finishing triumphantly—"the snows of June!"

A door left ajar, his father's voice, and one knows that life is merely death, slightly out of focus.

"Who are you?" he asked her, playing the game as well as he could.

"Demeter, the earth goddess."

"And who am I?" They were in the orchard, under the apple trees that seemed with the whiteness of snow to be in full bloom.

She embraced him, smiling and serious. "You are my dear, dear brother Robin. I don't know for sure which god you are—all of them, I think— Oh, Robin," she cried out, young and joyful, "let's vow never to grow old—"

He saw that there was no way to escape exchanging vows with her so long as he lived. He fell heavily, and over her laughing cajolery he heard his father say, "Where have you planted your seed?" and he answered, making no effort to get up because he knew, at last, where he was, and in naming the place he also answered his father's question. "Here," he said, making retribution for condemning the land.

When she could not make him move or respond, she lay down beside him, snuggling against his back, caressing the red velvet of his coat. She talked to him happily and eventually drowsily. She spoke of the warmth of the sun, and in her closed eyelids she saw him standing with his arms around the neck of his horse, beside the brook, and she imagined that her bare foot swept the surface of the water like a little brown broom. This, she thought, feeling the sun on her back, is God's favorite hour, when He walks His meadows, and Robin and I are a circle—an infinite number of straight lines that finally do meet—and this is my happiest day. She heard an automobile in front of the house; soon she would get up and see who it was, and make them welcome.

A little wind, gentle as June, blew snow from the trees in a drift as light as motes in a sunbeam, and they were veiled in white.

Handy went through the house, calling their names. He looked in family rooms and bedrooms and closed-off rooms in the house he had seen only from outside, the house of his best friend, without success. On the bed in the room next to the kitchen, he found a black suit with a piece of paper pinned to it and written on the paper the words SEND TO: and a name and address in New York City. It was a mystery to him, a white man's mystery. He settled down finally in the only room that was halfway warm, to wait for the return of the others, the way Priscilla had asked him to—"If they can't come," she had said, "wait there with them." He had not told old man Logan that he was coming, so if he got in trouble let the McChesneys patch it up, since one turn deserved another—though his experience told him they might not see it that way.

He sat smoking, dribbling flecks of gray and red ash on the carpet that to Robin's grandmother had stood for all she had given up in exchange for this grave-raw but somehow inaccessible land. Sleepily he thought that if Robin and Erin were not with the others, if they had not found some other way to get there to the death-place, he could only tell the others what it occurred to him was the truth of his life with them, and what could be the truth of their lives as well, together and apart, for all he knew: "I tried—I looked—I called—but nobody answered me. I could not find them at all."

ABOUT THE AUTHOR

Coleman Dowell was born in Adairville, Kentucky, in 1925 and died sixty years later in New York City. After service in the Army Medical Corps during World War II, he settled in New York, where he worked as a writer and composer for the DuMont Television Network. During the late 1950s and early 1960s he authored several plays, including the musical *The Tattooed Countess*, based on the novel by his friend Carl Van Vechten. *One of the Children Is Crying*, his first novel, was originally published in 1968. It was followed by *Mrs. October Was Here*, *Island People*, *Too Much Flesh and Jabez*, *White on Black on White*, and, most recently, *The Houses of Children: Collected Stories*. At the time of his death, Coleman Dowell was working on a novel, *Eve of the Green Grass*, and a volume of memoirs to be entitled *A Dark Book*.